THE ANGELS' SHARE

THE ANGELS' SHARE

A NOVEL

JANE BOW

Red Elixir
Rhinebeck, New York

Paperback ISBN 9781966293309
eBook ISBN 9781966293316

Library of Congress Control Number 2026900199

Book and cover design by Colin Rolfe

Red Elixir is an imprint of Monkfish Book Publishing Company

Red Elixir
22 East Market Street, Suite 304
Rhinebeck, New York 12572
(845) 876-4861
redelixirbooks.com
monkfishpublishing.com

For Grant

Crete's sense of history is extremely deep. Whoever sets foot on this island senses a mysterious force branching warmly and beneficently through his veins, senses his soul begin to grow.

NIKOS KAZANTZAKIS, REPORT TO GRECO

Terroir

Watching
granite, quartz, limestone, lava
scraped off mountains
by glaciers, wind, rain and snow
leach minerals
into clay-held moisture where
bacteria, beetles, mites and worms
turn rotting vegetation into soil,
and yellow-headed fennel drops
her frothy skirts
and sage, oregano, rosemary and thyme
fruit the air —
all this creating character
in a grape —
the angels wait.

i.

Dion shrugs off her knapsack. Crete's late afternoon sunshine is deliciously warm in March and this gully, carved out of the overhanging bank of a dry stream bed behind her family's vineyard, is visible to no one. No paths thread through the jumble of rocks and wild greenery below it. Bells tinkling in the distance belong to sheep who, grazing on a nearby mountainside, don't care what she wears – or doesn't – and a castle overlooking this valley has been a ruin for centuries. Still.

Spreading her rug, sitting down, she pulls her t-shirt up over her head. Wants to unhook her brassiere, but never in all her thirty nine years has she exposed her breasts out of doors in daylight. People in the places she knows – England, Canada, the United States – don't generally do that.

"So?" says Teddy's voice.

Poppies, daisies and milk flowers in the stream bed below her nod in a wisp of breeze. Dion scrutinizes shrubs, bushes, trees. Nothing moves. Then oh, the freedom!

She lies down, the rug soft under her bare back. Sunlight caresses the white mounds of her breasts. Bees buzz, birds chirrup. The breeze tightens her nipples. Her thighs feel too hot. She turns her head, scans the deserted stream bed again. A bird hops through the branches of a shrub on its other side. Bending her knees, she lifts her hips, pulls off her leggings, then her thong because why not? The tricksy breeze tickles her thigh. A giggle bubbles up.

Her body is stark white, her breasts a little fuller, her hips are a little wider than she'd like but still a hum starts: Taylor Swift's *Shake shake shake*... One of her hip bones shimmies to the beat, the other one joins it.

Spring's afternoon light, angling lower, reaches the gully's ceiling where purple, green, rust, white pebbles were polished by water swirling through here thousands of years ago, long before Zeus, king of the Greek gods, grew up on Crete. Aphrodite lives here still. Dion has seen her down on the south coast, plucking white plumes off the top of the Libyan Sea and twirling them out on winds that Ares, god of war and her lover, sends from the north. Sometimes a rainbow appears, just for a moment, above the water.

Her breasts are tingling. Better roll over. Dion's hair, a wavy mess of gingery auburn, would curtain her face if she hadn't cut it all off before leaving Canada last November. Wash-and-wear hair, she thought. Four months later it springs out in whatever direction it likes. She lays her cheek on the rug.

Sunshine explores her shoulder blades, the small of her back, reaches in under her bum. Pleasure licks her. Aphrodite's son Eros makes fabulous love to Psyche, a lowly human in his myth, on condition that she never sees him. Is he here now, with her? Dion tilts her hips to him.

Inside her knapsack her mobile phone starts to quack. Her hips collapse.

One hour, is that too much to ask for? One hour in which ninety-four year old *Yiayiá* finds her own glasses and her father's news about his Russian investor bottles itself and Kokanakis Wines' other creditors suck rocks. One single hour between trying to keep her family from losing a home that has been theirs for nearly a thousand years and milking Aretha (named by her father for Aretha Franklin) then feeding the chickens then helping her grandmother with supper. Her phone stops.

Below her in the stream bed the poppies, glowing red now, are dancing. She flips onto her back again, closes her eyes, opens her legs. But Eros has left. Her sensory cells, shut tight as barnacles when the tide's out, trap her once again inside a self she tried to leave behind on her birthday last November.

Freezing rain was tack-tacking against her window as she booked her flight from Toronto to Crete. She told her journal it was to spend Christmas with her father and grandmother and help them sort out their finances.

'Yeah right,' it replied, dripping sarcasm. 'You quit your job, cashed in your pension and sold your condo to take a vacation.'

Okay, she argued, I'm following my dreams. Their parents had always told Teddy and her to do that. When she was little it was easy, she just followed her big brother into the shells of houses being built down the road from their commune on England's South Downs, creeping behind him and his friends, climbing half-finished staircases, peering down into two-storey chasms, thrilled by the horror of what would happen if she fell. Which she wouldn't if Teddy was there.

'What dreams?' her journal goaded. 'Teddy died sixteen years ago, and look at your life: Cardboard coffee, subway, phone, government cubicle, gym then home to veggie-take-out, boxed wine, calories recorded, tv online. Day after day after day. Writing environmental assessment reports nobody reads.' No mention of men or marriage or babies. And a year from now this ripe body of hers would turn forty. Halfway to nearly dead.

Once her family's finances were sorted her plan was to lie on a warm beach before looking for a new start in England or Europe or Scandinavia, where exciting new climate projects might welcome her environmental studies degree.

Well. She rolls onto her side in the gully. No chance of any of that now. The nest egg she brought with her is gone. Payouts the winery used to receive from Leonid Salin, their Russian investor, stopped two months ago and nobody had thought to tell her that Kokanakis Wines owes Salin two hundred and fifty thousand euros, the debt due in November. If they don't repay the Russian they'll be homeless. The thought sends a shiver through the sun's warmth. She opens her eyes, sits up.

A man is standing in the stream bed below, watching her. Young, thin, paint-splattered shirt, jeans ripped at the knees, curly hair wild.

Dion's heart thumps. Fear flushes into her chest, arms, legs as, fumbling for her clothes, she peers through the late afternoon light, trying to see his face, what he will do. But the sun is too low, his head a silhouette. A cloth bag slung over his shoulder bulges with what looks like *horta* (wild greens.) He raises a hand, palm towards her.

"*Yass'*." (Hi.) Then turns his back. Does not go away.

She pulls on her t-shirt, her leggings, stuffs her underwear into her knapsack, rage flaming now: Damn him, why didn't she bring a knife or pepper spray (though where would she find that in Crete?) or her Dad's shotgun (not that she has a clue how to use it.) Is there no place on this entire planet where a woman alone can feel safe? A loud voice is your best weapon, a self-defence instructor taught her once in downtown Toronto, but here who would hear her? She sees her body ravaged then left for dead, her father and *Yiayiá* out searching, calling her name. This gully down the bank behind a stand of oak trees at the back of her family's property is the last place they would look.

Shouldering her knapsack, bundling the rug into her arms, she ducks out of the gully. Will climb the stream bank, disappear into the oaks.

"Please, I was hoping we could meet."

English. She stops, turns. He comes closer. His face is narrow, the lines of his nose and jaw sharp. So young. Did he see her hip-dancing, meeting Eros' touch? Embarrassment heats her cheeks. Anger is right on its heels.

"Who says I want to be met?"

"I know, I know, I'm sorry." He shrugs the shoulder holding his bag of greens. "I was foraging. Also sketching." Clearly Greek though his English is fluent, east coast American by the slight drawl in its vowels. He takes another step towards her. "I'm Theo. And I'm hoping you'll let me draw you."

"Draw me?" A scrape of surprised laughter. "That's a new one."

"No, I'm serious." He drops his bag, takes a sketch pad out of a beat-up knapsack and holds it out to her. "I'm an artist."

She looks hard at him. Nothing but earnestness looks back. The sunlight, nearly horizontal now, is tinged with gold as she takes the book, turns its pages. Charcoal rendered poppies play in a ditch, a bee explores a thistle against a mountain backdrop, a ruined stone tower stands under a sliver of moon.

"Rough studies," he says. But she can feel the lightness of the poppies' movements, the bee's frenetic busyness.

"Where are you from?"

"Here. Crete."

"But your English—?"

"I went to high school in Boston. My father's American." His eyes are grey, watchful, perceptive. Hopeful.

She turns another page. The first few lines of a naked woman are reclining in a stream bank gully. Dion's head snaps up, her cheeks flaming again.

"I stopped, you can see that! And came out to ask your permission."

"To draw me naked." Her head is already shaking.

"Not naked, nude. There's a difference." Her head goes on shaking. But:

"What difference?"

"Naked is stripped of clothing, exposed, vulnerable. Nude is a state of grace. Think Botticelli's Aphrodite On A Shell."

Is she really in a remote Cretan valley with someone who knows Botticelli? Dion hasn't seen the painting but every Rethymnon gift shop carries knock-off metal sculptures of the artist's goddess of love. She hands back his sketchpad.

"Sorry Theo, I'm no Aphrodite and my body's not a still-life." He appears to consider this.

"I'm not into still-life either." He brightens. "But maybe you'll let me do a few sketches of you fully clothed?"

All she has to do is shake her head again and this ragged boy/man will go away. Except now shadows are fading the wildflowers behind him in the stream bed, and there are worse things than being looked at by an artist. And when was the last time she had a conversation with anyone under the age of seventy?

"You must know all kinds of younger people you can draw."

"I do," he says, "but that's not what I want. Tomorrow afternoon?"

Usually she takes her time walking up through the oak trees, loves their close-knit canopies, their branches' long grace, the shush of their leaves. Their acorns, shaped like little penises, usually make her chuckle. Today she doesn't notice the oaks. She'll think about it, she told Theo, she's very busy. Now, clambering over the crumbling stone wall between the oaks and the olive grove behind her father's vineyard, Dion tries to believe Theo is not on his way to his local *taverna*, where he'll boast about the naked cougar he found in the wild.

The olive trees' grey-green leaves are small, pointed, tough. Some of their gnarled trunks are hundreds of years old, living testaments to so many lives, so many stories. Beside them she feels like a trinket.

In the vineyard between the olives and the winery Romeiko vines, each growing in its own space, look like a crowd of green-leaf dwarfs taking the last of the day's sunlight. Bowie, her father's black and brown border collie/mutt, comes bouncing through them.

The barnyard's twilight lullaby of clucks and baas and coos as she distributes food, and the smell of fresh goat milk splashing into the pail calm her a little. Speakers at the back of the winery are blasting David Bowie's voice singing *Let's Dance* as she carries her pail of milk around the corner from the barn. Her father has turned on the patio lanterns, lit a fire in an outdoor stove against the evening chill, and is nursing a glass of his red Romeiko wine at one of the wrought iron tables set out under an ancient plane tree. Fifteen years after moving to Crete Alex Kokanakis' wavy black hair has gone grey. Shoulders that were broad when Dion was little slope down now, but he also has a new fluidity of movement, as if his joints have been lubricated, as if he no longer has to try in anything he does.

On the other side of the patio the winery is also his home. Some of its honey-gold and grey stone blocks come from the house *Yiayiá* was raised in here, some come from the same local quarry his ancestors used. Inside the house stone arches that have been there for several hundred years now support white plaster ceilings. New windows let lots of light into a kitchen where a wood-fired stove will be flavouring the air with whatever Dion's grandmother has bubbling on its burners.

"Let's sway..." sings David Bowie. Seeing Dion, her father gets up, relieves her of the milk pail and takes her into a waltz. Bowie the dog watches from under the table.

Her legs feel like sticks, her back is a wooden two-by-four but her father holds her, humming along with the music, and gradually his warmth loosens her muscles. His slightly musky fruit scent whisks her back into childhood – picnics at the seaside in England, Mom and Dad swinging her between them while Teddy ran ahead; Teddy boosting her up into a tree, or tying a rope around her waist to haul her up the garden wall, Dion laughing so hard she was afraid she would pee.

"... under the moonlight," sings her Dad, pushing her gently away, then pulling her close again. "Let's dance!" Dion's hips sway a little. When the song ends her father pulls her into a hug.

"We're going to be all right, chicken. Maybe, I think."

All right how, Dion wonders? Her father turns towards the kitchen door.

"Ma! Come and have a glass of wine, I have some good news!" He fills two more glasses, hands one to Dion. "Ma!"

"I'm coming!" Opening the door, wiping her hands on her apron, *Yiayiá* sounds annoyed. On the other side of the Atlantic her voice had a harsh American edge, her English perfected by imitating American radio programs after she and Dion's grandfather emigrated to the United States in the late 1940s. Dion was eleven before she met her grandmother. When her family moved from their English commune to Toronto, in Canada, her father drove them over the border to visit occasionally but her grandparents were always busy in their restaurant east of Detroit, *Yiayiá* too brusque to approach. Dion never knew, until recently, that her father was named Alexander for his Cretan grandfather but also for Alexander The Great, according to *Yiayiá*. Who, having raised three sons and a daughter in the U.S. and enrolled in business courses as soon as Alex, her youngest, was in high school, now wears a black dress, cardigan and boiled wool slippers, her American self all but erased.

"I don't want to be mistaken for a tourist," she snapped when her granddaughter dared to point this out. Dion suspects that really it's to camouflage sorrow that still drags at the edges of her eyes sixteen years after losing her beloved Gio, who died with Teddy in the summer of 2004 when a man screaming political gibberish drove his van through the front window of their restaurant. The judge called it 'senseless domestic terrorism' and sent the man to prison for life. Dion's mother tried to escape her sorrow at the loss of Teddy by leaving the family, taking a job in San Francisco. "You'll visit," she told Dion. But soon a new partner and then terminal cancer took her for good. Dion's father went back to the U.S. to help his mother rebuild the restaurant but wound up bringing *Yiayiá* to her ancestral home in Crete instead. The restaurant's insurance payout and the sale of the property funded the new winery's construction and first years of production. Fifteen years later, at the age of ninety-four, *Yiayiá* often mates her English with Greek, delivering odd Cretan-animated expressions and sentence structures that belong to neither language.

"What good news?" she asks now. "The chickens have laid extra eggs? Aretha has given us double cream?"

Her son puts a glass of wine down on the table for her.

"Leo Salin wants us to sign a new contract and as soon as we do he'll start our payouts again." Her father's joy is as pure as the spring breeze through the honeysuckle behind the patio. "He said he sees great things ahead."

Hoods come down over *Yiayiá's* blue eyes as, supporting herself with the table, she lowers her body into a chair.

"Meaning what exactly?"

"He says he'll bring the new contract over on the weekend, before he leaves to take possession of a new yacht. He wants us to stock all his European resorts with our wines. And it turns out he's a connoisseur of brandy too!" Her father must have told Salin about the antique copper still he bought last month with euros they don't have. He wants to try making a Romeiko brandy. "So we'll invite him for dinner, eh Ma? Kill a chicken, make him some *dolmades*, and *boureki* – Russians love potatoes. And we'll open a bottle of our prizewinning rosé." Her father raises his glass. "So *Yamas*! (cheers!)"

Alex Kokanakis, creator of wines that are a coalescence of artfully nurtured nature and science, likes to say he "puts spirit into his spirits" and every morning, sipping her coffee in the winery's office, ignoring a stack of unpaid invoices – blue (first reminder,) yellow (warning,) pink (ultimatum) – on the desk, Dion watches his beat-up straw hat moving through the vineyard on the far side of the patio. Behind him the grey-green olive trees whisper with the oaks as he bends to his vines, talking to them for sure, commiserating about last night's chill, telling them what weather to expect today. Or singing. She's heard him, sometimes it's a lullaby, sometimes rock n' roll, or deep-throated opera ("Figaro, Figaro...!")

"Soil, vines, weeds and humans, we are all sunlit energy interacting," he has explained to her, arriving back in the office, filling the morning air with new observations, unseen glitches and ideas on how to solve them. "Together we create whatever comes next in the miracle called life."

Whatever comes next. Dion thinks of herself this afternoon, lying naked under the sun. Wishes she had inherited her father's ability to go with the flow, each moment unbreachable by common sense or ambition or paranoia. Across the patio table *Yiayiá's* eyes are blinking.

"He wants wine for how many resorts? And brandy too? Where will we get enough grapes?"

Dion has been wondering about that too. One vine produces one bottle of wine, roughly, in years when nature co-operates, according to the winery's account books.

"We can negotiate all that, *Mamá*," says Alex. "What's important is that Leo wants to go on working with us."

"And our debt?" snaps his mother. "What about that?"

Goosebumps sprout on Dion's arms. A Google search she did on Leonid Salin told her only that he is a 'computer specialist' based in Moscow. A numbered corporation issued all payments to the winery. Now, after stopping their credit line for several months, he wants them to produce an impossible amount of wine. And a quarter of a million-euro obligation won't just disappear. But.

Her father's joy is contagious. She raises her glass, will trust for just a few minutes his blind belief in 'the miracle called life.'

"*Yamas*! To Alexander The Grape."

ii.

Sitting on the stone wall between the olive trees and the oaks, her knapsack loaded with her book, her journal, two oranges, a bottle of water, her rug rolled up and tied beneath it, Dion tries to ignore butterflies loop-the-looping inside her stomach. Because why would she go back to her gully, her private place? Until yesterday. Why would she meet an imp-sized boy/man who says he wants to draw her fully clothed when really he wants her naked – or nude? Whatever. If she meets him again he'll take that as acquiescence, obviously.

So? What have you got to lose? says Teddy's voice. Other than your life possibly.

Dion stoops, wraps her hands around the wings of a hen pecking through the weeds and flings it back towards the barnyard. Further down the wall Melodious, the winery's donkey, is grazing in the shade of a falling-down stone shed her father uses for storage. He does not look up as Dion heaves her knapsack and herself over the wall.

Theo is sitting on the stream bank outside her gully, facing away from her, his head bent over his lap. Same shirt and jeans. Brush tracks have tried to tame his hair. A twig snaps under her foot. He twists around, leaps up.

"You came!" He takes her knapsack, spreads her rug on the grass. Clouds scudding down from the north lay a shifting patchwork of sun and shade on it. Kicking off her flip-flops, she sits down. He stands away from the rug, observing the way the afternoon sunlight is striking her, then sits cross-legged on the far side and reaches for his sketchbook.

"Can you show me a foot?" She extends one towards him, skin winter white, toenails unpainted. "Good. Now pretend I'm not here."

As if. She watches his grey eyes move from foot to paper to foot to paper as if nothing else, not even the rest of her leg, exists. His fingers holding a piece of charcoal are long, thin, calloused, dirty. His body, bent to his work, looks wiry, slight but hard. A male, not unpleasant sunshine-meets-earth odour comes to her.

The foot he is drawing wants to move, her toes want to wiggle. Her instep starts to itch. On purpose for sure. Neither her foot nor the rest of her likes forced immobility. Or being on display. Too bad. She said yes, so stay still. Practise breathing. Twenty minutes later he looks up from his sketchpad.

"Thank you."

"Can I see?"

Her foot on the paper has a high arch, toes slightly pointed, bony ankle swelling into a lower leg tensed for flight. Around his foot sketch each of her toes also has its own drawing, big toe a hammerhead, middle toes following, baby toe curling into the protection of its closest sibling. Down near the corner of the page her ankle's underside, shaded around her heel, stirs something inside her pelvis. How did he do that?

He asks for her hand.

"Why, just out of interest? If you're not into still life."

An errant flock of vibes – arrogance, bashfulness, ambition, self-consciousness – chase each other across his face. One of his shoulders twitches. She waits, intrigued. A breeze hushes up the stream bed, gossips with the oak trees at the top of the bank.

"Desire," he says finally. "It's what my work is about."

Oh boy. Her laughter is a rusty hinge. What can this boy possibly see in her, or know about female desire? Women in movies rip off their clothes and reach orgasm in seconds but in the real world desire unquenched is a cruel beast. And the last thing Dion needs right now is for anyone to see her writhing in its grasp.

She used to blame her failure to reach orgasm on her partners: This one was too pushy, interested only in himself, that one was hot on the dance floor but in bed? A cold compress. Sometimes a relationship lasted a few months, even a year or two, sometimes she teetered on the brink of a climax, other times she faked it, and falling asleep inside the warmth of grateful arms felt worth it, for awhile. Lots of women can't reach orgasm with a partner, say the books and articles and podcasts she has consumed on the subject. What you need is the right partner, the right circumstances, and stimulation that works. Most of all you need trust. Which is found where?

"I'm way too old for you, Theo."

"No no no," he says, "you don't understand. Desire is about so much more than just sex."

"Oh?"

"Yes! Show me any movement, any thought, one single action of any living being that isn't based on desire: For sex yes, but also for food or power or escape, usually for some mixture of these." All the bones in his face are pointed, so intense, but also pleading almost for her to understand. "Desire is the greatest force on Earth and that's what I want to paint." His grey eyes, levelled at her, hold no trace of seduction. "With you."

"Why?" Creases are starting to wattle her neck.

"Because your body wears its energy in spite of you, and that is a gift to me."

In spite of her? She thinks of yesterday, her prone dancing, opening her legs for Eros. Theo must have seen it all. Heat blotches the aforementioned neck. If he notices he doesn't let on.

"Your hand," he says. "Can you put it on the rug please? Palm down."

Skin on the back of her hand is starting to wrinkle and she keeps her nails short for typing and gardening and barnyard chores. Hardly model material.

Theo draws.

"Now bend your fingers, make a claw."

Her hand follows his instruction. Aggression travels up her arm, pulls back her lips. Her teeth clench. She laughs, surprised. He draws.

"Now turn your hand over."

Aggression becomes offering, her palm a bowl for something delicate, an egg maybe. She feels its grace, marvels. Gives him a couple of minutes then straightens her fingers, makes them rigid. Her jaw contracts. She wiggles her fingers. Her jaw releases. Amazing! He reaches towards her hand. Stops.

"May I?"

She nods. He tilts her hand on the rug, thumb raised. Her fingers curl a little. Beckoning. Inside her pelvis something twinges. He draws. Her fingers ripple, teasing. Flirting. More twinges. How can that be?

He folds her hand into a fist, his fingers warm, strong around hers, a little bit electric. He goes back to drawing. Her fist unfurls slowly, her fingers like petals of a flower, their energy lifting the back of her hand off the rug. Watching this strange sensuous finger world, she marvels.

He draws her arm, her shoulder, neck and head.

"May I?" Turning her chin one way, then the other. Watching, sketching.

When he's finished he shows her the various ways to render what's in the bend of an elbow, a knee, the jut of a shoulder blade. Crows' feet at the outer edges of her eyes horrify her. But:

"No!" he says. "See the beauty in the story they tell about what it is to be you." His smile feels like new-clean rain on a hot summer afternoon. "Can we meet again tomorrow?"

No. Feet, ankles, fingers, face, that's all she has to give. If she wanted to get naked she should have gone to one of Crete's nude beaches, where oily-brown tourists from all over Europe roast themselves.

Not in March. Alone.

"Sorry, I can't," she tells him. "I've got an important business meeting to prepare for."

"Later then, this time next week or the week after?"

"I don't know," she says. And she doesn't, can't think. "If I'm here, I'm here, that's all I can give you."

iii.

Her father leads the Russian across the patio, past the plane tree into the vineyard. Dion follows, notebook in hand. Record everything, *Yiayiá* has told her.

"None of those trained-up-a-wire vines, marching one after another like soldiers at boot camp, for me," Alex tells his guest and Dion can't help smiling. Her father thinks each vine has its own personality.

Salin looks nothing like Dion's image of a Russian government 'computer specialist.' His grey hair is styled, his biceps rounded just enough under a pink polo shirt. Only a gold watch and ring advertise a level of wealth that has allowed him to buy a state-of-the-art sailing yacht. His "assistant," bringing up the rear of their little group, wearing a black suit a half-size too small, hair slicked back, flaccid face devoid of expression, belongs in a Cold War movie.

Leaning down, her father strokes a vine's ropy, grey-black trunk:

"Each of these fellows is busy pushing roots down into this rock-hard soil, searching for food, bracing against the brutal winds that funnel into this valley." He spreads a broad, newly unfurled leaf across his palm, strokes it. "But all these leaves want is sunlight." He looks at Salin. "Cultivating a grapevine is a relationship, Leo. Wild grape vines wander, latching onto whatever they find and grasping, pushing, reaching. Producing no grapes. But stake a Romeiko vine's trunk to help it grow straight, find the sun, then tame its energy by pruning wayward shoots, and this ancient grape'll give you a whole spectrum of unique essences." He pinches the new-green leaf softly between his fingers, feeling its texture, testing for moisture, then gives Salin the easy smile of a man who has been communing with his soul since peace, love, rock 'n roll and righteous protests – against greedy fishing trawlers in the Atlantic, whalers in the Pacific, against baby seals being clubbed to death – ruled life in the English commune he once called home. When a government highway project expropriated them Dion's mother, who was British, got a job in Toronto, Canada. But even in the midst of city concrete, working in the kitchen of a downtown hotel, Alex Kokanakis had gone on caring for vegetables in gardens he created first on their apartment's balcony then behind a run-down suburban bungalow they managed to buy.

Aged seventy now, her father probably knows more about how all living things grow together than most people on the planet, thinks Dion. His journals contain only growth charts, grape yields, weather details, leaf measurements, sugar and acidity counts, coded wine production possibilities. Nothing in them explains how Greece's default on its European Union debts five years after his and *Yiayiá's* arrival here, or the austerity measures that followed, freezing bank accounts, raising taxes, cutting old age pensions, affected Kokanakis Wines; how unemployment skyrocketed, wealthy Greeks (who love wine) left, how tourism, Crete's main industry, all but died.

God must have wanted Kokanakis Wines to succeed however, *Yiayiá* has told her, because one day in 2015 Leonid Salin, the Russian, dropped in, tasted Alex's new dessert wine, ordered several cases, and then set up a five-year loan to the winery. In return Kokanakis Wines would supply a north shore Russian resort he owned.

Her father's journals do highlight his entering his Romeiko dessert wine in Europe's *Petit Vins* Wine Competition the year before last. It won a *Prix D'or*. Orders for it came in from all over Europe and when you have a prizewinning race horse stamping at the starting gate you have to let it run. Alex produced as much wine as he could but the costs of its production outstripped what the winery could charge for a bottle, driving them further into the red.

Liking Salin would be a good plan, Dion muses now, following her father and the Russian deeper into the vineyard. His starving them of cash flow just before presenting his new contract does not necessarily mean Salin is a despicable human being. Our attitudes can be choices, a therapist once told her. Maybe Salin's apparent wealth is a sham, or maybe he's dying of some terrible disease and the new contract will forgive their loan and bequeath them a future. They're not going to find salvation anywhere else apparently.

Her Dad's and *Yiayiá's* bank manager called yesterday.

"Even if we could manage a mortgage large enough to cover what you owe," he told her, "you would still need to finance your winemaking and living costs. So we're sorry Miss Kokanakis, a new loan is not something we can undertake at this time."

"A vine's large leaves act as both solar panels for photosynthesis and sun umbrellas to keep the summer sun from scorching its fruit," her father is explaining. "While each vine relates to every microscopic happening around it. If I keep wasps from devouring the sweetening grapes, nature will flavour them with each year's chemistry of soil, sun, weather and whatever else comes into the vine's realm." Dion hears the love in her father's voice.

Inside a pocket of his designer jeans Salin's phone dings. He stops, takes it out.

Her father waits while he reads a text then replies. Then, spreading a spray of tiny green knobs that will become Romeiko grapes across his palm, he waves at the sky.

"Some rain is good, especially in early spring and in this valley, where we're protected from the extreme summer heat threatening lower, more open vineyards and also from the coastal winds, our vines are doing very well." He smiles. "We're lucky."

Salin doesn't notice. His phone has pinged again. He reads, texts. Reads, texts.

"Excuse me," Dion can't help the slapping edge in her voice.

The Russian glances up, looks as if he's only just noticed that she exists.

"I just want to make sure you don't miss what my father is telling you." She tries to smooth her tone into politeness. "I thought, since you're investing so much in us, you'll want to hear what makes the grapes in our prizewinning dessert wine distinct."

Salin blinks, goes on observing her, saying nothing until her smile falls away, then finishes his text. Her father says nothing more until his guest looks up.

The early April afternoon has become uncharacteristically warm. Dion smells Salin's male-spicy cologne as they cross the patio, heading towards the fermenting room. Its overhead door is kept open during the day to let sun warm the room if it's cold. Shade from the plane tree overhanging the patio cools the room during the hot months. Inside, Kokanakis Wines' oldest wooden grape press, made for *Yiayia's* father at least a hundred years ago, looks like a giant-sized oak barrel with a handle on its lid that you turn to squish the juice out of the grapes. A larger generator-powered press, made by a local hooper, is also oak as are the winery's storage barrels. While tradition says French or American oak barrels produce the best taste, Alex explains that a few of his barrels come from oaks that lived right here with his vines.

"We know that trees communicate with each other through root networks that go back hundreds, if not thousands of years, so why would they not also communicate with neighbouring vines?" Dion hears his pleasure.

Salin's phone rings this time.

"Excuse me, I have to take this." He moves away, out past his "assistant" who is hovering in the doorway. Silence, then quick, impatient, low-volume Russian comes to them. When his investor returns her father explains his fermenting process.

"I don't just stick to the old ways." Alex is standing by two ceiling-high, pipe-fed stainless steel tanks. They make a third, barrel-shaped, wooden tank with a ladder up the side look like a dowdy country cousin. "Steel provides my white wines and rosés with a container that does not leach, so that they can become their own best selves." He launches into details about grape skins and tannins, timing and temperatures.

Salin asks no questions, clearly could not care less about her father's winemaking process. Until her father points to his new, gleaming copper still, bought for a brandy that so far is a product of his imagination.

"Ah," the Russian brightens, "I look forward to seeing how your first babies age, Alex."

Dion makes a note. If well-aged is what turns their investor's crank, maybe he'll come alive in the winery's underground aging room where, inside mould-painted rock walls, time and the angels are working their magic on barrels of her father's Romeiko reds. But.

"I'll leave you," she says. Working alone in the kitchen, her grandmother will be fussing over the dinner.

Smells of roasting chicken and fresh herb bread greet her but poor old *Yiayiá* is standing by the table drying her hands over and over on her apron.

"Artichoke and stuffed eggplant appetizers, Greek salad, then roast chicken, *horta* and *boureki, baklava,* what have I forgotten?"

"Nothing," Dion smiles. "Everything smells delicious." Coming around the table, she slides *Yiayiá's* potato *boureki* into the bottom of the kitchen's wood-fired oven and checks the heat setting. *Yiayiá's* homemade *baklava* lies cooling in its pan.

"And the table is set?" her grandmother asks needlessly.

"It is," says Dion. Her father brought a folding table into the showroom at the front of the winery yesterday and she set it with an embroidered tablecloth, linen napkins while *Yiayiá* polished wedding silverware she must have carted across the Atlantic to the U.S. more than seventy years ago, then back here again. Her father gathered a lovely spray of roses this morning for the centrepiece. Shelves above the counter on the far side of the showroom display bottles of the Kokanakis Winery's latest wines. Her father's *Prix D'Or* rosé has a plinth of its own.

Dion watches Salin enjoy his dinner, compliment *Yiayia* on her cooking, comment on Alex's choices of wines to accompany each dish. His English, learned in school, practised during a language internship in Britain and a career spent hopscotching around the globe (according to *Yiayia,*) and inflected with Russian intonations, is beguiling, his smiles appreciative. Dion clears the table of everything except the tiny glasses Cretans use for the island's traditional liquor called *raki.* The Russian knocks back a second round vodka-style then, sitting back in his chair, tells them the Kokanakis Winery they know and love is about to disappear.

"We will expand your vineyards and grow your operation so that guests at all my resorts, and as many others as we can reach, can experience wine produced under your *Prix d'Or* label.' Salin's English, clipped now, makes the transition sound inevitable, a reality in the making.

"How many resorts do you own?" *Yiayia* asks.

"Nine, in Greece, Croatia, Italy, Spain, five more opening next year."

"Fourteen resorts?" Dion looks at her father. "We can't produce enough wine for fourteen resorts, can we Dad?'

"With your present resources no, you can't," Salin says, "without more land and an updated, digitally-automated plant." As if her father has not spent the afternoon explaining the intricacies of his nature-based winemaking. "We'll build it behind the vineyard we were in this afternoon."

Alex's big head is already shaking.

"Nonono. Cut down my olive trees, and oaks older than my great-grandfather? Absolutely not, Leo. Those big old oaks suck carbon dioxide, the stuff that's killing our planet, out of the air. We know that. My winemaking process could be expanded a little without risking the quality of my wine but the soil, home of my vines, is a living organism. Forced growth will kill it. No, mechanization is not what Kokanakis Wines is about, Leo. Surely after this afternoon's tour you understand that?"

"Mechanized, digitized," Salin's hand sweeps the words aside. "These are just terms for more efficient ways of doing what you do."

"No," Alex says again. "Can't you see, Leo—?"

"It is you who has to see, Alex," the Russian cuts in, his words and his smile razor-sharp now. "Kokanakis Wines will join the 21st century with or without you, my friend."

He will drop off a new contract next week.

iv.

Sitting on the side of her bed in her nightie, *Yiayiá* looks at the wall opposite, where a crucifix hangs beside her wedding picture with Gio. She is not praying. She used to kneel by her bed as a child, on a rag rug her mother had made, so proud that she could recite Our Father Who Art in Heaven all the way through. You didn't think about what the words meant, you just recited them because God ruled all of life and having Him on your side was as necessary as breathing. Ninety years later she wishes she could still believe that.

"Because this mess we're in, all of it is my fault," she tells her beloved Gio. "If you could have seen that Russian sitting in his chair at the table, his belly full of *baklava* and *raki*, his mouth smiling. Not his eyes. Our existing contract will expire on November 30th, he said. He will email us the new one and 'will be honoured if we would allow him to entertain us with dinner at his villa to celebrate our signing it.'"

And what did you say, asks Gio's voice?

Yiayiá looks up at his picture.

"You know what I thought: Over My Dead Body."

Gio's chuckle ripples inside her heart.

Yiayiá was seventeen when war and a boy called Giorgio with wavy black hair started to crumble her belief in God. Two years earlier, on May 20, 1941, German paratroopers had dropped out of the sky above Crete, hundreds of them drifting down, silent as balloons, opening fire as soon as they were within range of the ground. Most of Crete's men were away, fighting on the mainland. Allied soldiers and the island's remaining men, women and older children fought back with rusty rifles left over from earlier wars, with pitchforks, knives, gasoline bombs, but there was no way to stop planeloads of Germans, tanks, trucks full of munitions from landing. After the Battle of Crete they took the islanders' chickens, eggs, lambs, sheep, cheese. By the winter of 1942 people were starving. God sent snails, thousands of them slithering along roads, paths, hiding under bushes, climbing walls, enough for every pot. Seeing this as a sign that she too must find a way to help, *Yiayiá* joined a resistance group taking food and medicines to high mountain villages, dodging German patrols, praying every step of the way.

Cherry blossoms were pretty white clouds in one of the villages' central square when Gio smiled at her. She may have just turned seventeen but she knew in that instant that he was her man. Less than a year later, hiding in a cave high up on a mountainside, she and Gio watched the Nazis herd all the men in a village below, mostly grandfathers and boys, into an olive grove. Their rifles pop-pop-popped in the crisp mountain air. Bodies dropped. Reprisals for a resistance attack on a nearby weapons depot, whispered Gio, holding her, both of them trembling. The only God she knew wanted her to push him away. But why should she obey an all-seeing, all-knowing Father who allowed this Nazi evil?

She and Gio married as soon as the war ended, then watched Greece's new British-backed government round up fellow resistance members who had been yesterday's heroes, declare them Communist enemies of the state and ship them off to labour camps as inhuman as any Russia's Stalin had set up. Managing to secure the papers they needed before being exposed, they fled to the United States. Detroit's Greek Orthodox Church sheltered *Yiayiá's* soul there for awhile but as her children grew in freedom and safety her mind began to sprout new ideas. Alexander, her youngest, crystallized them. While her other son and her daughter played, yelled, fought and danced, Alex sat in the grass talking to columns of ants, or taking a flower apart. When she and Gio insisted that their children secure their futures with post-secondary education, Alex joined the army and went to Vietnam – to see a wider world, he said – then became a hippy far away in England. Had his first baby without even marrying! How dare anyone decree which living beings are sacrosanct, he wrote in a letter home, answering her demand to know why. Leaving her no choice but to reject either her son or the God she had grown up with.

Now, sitting on her bed before going to sleep, the best moments of her day are these, shared with her beloved. "Remember, Gio?" she asks him, her mind replaying their first time making love in a mountain pasture. "Oh, and remember?" So many happy, carefree, excruciating memories come alive to chase away aches and pain and worry, so many worries, when Gio is with her, his love a flame inside her that does not go out, his voice as clear to her here in Crete as her own. Though after tonight's dinner it's hard to know how she can go on, how to find the strength.

"Oh Gio," she says, "I was a successful business woman for so many years, you know I was. So how could I have let this happen?"

Yes how, Gio echoes. When Leonid Salin first proposed the loan, you must have wondered why he was willing to fund your winery?

All she can come up with by way of an answer is what she thought at the time were the Russian's gentle eyes. Salin had built a villa down the road in the uninhabited heart of the valley, and said wines were his hobby, particularly those made with heritage grapes. Would they mind if he came back to tour the vineyards and winery? Two weeks later they celebrated signing their loan/supply contract with him at his north shore resort. His wife preferred to remain in Moscow where she had a law practice and saw to their children's needs, he told *Yiayiá* at dinner. His Cretan villa, built to his specifications, was his sanctuary. Lots of wealthy Russians lived in Europe, she thought. She could have asked him what a 'computer specialist' did precisely but computers and the internet interested her only as much they served her business needs.

'You must always be vigilant,' her father had hammered that into her during the war. 'Know who you can trust.' But she had not been careful enough.

"I guess I never doubted that we would be solvent," she tells Gio, "because why would Salin invest if we were not rock solid? I thought the clause that gave him our land and business, should we renege on our responsibilities, was just there to protect him from our running off with his capital. So short-sighted of me, so stupid—"

Stop it, my love. Five years ago you were eighty-nine. Where was Alex in all this?

"Pfff, Alex would have signed anything that allowed him to go on making wine." She thinks back. "Also, I think my guard was down because of Salin's upbringing in what was then the Communist Soviet Union." She can still hear the Communist leader of her wartime resistance unit asking rhetorically: 'Why do we take back this town, these munitions, these stolen chickens and bread? To eat them ourselves or sell them, to make ourselves rich? No! To share them equally amongst all of us.'

Gio snorts. Ask a peasant family in Siberia how much of his wealth Joseph Stalin and his henchmen ever shared.

In the kitchen, on the other side of the wall *Yiayiá* can hear Dion filling the kettle.

"I'm so glad to have my granddaughter here with us, Gio. She was so alone back there on the other side of world, so bound up by I don't know what. All winter the only times I have seen her smile are when she comes out of the barnyard with a basket of eggs. And now what will happen to her?"

Yiayiá was relieved to hand over the winery's bookkeeping accounts to Dion. Her ankles swell when she stands for too long at the stove. Acid scours the lining of her stomach. For the last few weeks she has seldom walked further than to Irina's garden down the road.

"All I want now is to be with you," she hears the wail in her voice. Gio hates the sound of wailing. "But first, I made this mess so before I go I need to fix it somehow. For Alex and Dion."

Gio is silent, thinking in the slow way he used to when they had a problem to solve so she waits, her spine aching now with the strain of sitting upright on the bed, until:

There's always a way to get what we need, it's just a matter of seeing it, her husband tells her. Good and bad live back to back, flip sides of the same coin, we know this my darling, you and me. War wipes out a village. A screaming maniac destroys a beautiful young life. And still new futures grow. So get into bed, my sweet Dionysia. Forget everything for now and sleep, knowing that more possibilities exist in every moment than anyone can see. Until we do.

Laying her head on her pillow, *Yiayiá* smiles a little in spite of herself, because Gio is right. Destruction wreaks havoc everywhere and yet a flower is just right for the bee buzzing into it. Winds demolish whatever lies in their path but also scatter next year's seeds. And through it all Gio, bless his dear heart, remains with her, so close.

Vines

Roots reach for food,
rope-strong trunks twist
up to the sun,
florets open,
hermaphrodite vines
fertilize themselves as
leaves broaden,
their green deepening
as summer weather ripens
this year's grapes, and
angels hover.

i.

Dion stows *Yiayiá's* prescriptions and bags of sugar, flour, salt in the winery's Fiat, parked in a lot across the street from Rethymnon's Old Town lanes. It's a sunny morning and, errands done, she'll treat herself to coffee on her favourite cafe patio at a junction of cobblestone lanes where an ancient Roman fountain still pours water out of the mouth of a concrete lion. She needs to think about finances, how to interest a new bank or a government or European Union development agency in a climate-conscious winemaker.

Proprietors are rolling up their *tavernas'* metal shutters, delivery men are unloading dollies stacked with cases of food and beer, a few tourists are photographing themselves beside the fountain.

Guessing where they come from can be tricky. Two big guys strolling by, wearing baseball caps and basketball shoes, may not be Americans; a pink-skinned man in flapping shorts and a woman wearing a serviceable cross-body handbag might not be Brits; and that uber-fit, mirthless couple striding one behind the other in shapeless cargo pants are not necessarily German; style and what comes across as exclusionary hauteur do often distinguish the French but Finns, Swedes, Italians, Norwegians, Danes, Romanians are a challenge. As for the group of twenty-something travellers striking poses with the concrete lion now, their long hair and jeans, flip-flops or sandals, tank tops and ear buds make them impossible to pigeonhole.

A pair of local business men — fitted suits, open-necked shirts, briefcases — walk by, one of them bald, looking at his phone. The other, tall, his salt and pepper hair blown dry, sends her a smile. Good looking Greek men in tourist squares often like to connect, if only in a moment of fantasy, with a woman sitting alone. No thanks though. Dion's body is no longer a playground. The only man she can imagine bedding now would have to be so much more than good looking. Strong, virile, sensitive, intelligent, is there a man anywhere in this crazy-violent mythless world who would know how to lay her open, to enter the very centre of who she is, where ecstasy must live?

Movement at the corner of the little square catches her eye. A woman covered from head to toe in a black abaya and a face *niqāp* has crept out of a side alley, staying close to the wall. Dion watches her look behind her then around the square before scurrying into a lane that leads down to Rethymnon's harbour. Not a tourist.

She can't be from Crete though. This island in the middle of the Mediterranean, so close to Europe to the north, to Turkey and the Middle East, and to Africa just three hundred kilometres to the south, has a complicated history. Canada has one of the world's most diverse populations but news from places so many of its people came from always felt as if it was happening far away. Here it defines every day. Millions of migrants who walked thousands of kilometres to Europe five years ago are living in a refugee camp on the island of Lesbos, others still try to steal ashore in boats. Not identifiable Muslims though. A hundred years ago the Ottoman Empire and Greece exchanged Muslims living in Greece for Greek Orthodox Christians residing in Turkey. Muslims still do not walk Crete's streets. And strict Muslims don't allow their covered-up women to go out alone. This one is moving fast. Scared.

Dion fishes some coins out of her jeans' pocket to cover her bill and follows the woman into the alley. Curious, but also to make sure she's safe.

The black-robed figure hurries past jewelry, leather goods, postcard stores, a *taverna's* outside tables, chairs tipped against them at mid-morning. She crosses the street above the harbour. People on the sidewalk stop to watch. Dion crosses after her, to see if the woman is meeting someone.

A shadeless quayside plaza beside the harbour's ferry dock is empty. The woman chooses a bench beside a ticket and snacks kiosk that is closed. The overnight ferry from Athens is docked at the pier, taking on cargo for its return trip tonight. Is the woman going to sit here for the next six or seven hours, waiting to board? Is someone going to bring her luggage? She must be roasting inside all that black. Dion saunters into the plaza as if taking a stroll on a sunny morning. Comes close enough to see how grubby is the woman's abaya. She's here alone, Dion can feel it.

"*Kali méra,*" she says. (Good morning.) The woman's eyes, all that is visible of her face, are large, brown, expressionless. They flick away, but not before Dion picks up fear. She stops. "Speak English?"

The woman ignores her. Dion can take her cue and walk away, leave the woman to whatever fate awaits her, or she can probe a little. She points to the bench.

"Mind if I sit?"

Long pause, then:

"It's not my bench." Voice husky, English fluent but odd. Dion sits down a few feet away.

"I saw you up the street and just want to make sure you're okay."

No response.

"I'm Dion."

Maybe a sniffle, nothing more.

"Are you hungry?" Because dressed like that, sneaking through the streets, how could she have eaten? Where did she sleep? Several stories on the BBC World News recently have been about Arab women escaping their shut-down lives and if this is one of them, then the least Dion can do is help her. "I have some euros and there's an out-of-the-way cafe up an alley on the other side of the road," she says. "We could get breakfast."

No response. Dion shows no sign of leaving. Hears a sigh finally. Brown eyes behind the *niqāp* turn towards her, flashing hunger, need overlaid by suspicion.

"It's okay," Dion tells her. "I'm in town shopping and I saw you and," Dion makes a face, "if you're in some kind of trouble you're pretty conspicuous out here."

The woman nods, does not look at her but gets up.

Except for a couple of ancient Cretan men and the husband and wife who run it, the cafe is empty. Dion orders a huge spinach and cheese breakfast pastry and coffee. The woman unclips her *niqāp*, eats quickly. Her face, under its headscarf, is oval, her skin golden. Hard to tell her age. Mascara applied at least a day ago has smudged below her eyes. Why would a woman hiding her face wear make up, Dion wonders? Satiated finally, the woman sits back in her chair.

"Thank you, Dion." She does not smile. "My name is Amina."

Over by the kitchen doorway the cafe's owner and his wife have begun to shoot glances at them, spitting staccato Greek at each other, their whispers elevated by something not friendly. The two ancients are also eying Dion and her guest.

"I'm sorry to say, but the abaya is a bit of an eyesore around here," says Dion, "especially if you're trying to hide."

Amina looks around fearfully then unwinds her headscarf. Long, black, lustrous hair is revealed. The cafe owners' voices pause, mumble.

So, she can't be too devout, thinks Dion.

"Any chance you can lose the rest too?" She nods towards some stairs at the back of the room. "There's a washroom up there."

Ten minutes later Amina comes back down with the abaya bundled under her arm and an expensive leather handbag over her shoulder. She's wearing a pink silk blouse and ankle-length white capris. Freshly made up, she would have the body of a model except that, uncovered now, her shoulders are rigid, her chin a little too defiant.

"I was going to put this in the trash but—" Her eyes dart towards the cafe's owners, who are starting to spit words again.

Dion gets up, crosses the room to pay their bill. News doesn't take long to spread, especially when it involves a beautiful woman who is obviously on the run.

A boutique hotel on the seafront has clean cubicles, toilet seat covers, soft paper, wrapped soaps, individual cloth towels, good mirrors, easy chairs. Dion often stops here before her forty-minute drive back to the winery. Today she makes sure the cubicles are all unoccupied before using one, washing up, checking her hair. Amina just stands there holding her bundle.

"You could get rid of it in there if you want to," Dion indicates a white plastic-lined wicker garbage container by the sink. "By the time it's emptied no one will connect it to you."

Amina stuffs her abaya, *niqāp* and scarf into the garbage then washes her hands. For too long, obsessively rubbing them with soap, rinsing, rubbing them again until Dion puts a hand on her arm, hands her a towel then takes her to one of the easy chairs, and sits down in the other one. Because who is this woman, and what should they do next?

"If I am found and taken back, I will be locked up in the dark, for years maybe, or my whole life," she tells Dion. "That's what they do to wives who try to leave."

"Who's they, the Saudis?" One of the escapees Dion read about was from there. Amina nods.

"Not that I'm a Saudi... except technically."

"A technical Saudi? What's that?"

"A person too stupid to know what she was doing," says Amina. Her face looks about the same age as Dion's. If it were not harshened by anguish it would stop traffic. It might anyway.

"Okay look," says Dion, "let's trade stories. I'm Canadian. I gave up a government career six months ago to come and live in Crete with my father and grandmother, to try and keep their winery in a mountain valley west of here from going under." Nothing from Amina. "You? Do I hear an American accent?"

The tip of Amina's tongue flicks out, runs around her lips, distrust still flickering in her eyes. Dion smiles, waits.

"Yes, you do, a Philadelphia accent originally but," she sighs again, "that was twenty-two years ago, before I married. I was eighteen, he was thirty-eight. My parents arranged it."

"An arranged marriage in the U.S.?" says Dion. "I didn't know—Sorry, it's not my business."

"It's okay, it's a good question. My parents are devout Muslims. They did everything for me but refusing them was not an option. Anyway, I didn't want to say no! My Saudi fiancée was good looking, exotic, polite, rich, and so much more of a man than any of the boys I knew."

"Your knight in shining armour?" Dion pictures a Philadelphia bungalow, prayers five times a day, a young girl's claustrophobia.

"In tin armour as it turned out, who swept me off my silly little teenaged feet." She tells Dion about the lavish wedding he paid for, and about arriving at his Saudi palace on the outskirts of Riyadh, where all these women and children were living behind a grill, out of sight, speaking a language she barely understood. "I thought they were relatives," she says. "And at first it was good. My husband taught me about sex, how to please him, how to enjoy it. No babies came though, and one night I saw him go into another woman's room. That's how I discovered I was one of several wives. No one had told me. Most of the kids in the palace were his! So I thought okay, I'll become his most desirable wife." Amina keeps glancing towards the door.

She's right to be afraid, thinks Dion. Who knows who has followed her to Crete, and if they stay too long in the washroom someone will come to check on them. Will be able to describe Amina to anyone looking for her.

"Do you want me to book you into a hotel, or an airbnb?" Dion asks her, "Or drive you to the airport in Chania?" Amina shakes her head.

"To do any of that means using my passport, and my husband will trace that."

"So how did you get this far?"

Accompanying her husband to Istanbul two days ago, Amina knew she was leaving, so watched him lock their passports and a manilla envelope full of American dollars in the hotel room safe and memorized his pass code. Later, pleading a need to rest while he was in a business meeting before dinner, she opened the safe, hid herself in her abaya and *niqāp* and fled. Lots of unidentifiable Muslim women were boarding Turkey's coastal ferries and Amina would not have to use her passport for domestic travel in Turkey. A second, smaller ferry took her to an offshore island. From there a wad of U.S. dollars found her a fisherman willing to smuggle her into Crete. A bus brought her into Rethymnon early this morning.

"And if there really is an Allah or God or Whoever receiving prayers up there," she says, "surely He or She doesn't want me to have to go back and spend my one precious life locked up, my husband's slave?"

Emotions fleeing across Amina's face as she tells her story make Dion believe what she's hearing. And damn it, this is one problem she can do something about.

"Come with me to our winery," she says. "No one will find you there and it'll give you a safe place and time to think."

"No no, I couldn't do that."

"Sure you can. There's a spare bedroom we use for storage and my father would be the last person in the world to object." *Yiayiá* will listen and watch before casting judgement, then will give Amina a bed.

Pines along Crete's north coast highway flash by but not until they turn off onto the road into the White Mountains' foothills can Dion be sure they are not being followed. A village comes up. Dion stops, backs into a side alley, kills the engine. Half an hour later four farmers' and shepherds' pickup trucks, one donkey laden with firewood, and one bus have passed them. Her passenger must be safe.

Winding deeper into the hills, she asks why Amina left.

"Did you not succeed in becoming your husband's favourite wife?"

"Oh sure, doing that wasn't hard. What a man like my husband likes most is to see his woman writhe under his touch. But still I didn't get pregnant. So then I painted pictures for him on the pillow of how my studying business, combined with my English, would be useful to him on business trips, and with my body and face covered, what harm could come from it? And he allowed me to go to university in Riyadh."

Dion's eyes leave the road to glance at her passenger. Her tone of voice and colour seem to be reviving. Gestures begin to join her flow of words.

"After I graduated with a Masters of Business Administration my husband started taking me with him all over the world. To translate memos, reports, contracts during the day, then keep his bed warm and interesting at night." Amina looks out the car window. "A win-win, he liked to tell me."

Dion glances at Amina's slim body and long graceful legs as she turns onto a road that twists into an inland valley. Pink oleanders are blooming on its shoulders, poppies, daisies bobbing among the wildflowers colouring its ditches.

"So why did you leave?"

"A win-win for him. For me not so much. Don't get me wrong, I like sex and he was good in bed, but at home the other wives were jealous. And when we travelled I was never allowed to go anywhere by myself, to shop or eat or sightsee like women I'd see in London or Paris or Moscow." Amina looks out the window. "Then a couple of months ago a new thing happened. A business associate of my husband's, an Australian closer to my age than his, came to a conference in New York and looked at me. I mean really looked into my eyes when my husband was not noticing, and it was as if he could see me right through all my coverings." She turns to Dion. "Are you married?"

"No." Another village, roadside shops, houses, a church. Dion slows the car, checks the rearview mirror. "Why?"

"Well, I wondered if you know how it is to have someone see right into who you are. When the Australian did that something inside me did a somersault and I was so afraid my husband would pick it up, but he went right on talking to a man across the table from him. So, to make a long story short, the Australian came to our hotel room while my husband was tied up in a meeting and thought I was resting and changing for dinner." Amina laughs, a bit maniacally. "And I opened the door even though I wasn't covered. He'd brought a mini-bar whiskey for himself and an orange juice for me and just wanted to chat, he said, to know me. And he was tall and funny and I heard myself laughing with him. Enjoying myself. But, 'I better go,' he said after a bit, and the next day he went back to Australia." The Cretan village disappears behind the Fiat, vineyards on one side of the road now, olive trees on the other as they wind further into the valley. "Which was probably good because I had been imagining all these sexy scenes with him." Dion takes her eyes off the road again to glance at her passenger.

"And you've left your husband to follow him to Australia?"

"No no. Well, I don't know," she says. "Freedom, that's what I tasted in my few moments with him. And I want more of that, want to wear and eat and drink and work and play however and wherever I want. And I want it now, before I'm too old or sick or stuck in my life to make it happen."

Dion thinks of her gully, of Eros' visit.

"I hear you, sister."

Her husband will be outraged, dishonoured, vengeful, Amina knows that. He will cast his net widely to find her.

"And he has the ear of governments and business interests all over the world."

"Not in our valley." Dion smiles. When next she looks, Amina's eyes are closed, her head lolling against the back of the passenger seat, fear and obstinance and courage painted into a face that in repose mirrors all of its forty years.

Under them the Fiat's engine purrs. Dion shifts down, turns into a side road. The winery's stone building is just ahead. Dion gears down again, turns into the driveway and cuts the engine. Amina wakens, startled. Looks around in fear.

"It's okay," Dion tells her, "we're home. But listen, I don't use social media at all here. Back in Canada I used to check Facebook, Instagram, Twitter about every five minutes. For what, I mean really? Now all I use my phone for is to read the news. And I've been thinking, while you're here you better not post on any social media sites either, right?"

Amina nods.

"I left my phone in Istanbul. My husband has a tracker on it."

Yiayiá serves sweet bread and coffee, listens to Amina's story then instructs Dion and her father to convert one of the winery's storerooms into a bedroom.

"You take as long as you need," the old lady tells Amina, "to feel safe."

ii.

Dion is at Kokanakis Winery's computer searching for grants or loans or any other way to leverage the winery's assets to find capital. Outside the office window *Yiayiá* is teaching Amina, who is kneeling in the vegetable garden in a t-shirt and a pair of Dion's jeans hitched at the waist with a belt, how to find onions that are ready to be pulled.

"The bulb might be showing a little, might be a little purple. Yes, that one. Now tug. Harder, to break the roots."

A week after her arrival at the winery Amina spends most of her time with *Yiayiá*, listening and watching as the old lady shows her how to roll out phyllo pastry, prepare the filling for the morning pastries. Yesterday Dion came out of the office to find them painting *Yiayiá's* nails with polish Amina must have brought with her. Why hadn't she thought of that, Dion wondered a little enviously? Not that the old lady would ever have allowed it from her.

Late at night, after the oldies have gone to bed, she and Amina have started to share mugs of Cretan herbal tea in Dion's bedroom, Amina curled up in her easy chair wearing one of Dion's nighties, the world theirs to dissect.

Now, outside, a car engine comes into the driveway, shuts off. Dion leaves her desk to look out the window.

"Good morning." Leonid Salin is coming towards the garden, holding a leather file folder.

The original plan was for Amina to hole up in her bedroom while she was hiding here. Her husband would not embarrass himself by releasing the news that his wife had run away, she said, but he would not stop canvassing trusted contacts to look for her.

"Well then maybe it'd be safer for us to hide you in plain sight," Dion said at the family's midday dinner a couple of days later. "Because if someone should drop by unexpectedly and see you, and word gets out that there's a woman hiding at the winery... The last thing you want is for people like Leo Salin to start asking questions. Why don't we say you're a friend of mine from the States?"

"No no, I can't do that." The fear Dion had seen down at Rethymnon's harbour was not far below the surface.

"You can't hide forever, dude," said Dion. "What do you think, Dad?"

Alex put down his soup spoon.

"It's a good idea Amina, and sustainable for as long as you like." He gestured at a bowl of roses Amina had arranged in the centre of the table. "We'll call you Rose."

"And we'll make up a whole backstory for you," said Dion, "where and how we met, why you're here."

They have not had time to practise using it though. And this must be the first time in her adult life that Amina has met a stranger without the protection of a mask and shapeless black robe. Dion races out of the office, through the kitchen.

Salin has reached the vegetable patch.

"So, who do we have here?" He runs an eye over Amina, who is on her feet now, wiping nervous hands on Dion's jeans.

"Rose," *Yiayiá's* chin is raised, imperious, "a friend of Dion's from America."

"Hello," says Amina. Salin smiles, then turns to *Yiayiá*.

"Is Alex around?"

"No."

"He's working in one of his other vineyards," says Dion, joining them. "Can I do something for you?"

Salin holds the folder in his hand out to *Yiayiá*.

"I've brought a draft of our new contract. I'd be grateful if you and Alex would review it and then come for dinner at my villa to sign it."

Yiayiá looks at her granddaughter. Dion takes the folder.

"I have to go away for awhile," says Salin, "but I'll be in touch." He gives Amina another smile. "Perhaps you'll join us for that dinner, Rose, if you're still here."

Alex opens the leather folder before sitting down to dinner at midday, glances at its contents, then relegates it to a sideboard where invitations to wine shows he can not afford to attend and keys and random bits and pieces of paper are ignored.

iii.

Melodious the donkey is chewing steadfastly late one afternoon when Dion leaves her paperwork to climb over the stone wall. The two weeks that have passed since she posed for Theo feel like a century, in a different world. He won't be there today, of course he won't, and that'll be fine. Last night she told Amina about sunbathing nude in her gully and Theo's appearing, about his desire to paint desire.

"Interesting."

"No it's not. I never went back."

"What? I thought you said that gully is your special place! You have to claim it back." Amina wriggled deeper into her chair, warm bedroom light picking up an impish curve in her cheekbones as she looked at Dion over her teacup. "I can wait for you in the oak trees if you want, so you'll feel safe."

"No need," said Dion, Theo's rain-clean smile springing up in her memory, his voice describing her crows' feet: *See the beauty in the story they tell, about what it is to be you.*" He'll be long gone now, off to find his muse elsewhere. Still, she would like to spread out her rug again, maybe read or dream or play with Eros in her gully's sunlit privacy, and Amina will know where she is.

He's sitting in the same spot, his body bent to study something in the grass.

Hearing her, he leaps up, grinning. Has been coming here every day, he says, waiting, hoping.

"Seriously?"

"Why not? There's a lot here to gather for dinner, and to draw." He takes her rug, lays it out.

Sketching days turn into a week, two weeks, three. Theo doesn't like to chat while he draws, answering questions with monosyllables. At first her mind flaps like a trapped moth, trying to escape the silence. Gradually though her need dissolves, freeing her to notice the way the breezes play with the leaves on the bushes below them, the way Theo's facial expressions shift slightly as he draws, the way her neck, her back feel under his gaze.

She never knows if he'll be at her gully. April storms sometimes sweep through this valley, bringing winds and rain and sometimes even reddish Sahara Desert sand from the far side of the Libyan Sea to the south. Sometimes without explanation Theo is just absent.

He will eventually ask for more of her body, she knows that. Desire is what he wants to paint, and there's a pot of that inside of her, bubbling away now. Which is strange because, sweet as he is, pointy-boned, intense, impossibly young Theo is not her kind of man. Which is lucky because once she's given him what he sees in her, he will tire of her. And young, beautiful women all over the island will model for a lithe young artist with curly hair and seemingly unlimited energy, and do whatever else he wants.

The afternoons warm up. Sometimes, as she hurries through the vines, Bowie tries to follow. She shoos him back towards the house. A wet-tongued dog is the last thing she wants to add to her gully now. Birds' wings thrum, sapphire-blue bumble bees buzz while she poses in tank tops and cut-off jean shorts, her body and Theo's and a spiked purple stink weed down in the stream bed emitting a panoply of odours. She begins to observe more closely how the set of his shoulders and head, and the loose lankiness of his legs, folded to make a support for his sketchpad, reflect Theo's moods, how the sun brings whatever part of her he is drawing to life, how it highlights the colours of the pebbles imbedded in her gully's walls, how her neck, her shoulders, her ears, the underside of her arms sense the world around them as he draws, the way their expressions shift as she moves. Sometimes, even as Theo draws a part of her she does not associate with sex — an elbow, a knee — subtle, unmistakable, inexplicable desire flutters down inside her belly.

One day she brings a half-full bottle of leftover wine with snacks she has taken to packing. Theo spreads her rug inside her gully, where the sunlight is gently diffused. Her cut-offs' fringe is a few inches from the top of her legs. He asks her to lie on her side so he can focus on her thighs. She runs a surreptitious hand down her upper leg. Last time she had a shower she noticed a few cellulite pockmarks.

"It's okay," he says, sensing her self-consciousness.

No it's not, but what can she do about that now? She lies back on the rug anyway.

When finally he puts down his charcoal she hesitates to look at his work. Her leg in his first sketch is invested with sinuous energy. His second, third, fourth drawings extend the thigh, lightening it, lifting its energy off the page. In the last one he has thickened it, making it heavy, fecund, hungry. A drawing of what he must have seen. Her face flushes.

She busies herself unwrapping a package of *Yiayiá's spanakopita*, hands him the wine bottle. Asks him where he lives.

"On a mountain top," he says, "in a pirate's castle."

"Oh?" She points in the direction of the ridge top overlooking the valley. "Up there?"

"You know it?" He grins. "And one day I saw you come out of the olives—"

"You saw me? You mean that day, when you came by, you were stalking me?"

"No! I just..." Rabbit holes open inside her brain: How many times has she read about lonely middle-aged women being lured gradually, seductively—

"I'm an artist, I can't help looking, wanting to see."

And a conman or potential who-knows-what wouldn't have admitted spying on her. And in the end the only way to avoid living inside any of the many mental prisons life makes for women is to to rely on your instincts.

Theo tries to soften her distrust by telling her about his life. His uncle owns a *taverna* in Chania and lets him work a few shifts when he needs money for food or art supplies.

Snacks at the end of their sessions – rusks dipped in olive oil flavoured with oregano or rosemary, *Yiayiá's* pastries, carrots from her garden, wine or *raki* – and chats become part of their routine.

Theo tells her he is twenty-eight, and has been drawing since the age of eight, first tourist portraits down at the harbour in Iraklio (Heraklion in English,) where his mother works as a jewelry maker. By the age of ten he was selling his work to its subjects.

"There must be photographs of little me in Spanish, Japanese, Israeli, Brazilian living rooms," he laughs. His father, an American serviceman stationed in Germany in the 1980's, who had a holiday fling with his mother, took an interest when Theo was in his early teens. "Who knows why," says Theo. "A midlife crisis maybe? He paid for me to come to Boston, where he was stationed then, so I could study at a high school that specialized in the arts." Theo was supposed to go on to university but he didn't like his macho military father much, and in high school he discovered El Greco. Who came from Crete! By the time Theo graduated he had his heart set on studying in Venice, following El Greco's footsteps. A scholarship allowed him to leave the U.S., study and live on tips he earned as a late night bartender in Venice's Piazza San Marco. Then in 2010, two years after the world economy crashed, Greece's debt load and the austerity measures that followed threatened to put his home country out of business.

Dion nods. When her father brought *Yiayiá* home to Crete and revived the family vines to help both of them heal, he knew nothing about the tax evasion, government corruption and blatant dishonesty that forced Greece to beg the European Union for debt relief. When Dion arrived late last year and saw the devastation that had resulted in Kokanakis Wines' account books, she was appalled but, sitting over an after-dinner glass of *raki* at the kitchen table, her father just shrugged:

"Your island is occupied for hundreds and hundreds of years by Venetians then Turks then Germans. They rule your life, take everything that's yours, leave you with nothing. So, when finally you regain your country and achieve independence, what do you know about fiscal responsibility?"

"Baaf," said *Yiayiá*. "It's simpler than that. Stone martins in the hen house, how can they help themselves?"

Tourism's shrinkage meant Theo's mother couldn't pay her rent. Theo faced two choices: join Venice's army of full time waiters and bartenders catering to herds of tourists flocking off ten-storey cruise ships, and hope to make enough to support his mother and himself with no time for art, or come back to Crete, live with his mother, scratch out a living doing odd jobs, sketching, whatever would pay him enough euros for their rent, and also, hopefully, do his own work. When German holiday makers began to return to the island, wanting gold necklaces, rings and earrings, and cruise ships started docking again in Iraklio, Theo felt free to leave the city on an old motorcycle with nothing but a knapsack full of pads, pencils, paints and a change of clothes. The castle ruin overlooking Dion's gully has been his home ever since.

"Except when I'm working for my uncle, or hanging with my friend Kiri, whose father supplies my uncle with fish, or helping another uncle harvest his strawberries or oranges, or olives later in the year. The rest of the time, up in the castle, I try to paint like El Greco," his smile is lopsided. "You know, what lies deeper than the surface of a subject. And you? What's your story?"

Her *curriculum vitae* sputters out.

"Is there a man?" he asks.

"Is that your business?" she counters, because to answer 'yes' would be a lie. Where is this man, he would ask? And another lie, a whole web of them, would be required. Answering 'no' would trigger questions that, even if unasked, would hang in the air: Why not? Are you not interested in men? Or is there something wrong with you?

The therapist she visited a couple of years after Teddy died suggested that her failure to build a satisfying love relationship might be collateral damage caused by her family tragedy. Perhaps the pain of loss is making you afraid to risk closeness, she said. Dion has no idea what to do with that. Understanding does not equal healing, anymore than running, weight-lifting, Omming through meditation classes do. Facts are facts, they make you who you are. And pain is pain.

She finds herself telling Theo about Teddy, how he built a pair of cardboard wings, jumped off the roof of the chicken coop and broke his leg when she was about five. She would carry a glass of lemonade to him on the couch, admire his huge white cast full of multi-coloured drawings his friends had made. Later, studying aeronautic engineering at university, he took up hang gliding: jumping off mountains to float on airstreams under a multi-coloured canopy. "Oh D," he told her, his voice so excited on the phone from Vancouver, where he was working one summer, "you gotta come out and try it. And go surfing on Vancouver Island, and hike into forests so old no one's probably ever been where you're standing." So of course, visiting him, she had to strap herself to him in his hang-glider, throw herself off a cliff into the sky with him. The purity of awe and her breathing and the rush of air as far below the sea broke against the coast is a feeling she can still summon. Back in Toronto, riding the subway every morning then an elevator up into a government labyrinth of office cubicles began to feel like claustrophobia. Maybe she would quit her job and join Teddy, who had just landed a tech job in Vancouver. She would talk to him about it when he came east to spend a last holiday weekend with their grandparents outside Detroit.

"But before I could do that a madman in a cube van jumped the curb and smashed the front window of in my grandparents' restaurant while Teddy and my *Pappoús* were playing backgammon in a front booth." She doesn't talk about daring the world to knock her down too after that, by hanging off the roof of Toronto's CN Tower, one of the tallest structures in the world, on a guy wire, or by testing her little red Toyota's capacity for highway speed in the wee hours, or by drinking, dancing, smoking weed but the fact is that she is not a daredevil like Teddy. She does not want to die and the high wire between ecstasy and hopelessness has no safety net below it when you've lost your big brother.

Sometimes now, working alongside her grandmother in the kitchen while *Yiayiá* is busy cooking, Dion tries to get her to talk about her loss of *Pappoús*. Maybe sharing their grief will help them, and ease a strain that has always bristled between her grandmother and her father. But *Yiayiá's* lips remain tight closed around the shell guarding her pain.

"Then last November I turned thirty-nine," Dion tells Theo. He might as well know the hollow, middle-aged husk of loneliness he is drawing. His only response is another question.

"Friends?"

Her shoulders lift. Back in Canada she had a few coffee shop pals from work. Her university friends have dispersed into marriages, children, faraway home towns.

"Canada's a big country. To see each other cost more than any of us could afford." Here her friendships with Cretan women are about food, trading eggs for tomatoes with Maria down the road, accepting homemade yogurt as a gift from another neighbour, reciprocating with her grandmother's dynamite egg bread, sharing the occasional coffee with *Yiayiá*, her friend Irina and Irina's pregnant granddaughter Georgina. Dion says nothing about Amina. "Sometimes though I feel like my best friend is the peace I can find sitting in that tiny church carved out of the rock just outside our village. Neither my Dad or *Yiayiá* are religious but my grandmother says it's been a place of worship for thousands of years, that the griffin on top of the iconostasis and the seeing eye painted on the ceiling came down from the ancient Minoans who once lived here. I love that." Theo nods.

"Some say the Virgin Mary represents the ancient goddess, Sofia, who was queen of wisdom, before priests and religion and politics started messing with people's heads. For me there must be no dependence on any kind of thought prison, religious or political or personal."

"Oh? What about your El Greco, wasn't he a religious painter?" She remembers seeing his oddly elongated saints in a university art history course she took.

"He was a man of his time, yes, but so much more also, the way his paintings used line and colour to go down into places the church will never talk about."

She chews on a rusk.

"What about your friends, is a girlfriend a personal thought prison?"

He catches her eye, its smile.

"Sometimes." He packs their leftovers into her knapsack, leaving her no wiser about his love life than he is about hers. He looks up. "Will I see you tomorrow?"

She nods. It's his turn to smile.

"We've been doing this for awhile now. Do you think you might feel safe enough to make like a tourist on our beaches and let your breasts out of their prison?"

iv.

"Something about you is different." *Yiayiá* rolls out pastry on the kitchen table, pretending not to look quizzical while Dion drinks her coffee in the early morning coziness of the wood-fired stove/oven. Scrap wood from olive trees and vine pruning and fallen branches from a long deceased oak at the back of the property are piled in a bin beside it. "Is there a lottery you've won?" The edges of *Yiayiá's* lips quirking up tell Dion that Amina has told her about Theo and Dion's modelling sessions. Bowie, lying on his mat by the stove, looks up as if he too is wondering.

"I wish," Dion aims her tone of voice towards casual, as if taking off her t-shirt and bra under Theo's gaze were natural as a bee's flight. Because it turns out Theo's right. Finger stumbling nakedness and the rightness of nudity have nothing to do with each other. Even clothed now she can feel the skin of her breasts. A good feeling. So she might as well admit to her project with Theo, explain that he's an artist and she's his model.

No need to mention desire, how Theo positions her body to let late afternoon sunlight and shadow play across what he wants to explore, maybe the curve of her waist or the roundness of a single breast, how his breath jags a little sometimes as he draws page after page, reaching out now and then —"May I?" — before readjusting one of her limbs, his fingers lingering a moment longer than necessary. Or how her skin's nerve endings felt sensitive as a sea barnacle's fronds under water as his left hand hovered over her knee: "May I?" She nodded and then his finger, light as a feather, traced the line of her leg, calf, ankle, foot while his right hand drew and the barnacles turned into slow-moving fire inside her lower abdomen, which she must somehow manage to contain without moaning or moving. Without letting on how pathetically needy she is. Only later in her bedroom, reigniting the sensation with her older, graceful and sanguine imaginary lover, can she relieve it. None of this can she speak about to her grandmother. Still:

"It's amazing how he sees beyond what's in front of his eyes," she explains.

"Ah," *Yiayiá* aims her amusement at her sheet of pastry dough. "I see."

"No you don't, *Yiayiá*! He's twelve years younger than me and not even remotely my type. If we were in a bar or at a party I wouldn't give him a second glance and he'd be dancing up a storm, wouldn't even notice I exist."

Her grandmother cuts her pastry into squares.

"Well why don't you invite this boy artist for dinner," she says, "so we can see for ourselves what type he is?"

When Theo arrives at the winery Dion's heart goes out to him. His shirt is still creased from its box, his jeans pressed. Costing him how many shifts at his uncle's *taverna?* Wild hair trimmed, cheeks shaved, he almost looks like a person she doesn't know. She introduces Amina as Rose, a family friend from the U.S.

The kitchen table is laden with a stew *Yiayiá* has made with a rabbit her friend Irina's nephew gave her in return for strawberries, homemade bread and wine. Sitting at one end of the table, with Alex at the other, Dion's grandmother watches Theo's every move and mannerism as Dion and Amina chat with him. Her face gives nothing away.

It's her grandmother's way of dealing with a world she has never been able to trust, realizes Dion, who also can't stop watching, gauging, trying to perceive what everyone at the table thinks/feels/needs for the same reason. She waits on tenderhooks for her father or *Yiayiá* to ask to see Theo's sketches of her but Alex the Grape seems content to put on a Mozart CD, pour wine, discuss Crete's history with Theo.

"Did you know that your castle was built by a Byzantine pirate?" he asks.

"Yes," says Theo, "in 1185. I looked it up in the library in Chania."

"So did I, when we came here," Dad turns to Dion and Amina/ Rose: "Piracy was big business in these parts for thousands of years, right back to the Minoans and Egyptians, maybe even earlier. Gold, gems, grain, slaves was what they came for, especially slaves. That's why villages on Crete's south coast were built high on the mountain-sides, one house leading into the next so people could see their ships in time to escape unseen up into the heights. Theo's pirate would have stashed his loot here, inland, in a castle protected from the south coast by mountains, and where he could see anyone landing to the north."

"Also, his brother lived here, right below his castle," says *Yiayiá*. Alex and Theo look at her, surprised. Dion's grandmother smiles, enjoying ancestral knowledge that does not come from history books or data bases. "He was abbot of a monastery at the top of our valley. There's a church there now but the place has been holy for four thousand years. There's a natural spring, and Minoan steps leading up to a carved sacrificial stone cup."

"Really! Did the pirate come down at Easter to make his confession?" Dion laughs at the thought and then they are all laughing, even *Yiayiá*, and looking around the table at what feels a bit like a rag-tag family of strays, Dion feels a little well of happiness opening.

"Easter is a big deal in Greece," Theo explains to Dion and Amina/ Rose, "and it's next weekend. So why don't you two come up to the castle on Saturday? Some of the coastal villages send up fireworks at midnight to celebrate Christ's resurrection. They'll be spectacular from up there."

"Well," *Yiayiá* levers herself to her feet. "Tonight you must stay with us," she tells him. "You can't be hiking up a mountainside in the dark." Dion can put a pillow, some sheets and a blanket on a couch/ futon under the window in the fermenting room.

v.

She rides helmet-free, in t-shirt and jeans, behind Theo on the passenger seat of his motorbike, holding onto his ropy-lean chest. Under one of her knees a roll of screening wrapped around long thin slats of wood has been strapped to the side of the bike. His knapsack, heavy with bottles of water and who knows what else, and his usual bag of *horta* are tied behind her on the other side. Dion's pack, on her back, is stuffed with cheese, sausages, a loaf of *Yiayiá's* sweet Easter bread and traditionally dyed hardboiled eggs, wine, water, an extra sweater. Wind tugs at her ponytail. Amina/Rose has stayed behind, pleading a need to rest before she continues her journey.

Theo hides the bike behind some bushes off the road and shoulders his load. The pirate's mountain looks like a rocky hill from her gully but the goat's path they follow is steep. Theo stops, leans down to pluck a dark green shoot out of the weeds.

"Wild asparagus, for our dinner." He puts it into his bag. Another few metres and he stops again, this time to pick a mauve-white, daisy-like flower which he holds out to her. "Milk flower. Bite down on the stem." Thin liquid sweet as a nursing mother's milk trickles onto her tongue. No wonder he can make a life for himself in the wild.

"How do you know all this?" she asks. He grins.

"It's in my blood, I think."

Scents of sage, oregano, rosemary perfume the air as they pick their way up the goat path zigzagging between thorny bushes and a jumble of boulders that must have broken off and rolled down here many millennia ago. Easter church bells ring out across the valley below. Families

Dion knows have all been baking Easter bread, dying hardboiled eggs red, making a traditional bean soup for later tonight, preparing to roast lamb on a spit for tomorrow's celebration feast.

"And you can bet that after tonight's midnight masses guns will be fired into the darkness to celebrate Christ's rising from the dead," Theo tells her as they climb. He does not know that, after their dinner with him, *Yiayiá* morphed into a pious Cretan crone, trying to keep Dion from spending the night in Theo's pirate castle by asking her to go to midnight mass with her.

"Why?" said Dion. "Never once in all my life have I seen you care about Greek Orthodox Easter." The old lady had enough grace to look sheepish.

"I like the way they light candles in the church's chandeliers and swing them, and I'd like to carry a lit candle home afterwards for good luck, the way I did as a girl." What she really wanted was to prevent Dion from having sex and then getting hurt, Dion knows that. But Dad can go with her, and maybe they'll use the occasion to pray for a safe future, because hours at the computer have made clear that there are no grants Kokanakis Wines can apply for, no government incentive programs, no fairy godmothers anywhere out there.

The sun's heat brings beads of sweat to Dion's temples. Theo's sandalled feet grip the steepness ahead. Until a tree, mostly hidden from below by gorse and other prickly bushes, appears above them, its roots anchored under what was once a stone tower. The path circles the base of two ruined towers, the incline nearly vertical. Theo reaches down to give her his hand, then pulls her up onto a green carpet of grass at the top of the world.

Northeast of them Mount Psiloritis, Crete's highest peak, is wreathed in clouds. Below them to the north the valley is a green rug rumpled and creased by hillocks and gorges all the way down to the Aegean Sea, where the sun, descending now towards Crete's snow-covered White Mountains, is laying a path of light to the horizon. Teddy would love this Cretan mountaintop. She pictures him gliding out over their Kokanakis Winery, over a patchwork of vineyards that look magical in this late-day light, their free-growing vines alive in the sun's glow. She would have looked small as a doll when Theo first saw her from up here.

More than eight hundred years of wear and weather have brought down the castle's exposed north and west walls. The south-facing one behind her, about eight feet high, is protected by a platoon of rocky sentinels rising out of the mountain behind it. Sunlight slanting across the grass lands on the east wall: Theo's art gallery. A hand, arm, shoulder, breast, a foot, leg, a curving thigh each have their painted place on pieces of board Theo has hung on nails hammered between the stones. All of the body parts are hers. Centred among them and much larger, sketched and half painted on what looks like paper or canvas, a female body is lying on her side facing away, the muscles of her back taut above cut-offs that accentuate the fullness of hips she has not shown him, yet. Her face, looking over her shoulder at the viewer, is Dion's. Heat prickles her skin, nothing to do with sunshine.

She can't look. Can't not look. Goes closer, can't help herself, her eye judging, finding fault. Unable to accept that this earth-solid, sexually suggestive play of light and shadow could be her. Her throat tightens.

Theo moves to the wall, rubs the edge of the painting between his fingers.

"I made this paper — a printer in Rethymno gives me his scraps — and I love its silky rough texture. Next I'm going to make a one-and-a-half by two-metre canvas with that," he points towards a stack of sticks and a rolled up screen stored under a tarpaulin that, stretched across the top of one of the towers, also protects his paints, brushes, buckets, paper frames, plastic bags stuffed with paraphernalia. Beside them a little gas cooking ring, a pot, utensils, a wash basin with soap and a carefully folded towel make up his living quarters. The nearside corner of the tarp is angled down to funnel rainwater through a pipe into a large plastic barrel. A single mattress covered with an old blanket and a rolled up sleeping bag lies out under the stars, against the west-side stone wall, which is too low to be of any other use. Theo turns to the castle's south wall. "That's where I'll work once the spring rains stop."

She can not find words.

"This light, this air," his bony arm pivots towards the sky, the mountains, the valley, the sunlit sea. "Do you see how powerful they are? It's why the Minoans were worshipping a goddess long before Zeus and Apollo and all the rest came along." Giving Dion time to steady herself.

Not possible. His sweet compassion confirms her need for it, her whole carefully composed outer self threatening to shatter, to leave exposed her naked, snivelling bundle of needs.

"What do you use for a bathroom?"

He points towards the jumble of rocks and bushes behind the castle's south wall.

"Help yourself. I do what the pirate would have done, what humans have done forever really, dig a deep hole, put a log across it, fill it in after awhile and dig another one. For showers there is always the sea, also I have my uncle in Chania..."

When she returns the sun is about to drop behind the White Mountains, shadows darkening, elongating in a light that is almost horizontal. Theo has taken out his sketchpad. Can they use this last hour to work?

"I could lay my blanket on the grass for you."

The woman on the gallery wall trembles as a breeze lifts her paper. Dion sits down, takes off her running shoes. The grass under her feet is soft.

"I don't need a blanket."

Shedding her t-shirt and bra is routine now. A frisky breeze plays across her back, her breasts, nothing but rock, stone, sky watching with Theo. Who, sitting crosslegged now, preparing to draw, looks at wrinkle-eyed, white-skinned her and sees the woman in his painting. Golden sunlight angles lower, begins to leave the woman on the wall. Another gust of breeze rustles the needles of a twisted pine between the towers. She turns to it. Just her and the sky and mountains and breeze. Her arms rise, her bare feet wriggle in the grass. She wants to drop her jeans, her underpants so the mountain air can stroke her belly, her bum. So he can see the line of her buttocks and thighs. Her hands come down of their own accord to undo her fly, pull down her jeans. Stepping out of them starts a tremor inside her belly. She lifts a shoulder. The other one follows. Her eyes, closing, shut out everything but her body's swaying, her hips circling now in curvy freedom to wind-or sun-or grass-made music beyond the reach of her thinking brain. Her bare sides greet the frisky breeze. Which suddenly leaves, replaced by air that carries scents of herbs and flowers and sounds of twittering birds and sheep bells up from the valley. Weight leaves her body, her every cell vibrating, lifting her right leg, toes pointed, ready to step into—

Her eyes, opening to look, see Theo watching. Her leg drops, heavy as lead.

"No," Theo cries, "keep going!"

But her foot, planted in the grass now, does not know any way out of embarrassment, back into that airy lightness. And the sun is behind the mountain now. Chilliness clenches her nipples, raises goosebumps on the skin of her stomach. She crosses her arms, hugging herself. Theo jumps up to get his blanket, wraps her in it.

His fire pit is a circle of stones. He bunches some scraps of newspaper, covers them with twigs and small logs from a pile in the corner. Snuggling in her blanket, she watches the sun send a last, peach then purple hurrah into a few puffs of cloud above the castle. Flames from Theo's fire create a circle of warmth in a gathering darkness that is growing colder.

"What do you do in winter?" she asks. He points towards his bed.

"My sleeping bag's down filled, left over from my American life. Painting is hard in the cold so I tend to work on small pieces, but that's not a problem now." He leaves the circle of firelight, returns with a mug, a glass and a small plastic bottle. "*Raki.*" His uncle makes it. Everybody's uncle or father or grandfather does. Dion has gone exploring with her father enough times to have discovered that no Cretan problem exists that *raki* can not alleviate. Burst a car tire or drive into a ditch or hike into a remote village, and someone will call out "*Raki!*" Now, sitting by the fire beside her, Theo holds his mug out to clink her glass.

"*Yamas.*" He smiles, something Theo doesn't do often. The liquor heats her insides. "You were free there for a moment," he goes on. "Beautiful." She does not reply. He's saying what he thinks she wants to hear. "It must have felt good?"

Still she says nothing. Of course it felt good, more like Great! Amazing! Inhibition, isolation, useless carnal alienation all danced away in one miraculous moment. But even sitting naked inside a blanket that, soft around her body, smells of Theo and earth and a whole stew of unnameable, not-unpleasant pungencies, she only knows how to live inside her one-size-fits-all packaged self. She swallows another swig of *raki*. Theo leaves the fireside again, returns with her clothes and knapsack.

"You should get dressed. It'll be cold tonight."

The night darkens. A crescent-shaped Easter moon takes over a blue-green sky framed by silhouetted mountains to the west, castle towers to the north with the sea, moonlit now, beyond them. Stars pop out. Theo lights a kerosene lantern. Dion lays out the food she brought, and a bottle of red Romeiko wine.

"Dad's contribution."

Theo uncorks it, sniffs it, then takes a sip, swishing it around his mouth like a connoisseur.

"This is awesome."

"I know." Dion tells him about Alexander the Grape's love for his vines, how he won't let pesticides or any other kind of man-made chemical taint his vineyards, won't allow any cost saving measures to intrude on the subtleties of his winemaking, and inside the evening firelight she hears sadness in her pride.

Theo must hear it too because he tilts his head, questioning, and then the whole story spills out: how close the winery is to bankruptcy, how the Russian 'computer specialist,' to whom they are deeply indebted, who couldn't care less about wine, wants her father to make more than the Kokanakis Winery can possibly deliver. And Dion can't remember the last time she talked this much. It feels so good to let it all out, to hear the veracity of her worries. But, is she betraying her father and grandmother by speaking about their situation, wonders a fringe of worry at the edge of her mind. Could it hurt them in some way she can't foresee?

Theo nods to show he's been listening, takes another swig from the wine bottle, but has nothing to say.

Of course he doesn't, thinks Dion. He's twenty-eight, still at life's play stage. She takes the bottle from him, should have kept her mouth shut.

"I may be able to help you find out about the Russian," he says.

"You?" A vagrant artist five minutes out of boyhood? "How?"

"I know something about computers from my Boston days, and I still have friends there." He tells her about landing in a Boston school yard, not a healthy place for a slight, swarthy-skinned fourteen-year old whose broken English came from the other side of the world, where terrorists live. Pubescent girls watched, some of them giggling, as day after day a group of boys taunted him then, when he didn't respond, beat him. "Man up," said his military father. "Fight back!" As if one against five was a sane option. Luckily Boston had a Greek community. One of Theo's classmates took him there and, in the basement of a restaurant probably much like the one Dion's grandparents owned, he found friends who were obsessed with computer hacking.

Gaining access to games you were supposed to pay for was fun then, over the next four years it morphed into finding ways into other people's computers, slipping behind firewalls, outfoxing personal, then industrial, then government security systems. Theo never learned more than basic hacking skills but he knew the world beyond Boston and he had a creative mind and his buddies were savvy and slick enough to use this to get them undetected ringside seats as FBI cyber-terrorism investigators circled Chinese and Russian cyber-serpents that were co-opting computer systems across the world, creating false identities and thousands of fake social media accounts and news sites that looked legitimate. Marshalling forces of misinformation designed to take over the disgruntled minds of unsuspecting voters, to sway elections, destabilize entire countries.

"Think Britain's Brexit," Theo tells Dion. "Or the last U.S. election. World leaders are clueing into the cyber-swamp now but this Leonid Salin is probably capable of crawling into the private digital life of any person or company anywhere in the world. My friends can find out if his name is listed on any roster of Russia's FSB security service at least."

"But why would the Russians want anything to do with our little winery?"

"Who knows. Maybe this Salin just likes your Dad's wine," says Theo. "Let me see what I can find out. Also, for what it's worth, I think your Dad and what he does are amazing. If I can help him and your *Yiayiá* anytime, let me know." His sharp-edged face looks pixie-sweet as he lays a metal rack on the stones of his fire circle and heats olive oil in a pan for his wild asparagus and other greens from his bag.

Dion cuts cheese, puts bread and sausages onto two plates. Theo adds his greens. Dion pours wine, and realizes she's ravenous. Also happy up here inside this little circle of firelight in the pirate's castle.

They are finishing some of *Yiayiá's* Easter pastries when church bells peal somewhere below them. Theo raises his mug of wine.

"Here's to you, Jesus." He turns to Dion: "And here's to you. 'Dion,'" he muses, "that's an unusual name."

"It's short for Dionysia, my grandmother's name."

"Dionysia?" Theo starts to laugh. "You?"

"Yes, all the women on *Yiayiá's* side of the family were called Dionysia, probably because they've been winemakers since forever—"

"But Dionysia comes from Dionysus, god of wine but also of orgies!" He goes on laughing. "And you are not one for orgies."

Cocky bastard.

"How would you know?"

He hears her rancour. Looks at her.

"What I know is that you don't know your body very well."

"What are you talking about? I've been living in this body since long before you were born!" A log in the fire shifts, crackling, sending up a shower of sparks.

"And in all those decades has anyone ever properly explored the landscape of your skin?"

He passes her the wine bottle but Dion's throat has closed. Because breasts squeezed, nipples sucked, stomach kissed, fingers roaming, she has had her share of explorers. The river of foreplay has always been hurried though, on its way to a waterfall whose rush she can hear, she can even feel its spray sometimes but—

Theo is peering at her through the firelight.

"Your body is beautiful but it's like you're trussed up, like a chicken on its way to market." He takes back the wine bottle, tips it up into his mouth.

She sees an old hen, strung up by her grizzled feet—

"With me you can relax though, feel free, like you did earlier," he takes another swig of wine, "because I will never try to have sex with you."

There it is, a bald truth. She nods at it:

"I know. Because who gets turned on by a trussed up chicken, right?"

"No!" cries Theo. "See, that's what I'm talking about. You're old, you think, you're wrinkled you think. Think, think, think, you never stop, are never able to just be." One of his hands crosses the space between them, takes hold of her chin. Glass clinks against her teeth as he pours wine from the bottle into her mouth. "Do birds and beetles and the green earth think they're too young, too old, too thin, too fat?" And there is something in this move, her chin tilting up in his hand, that comes alive down inside her nether regions. He brings his head close as the wine slides down her throat. "I won't lie with you because I told you, desire, yours and mine, reaching for each other is what I want to paint."

He desires her, a trussed up chicken? Come on, she wants to say. If that were true, if they're both sexually starving, why don't they do it right here, right now, while he's not painting?

Because desire, the most powerful force in the world, is what interests him, nothing else. Not her, not a relationship. Which is fine. Because why wreck whatever this is?

"Don't worry," she tells him, "meaningless sex doesn't interest me."

He laughs.

"Right, why spray graffiti on a wall when you can paint an El Greco!" He tips the dregs of the wine into his own mouth and picks up their plates.

And where, she sighs to herself, will I ever find my own, real El Greco?

He comes back dragging his mattress.

"Why don't you lie down, get a little sleep before the fun begins?" Across the fire from her he rolls himself into another blanket.

Bells ring out all across the valley: Midnight. And here is Theo, leaning down to take her hand, leading her to a spot on the north wall between the castle's two guard towers. A dot of firelight punctures the darkness on the far side of the valley.

"They're burning a straw effigy of Judas." He passes her the bottle of *raki*.

A series of bangs punctuates the bellringing: guns being fired into the sky. A more sonorous bang followed by a whistle sends a ring of colours into the blue-black sky to the west, in the direction of Chania. Another follows, another, another, blue, white, green, purple, red pinpricks of light exploding. Over in two minutes. A spray of bang-bang-bang children's firecrackers, then silence.

A second fireworks display starts closer to them, in Rethymnon.

Smaller towns follow it, plumes of colour bursting into the sky all along the north coast.

Dion is not sure what she believes about the Jesus and Judas story, about Jesus's resurrection. Her father's divinity is Nature. *Yiayiá* claims that she gave up her belief in God The Father long ago – except at Easter apparently. But now, listening to church bells and celebratory guns, watching fountains of light colour the starry heavens, none of that matters. The joy of rebirth, of renewal coursing through her has nothing to do with any kind of thought structure.

"*Kálo pásca!* (Happy Easter!)" The sun has long since breasted the top of the eastern mountains when Theo delivers a mug of instant coffee, segments of orange, *Yiayiá's* Easter bread and a red hardboiled egg to her mattress. He's wearing jeans, a clean white t-shirt with a happy chick peeping out of a broken eggshell, and a beat-up Boston Red Sox baseball cap. His hair, spilling out from under it, makes him look like an overage skateboarder. "Come on lazy bones," he unzips her sleeping bag and peels it away. "Time to get undressed."

Easter Sunday's morning sky is crystalline blue. Herb-perfumed warmth, coming up the mountain, dissolves the night cold. Theo sits on the grass below the blank stone wall where his new work-in-progress will hang, his sketch pad ready. Sheep bells tinkle in the distance as she steps self-consciously onto the patch of grass in front of him. Naked under a glaring sun.

"Good," he says, "now move freely, like you did yesterday."

As if. Harsh morning light picks out the cellulite pocks on her thigh. And what on earth does her hair look like? She packed a brush, a mirror. Better go find it—

"Think think think," Theo taps the side of his head. "Stop it."

Easy for him to say.

The breeze sneaks in under her mess of hair. Her skin picks up its lilting signals. And look, here now is her grizzled foot lifting like a hen's. Part of her watches incredulously as it takes a step towards him. Reaching down, she plucks his Boston Red Sox cap off his head.

"Hey!"

"Hey what?" She jams the cap onto her head. "You want to paint desire? So you get naked — I mean nude — too." Hearing herself laugh, she's as startled as he is.

He jumps up, peels off his t-shirt, drops his jeans. Isn't wearing underwear. His body is dark skinned, muscle on bone, his collarbones, elbows, knees, ankles sharply defined by relentless sunlight. Taut with youth. His cock rises, pole straight, out of a pubic bush as black as his hair.

Pleased by this, she stalks away on her chicken feet, flapping her untrussed chicken wings.

"R-pukpukpukpuk."

Stops by the mattress, picks up a segment of orange left on her breakfast plate and, turning back to Theo, watches herself raise it to her lips, sucking, licking, teasing. Nothing like a chicken. His penis jigs. She dances away with the breeze, towards the low wall between the castle towers, where they sat last night. Raising one leg, resting it on the stone, she lifts an arm to shade her eyes the way a pirate would, scanning the valley below.

Is she the first naked woman who's stood here looking out? The breeze brushes the underside of her raised leg. A medieval female Tunisian corsair once wrought havoc in this part of the Mediterranean, according to Alexander the Grape, but she would never have shown herself naked. And any 12th century women this castle's pirate brought here would have been kept behind stone walls. All of them, men and women, must have been tiny, five feet tall at most, judging from the height of window slits in the remains of the tower beside her. She stands tall as a Grecian statue, the breeze bathing her as she picks out her home far below, her father's vines, the winery, the barnyard clearly etched by the morning light. The olive trees' grey green leaves are trembling, the oaks swaying, and there's the stream bank where Theo first saw her. All of it a prize being eyed now by a modern-day Russian pirate—

Stop thinking! Beyond the valley a careless sea sparkles. She pirouettes back towards Theo, sunshine kissing her all over.

Sitting on the grass, he watches her, sketches, watches, sketches. Her arms rise, feel the air on their undersides and free themselves. Show her how tight her chest, her shoulders, her neck usually are. Trussed up. Not who she wants to be. Her left hand comes down of its own accord, cups the bottom of her left breast, lifting it as she dances towards him, offering it.

"Yes!" Theo's penis pokes up out of his lap as he draws. "Hold that pose and lie down, here in front of me, on your right side."

The grass is soft under her bum as she follows instructions. Theo crawls forward, plucks his cap off her head. Then:

"May I?"

She nods, desire pumping moisture into her vagina. He bends her top leg and pulls it gently towards him. Tufts of grass tickle the underside of her knee as her torso tips forward, her spine arching to maintain her balance. She thrusts her proffered breast forward. He sits back on his heels. Her nipples are tiny soldiers standing at attention, her stomach taut, her juices pulsing now as his eyes run over her, then close. He breathes in, out, then starts madly drawing, looking, drawing, ripping off pages, starting new ones.

Her left, breast-holding hand tires. She flops onto her back, raises both knees, feet flat on the grass to take the strain off her spine. Under her the earth, not yet penetrated by the sun's warmth, sends an electrical current almost too faint to sense up into her feet, her spine, her hands, the back of her head. The breeze finds her vagina, cools it. Theo is still drawing.

"This will be my painting!" She hears his excitement.

"Will you come up here again," he asks as they pack up to leave, "to pose for me? The late afternoon light is what I want."

vi.

Leonid Salin calls to invite them for dinner and to sign the new contract. Dion finds his leather folder under a pile of papers in the office. *Yiayiá* refuses to read it.

"I'm too old. My eyes are failing."

Alexander the Grape is buried in his vineyards.

Theo sits at a patio table with Dion and Amina. He came down to the winery a few days ago to tell them what his Boston buddies found out about Leonid Salin, and has not left. Alex has three vineyards of his own and three others he tends with a neighbour. Weeds are thriving in all of them in late April and Theo knows how to wield a weed-whacker. Alex has shown him how to prune vagrant vine shoots and Theo thinks it's the least he can do, given what Dion's doing for him. Also he likes these people.

A decade-old article surfaced in his Boston buddies' search into Russian computer companies, security specialists and social media misinformation campaigns: A Canadian newspaper investigating corporate corruption traced a series of bribes paid for 'internet influence' to an office in Belarus that nobody appeared to occupy.

"Internet influence means manipulating human psyches, making people think and say and do what you want," Theo explained after supper on the patio, where the family likes to linger over *raki* and conversation. The journalist set a camera to watch the office entrance and picked up a blurred but unmistakable shot of a younger Leonid Salin.

"Why would a man choose to live that way?" Dion wondered, looking at the picture on Theo's phone.

"That's easy," he said. "Desire for power."

Yiayia pressed her lips together, nodding.

"May be all he knows," said Alex, "like the scorpion and the frog on the riverbank. Do you know that story?" Theo, Amina and Dion shook their heads.

"Well," said Alex, who loves a story, "Frog is about to cross the river when along comes Scorpion. 'Will you give me a ride across on your back?' he asks Frog. 'Of course not,' says Frog, 'if I let you climb onto my back you'll sting me and I'll die.' 'No I won't,' argues Scorpion. 'If you die I'll drown.' This sounds logical to Frog so he allows Scorpion to crawl onto his back. Halfway across the river Scorpion stings him. 'Why?' cries Frog as he sinks into the water, dying. Just before he drowns, Scorpion shrugs: 'It's what I do.'" Dion's father looked around the table.

"I know!" Theo exclaimed. "Desire makes everything, turns plants to the sun, gets bodies to mate, run, kill, eat."

"Kicks aside whatever gets in its way," added Amina, surprising him.

Amina: Crazy-beautiful. Theo runs a hand over his newly shorn hair. Yesterday she sat him in a chair outside the kitchen and cut off his curls, her body brushing closer to him than hair cutting made necessary, her fingers sliding across his shoulder, nothing to do with hair styling. When he tried to respond she pulled away, laughing. Still, he had the feeling that anything was possible with this woman. Who's also a sweetheart. And ridiculously brave. She and Dion trusted him with her story this morning. Later, when he drove her to Rethymno to buy a dress, shoes, a handbag, a disposable phone, with a stash of U.S. dollars she has, she kept glancing over her shoulder, tight as a wound-up spring. Nothing like a normal American tourist out shopping. So Theo took her arm and held it against him the way a lover would.

He should have gone back to his castle right after telling Dion and her family about Salin. Passing clouds are close enough almost to touch up there, and mountaintop winds bring him all he needs from the world below. And roles are clear: Dion is his model. Golden, luscious, but that's all.

"I should leave," he said. "I need to plan my painting in a place where Zorba The Greek's 'whole human catastrophe' can't reach me."

"There's no such place," said Dion. "Like it or not, we're all part of the catastrophe."

"Not if we refuse to participate."

"Not participating is a form of participating."

Amina's head could have been watching a tennis match. Theo snorted:

"You're playing with words, which shut out everything but the puny thoughts they're trying to carry. Words are the whole problem."

Across the table *Yiayiá* said nothing. Reaching for an olive and a slice of sheep's cheese, Alex cocked an eyebrow. Dion's eyes flashed her impatience.

"Oh come on, you've told me all kinds of interesting things which then led to new thoughts, which built new ideas." Dion looked to her grandmother. "What do you think, *Yiayiá?*"

The old lady put her hands on the table to push herself upright.

"I think this old bag of bones has drunk more wine than she should. And may need help getting to her bedroom. Before I go though, I will say this: God gave us thoughts. If we do not put them into words, what use are they?"

"Exactly!" cried Dion. *Yiayiá* put up her hand.

"But if, on the other hand, our God-given thoughts are the consciousness of Earth, then what good can they do as long as greedy egos run the show?"

"*Ano!*" cried Theo. Yes!

Alex downed a last mouthful of *raki* and pushed back his chair.

"I'll help you, Ma. As for you two, in my book you're both right. Thoughts are like tangled vines endlessly climbing over each other, sometimes beautiful, sometimes choking out whatever is in their way. Needing pruning shears." Coming around the table, he stopped to lean down and kiss the top of Dion's head. "We are far more than our thoughts though, chicken." He turned to Theo. "As for you, please don't leave unless you absolutely have to."

Now Dion wants him to drive them to the Russian's villa. Her father will be too nervous to be trusted at the wheel in the dusk, and she needs to think. The trip won't take long. *Yiayiá* says she's not up to it and if all Salin wants from the outing is her signature on his contract, they'll just turn around and come home.

That won't happen, thinks Theo. The Russian will want to show off his power and Dion and her father will hope words can breach his wall of ambition. Theo will wait in the car with a picnic, his sketch pad, a book.

Alex, in the Fiat's front passenger seat, is a spruced up version of himself in a blue and white checked shirt and newly pressed navy slacks. Even in the dimly lit backseat AminaRose's new cream-coloured dress sets off her black hair and golden skin, though Theo can almost feel her quivering with stage fright before showing herself in public without her abaya, not to mention playing a carefree American tourist for a whole evening. To stay home with *Yiayia* was not an option though. Salin's interest in her, thwarted, would do nobody any good.

Beside her in the back seat Dion looks beautiful too, thinks Theo, tanned in an off-the-shoulder white embroidered peasant blouse that goes with a multi-coloured skirt. Her hair is long enough now to curl into ringlets. Such a gem. Complicated, confused, hopelessly inhibited until lately but so what? Her curvy body mixes authentic, unadorned energy she doesn't seem to know she possesses into dark, anxious hollows of hopelessness. If this moment in this car were a painting, she'd be the vibrance that draws the rest of the picture together.

The Fiat bounces down a dirt road into the heart of the valley as mountains to the west steal the last of the day's light, making shadows of oak trees that must be at least a hundred years old.

"Who are you?" Dion suddenly asks AminaRose.

"Rose Williams." Wrapping her shoulders in one of *Yiayiá's* many soft wool shawls, this one peach coloured, Amina doesn't miss a beat. Williams is a common name, chosen because Salin, who clearly is interested in her, will do a search. And must not be able to distinguish her. If he questions her at all she'll tell him her father changed the family's many-syllabled, unpronounceable name when they emigrated to the Unites States. Any further probing would be rude and can be shut down if necessary.

"Where do you live?" Dion shrugs into a rust-coloured shawl, also *Yiayiá's*. She doesn't own much more than a few make-up basics — most days all her cheeks get is a splash of water — but this afternoon Amina took all kinds of pots and tubes out of the handbag she had brought with her from Istanbul and started applying eye shadow like an expert.

"How did you learn," Dion asked, "I mean if your face was always hidden...?"

"Not from my husband." Amina surveyed her work in the bathroom mirror. "Or from myself. And make-up's fun, like my face is a canvas I can paint. Here let me do you too."

Foundation, mascara, eye shadow, it looks more like armour than art. Inside which Dion will have to find a way to probe the psyche of the man who is threatening to take away her family's home and property and business. To see how best to negotiate with him.

"I live in New York," AminaRose replies now, blinking eye shadowed, mascara-lined eyes at her, "when I'm in the U.S., which isn't often. I like to travel."

"Continuing what your family did when you were growing up," Dion prompts, because AminaRose's accent does not have a lifelong American's hard consonants. And Salin is a predator, will pick that up. "And we met where?"

"On Cape Cod." It's a place they both know, so her lies can be laced with truth. "You remember that summer?" A hint of playfulness. Theo sends a good-for-you smile through the rearview mirror.

The road ends at the Russian's villa, a white-washed concrete wall obscuring all but its roof. The Fiat's headlights pick up two large clay urns, on either side of a locked wrought iron gate, that are planted with peach coloured hibiscus. Before Theo can wind down his window to press the buzzer beside the gate it swings open, unlocked from inside. A semi-circular white stone drive leads to the front door of a pink stucco house with an oak front door, now open. Showing off a white marble statue of a male nude standing in the centre of a large, well lit foyer.

Salin's assistant is waiting to hand AminaRose out of the Fiat's back passenger seat. Dion climbs out of the seat behind Theo. Salin comes out to shake Alex's hand, then looks past him into the car.

"Your mother?"

"Sorry Leo, I'm afraid she is unable to join us tonight."

Dion watches the Russian's face shift consternation into concern.

"She is unwell?"

Alex smiles ruefully.

"My mother's ninety-four, Leo. My daughter Dion will act as her proxy, though she cannot sign anything. So if you'd rather cancel tonight—"

"No no." Salin tosses a glance towards Dion. "My assistant will drop by the winery with the papers for her to sign tomorrow." He aims a smile at AminaRose. "Let us go in."

Alex stays by the car, looking apologetic.

"I don't know if you want that, Leo. I'm afraid I won't be signing anything either tonight."

The Russian's expression shifts again. AminaRose moves closer to Dion, by the car, where Theo is still in the driver's seat. Salin makes a decision.

"This is a shame Alex, you should have told me. I have had dinner made. But never mind," he claps Alex on the shoulder. "We'll have a drink, eat, then perhaps you can sample one of my brandies while we have a chat." He moves ahead as if Alex's agreement is a done deal, and shepherds AminaRose towards the door.

Watching from the car, Theo takes out his phone, to snap a shot of the Russian. But.

"*Ochi vlakas!* (No, you fool!) Not here on the monitored driveway of a guy who can shut down banking, government, business systems, not to mention people.

Salin's living room, off the left side of the central foyer, is a breathtaking marriage of white-walled Greek architecture with what must be some of Europe's finest *objets d'art*. Questions, worries, strategies lined up in Dion's head are swept away by ancient vases, each one mounted on its own wooden plinth, a corner wrought iron sculpture of climbing leaves, and walls hung with paintings individually lit from above. What takes her breath however, drawing her into an intimacy of light and life and colour is a large oil painting hanging above a tiled fireplace at the end of the room. Two sofas face each other across a coffee table. Between them a well used leather armchair faces the painting of 19th century couples dancing under light standards set amongst the trees at an outdoor cafe, light coloured dresses and men's panama hats set against dark suits and coats, young people drinking at tables around which you can almost feel the nip of a Paris winter.

"A Degas?" asks Alex.

"That's right," Salin says. Dion hears his pride.

"Go get Theo, Dion," her father tells her. "He needs to see this."

"Theo, your driver?" asks their host.

"Yes," says Alex, still held by the painting. "He's an artist."

"Oh? Well then what is he doing outside?" Salin takes out his phone, punches in a number and speaks in rapid Russian. Then: "Please, also enjoy some other pieces. See here?" He moves to a small canvas on a side wall, a pub scene, tankards on a wooden table, a man's head being grabbed from behind by an attacker about to slit his throat. "A four-hundred-year old Caravaggio." He sweeps one arm towards the

Degas. "Grace." He points with his other hand at the pub. "And destruction." His smile broadens. "This is life." Out at the edge of Dion's brain, beyond blind appreciation, a *Yiayiá*-inspired alert lights up: ("Watch everything. Listen to what is behind what he's telling you." Showing off his treasures, Salin is enjoying himself but nothing men like him say or do is meaningless.)

Her father, Dion, and AminaRose move from one canvas to the next around the room.

"You have art worth millions hanging here. How do you keep it safe?" Alex wonders as they return to the sofas. Smugness rounds the Russian's smile.

"I am a computer man, Alex. Security is my livelihood."

"But here in Crete electrical power fluctuates so much—?"

"No matter," a shrug. "I have no need of Crete's electrical grid."

Rooftop solar panels heat everyone's hot water here, thinks Dion. Salin must be storing solar power in batteries, to run a back-up generator, alarms, cameras. Unobtrusive red dots of light watch from each of this living room's four corners.

Salin's man opens the door. Theo comes in, his ripped jeans and t-shirt and the annoyed look on his face at odds with everything else in this room.

"Ah," Salin smiles, "the artist." Alex points to the Degas.

"Theo, look! We thought you'd want to see this."

They watch him move to the painting, stand looking at it. Salin speaks to his man.

"And Theo," says Dion, pointing out the side wall, "there's a four hundred-year old Caravaggio over there."

Lost in the Degas, Theo does not speak.

"Please sit," Salin says to his guests. His man appears with a tray full of gilt-lipped shot glasses and a bottle of vodka. "Allow me to welcome you with a specialty of my country." Putting the tray on the coffee table, he pours and offers glasses. Theo moves away to look at other paintings: the Caravaggio, a water colour study of a ballet dancer – another Degas? – a landscape rendered in a unique semi-realistic, semi-impressionistic style.

"A painter I favour, from Georgia, not yet known," says Salin, suddenly beside him, handing him a glass of vodka. Dion watches from across the room as he puts a hand on Theo's shoulder and says something, inviting him to dinner probably because Theo is shaking his head, pointing down at his jeans, sandalled feet. She gets up, comes over to rescue him.

"What do you paint?" Salin is asking him.

"Nudes mostly."

"Ah. May I see them sometime?"

"Sorry, I'm not ready to show my work." Put off a second time, the Russian nods, as if considering this.

"You are from Crete?"

"That's right."

"A modern El Greco?" Mouth smiling. "May I ask how is it that a Cretan artist in torn jeans speaks English like an American?"

"Sure," Theo tosses back the vodka. "My father comes from there. I lived with him for awhile in high school."

"Ah," Salin relieves him of his empty glass. Moving back to the others, he picks up the vodka bottle and refills Theo's glass. "Anyone else?" AminaRose, her father and Dion shake their heads. Salin fills his own, then holds out Theo's glass. "Join us Theo, when you've finished looking. And please stay for dinner." Invitation issued in front of all of them, two choices available, clear as computer binary:

1: Insist on leaving, insulting the man she and her father are here to persuade; or

0: Stay, put his authenticity on hold.

Dion cannot watch him struggle.

"Yes Theo, please join us," she says.

"Please," AminaRose echoes from the couch. "I'd like that very much too."

Why, thinks Dion? Is Amina following her lead or making her own way here? This is her first uncovered social outing since her escape from her husband and look at her, sipping vodka as if drinking was normal, chatting with the Russian as if he mattered to her, so at ease inside her body. So what if the art on the walls of this isolated villa cost gazillions of dollars, says her smile, and who cares what he paid for it.

When dinner is announced Salin offers AminaRose a hand up, then slides it around into the small of her back and waits for Dion, her father and Theo to go ahead before propelling her towards the doorway. He stops in the foyer.

"Before we go through to the dining room, come," he opens a door on the other side of the foyer. "This room will interest you Alex, and you too Theo."

Floor to ceiling shelves are filled with books, most of them bound in red, green, brown, blue leather. Between them four burgundy leather wingback chairs are set around a round glass coffee table. The sun's last light, slanting through a side window, glows gold on the contents of bottles on shelves behind a polished wood bar counter at the left hand end of the room. Some are tall and slim, some squat, some round, some crystal topped by stoppers that look like crowns. Cameras, one in the corner behind the bar, another at the far end of the room, watch as they gravitate towards a single bottle, sheathed in silver and gold, that glitters on a four-foot olive wood pedestal between the chairs and the window.

"Diamonds," says Salin. Again Dion hears pride. "Six thousand five hundred of them set into twenty-four carat gold on one side, platinum on the other." Hedgehog-like knobs protrude from the sides of the bottle and the top of its stopper.

"What does it contain?" Her father bends to read the label.

"Henri IV Dudognon Heritage cognac, one hundred years old."

"So many diamonds!" AminaRose needs both hands to lift the ornate bottle off the pedestal. "It's heavy!"

"Please." Salin takes the bottle from her, feigns a smile. "Yes, it's heavy, eight kilos to be exact: a two million-dollar bottle of cognac."

AminaRose laughs, a low-pitched, breathy sound that manages somehow to be sensual. How does she do it, Dion wonders?

Answer: she doesn't. What she says, the way she sways, seeming to float when she walks, all come out of physical freedom Dion has only experienced, fleetingly, up in Theo's castle. Only once since they found her pose has she been able to go there again, to let golden rays of late afternoon sunlight work their magic as, sitting naked beside her on the grass, Theo asked: "May I?" and she felt free to let him trail a finger up the inside of her arm then down the side of her ribs, along her thigh, watching her eyes lose focus, her skin flushing as desire pumped through her, expelling her breath. So that he could draw, shade, tear off pages quickly before the light went. AminaRose exudes sexual freedom naturally, which is ironic in someone who has spent their entire adulthood cloistered, or inside an abaya. Or is it the result of that?

"Is the cognac any good?" AminaRose's hand tilts Salin's, better to see the bottle's diamond-studded glitter. "What's the point of having a two million-dollar bottle of anything if you can't touch it or drink it?"

Bad idea to be flip. An ordinary American woman would be impressed, not cocky. Still, AminaRose has nailed a feeling Dion has been ignoring since she walked into this house: the Degas, Caravaggio etc are all real, as are the books, this bottle and the others, but it's as if all of it is on display, designed to impress.

"Maybe one day I will drink it," Salin says archly, "when the right occasion presents itself." (A put down: the right occasion will not include them.) "In the meantime I like to look at beautiful things." He puts the Henri IV Dudognon bottle back and goes behind the bar. "Let me show you my other brandies Alex, then after dinner we will sample some."

Her father reads the label on a round, tapered bottle Salin puts on the counter.

"Ah, a J stamped on its side under the crown, Courvoisier's *L'Esprit de Joséphine*! Never in my lifetime did I expect to be looking at one of these." Salin's smile looks genuine.

"Beautiful isn't she? The bottle is crystal, one of only fourteen produced last year." He turns the smile to AminaRose. "Empress Josephine was Napoleon's wife, also a great lover of the arts, and of roses." Alexander the Grape is nodding.

"A treasure for sure. This cognac dates back to the 1800s, hence its name. It's also a wonderful example of what I'm all about, Leo—"

"Dad—" says Dion. Now is not the moment. But.

"No," counters Theo. "What were you going to say, Alex?" Dion catches a shot of pleasure Theo's angular face does not try to hide. "I'd like to know." And he's right, the Russian has been controlling them ever since they arrived.

"Only that the story of wine and her spirits reminds us that we humans are servants, not controllers of nature," says Alex, pleased to go on. "Cognac only exists because several hundred years ago Dutch traders wanted to take home wine from that region of France. But how to make sure it didn't rot in their ships' holds? Someone came up with the idea to distill it. And wow, did that taste good! So why not double-distill? Even better! Distillers set up shop in Cognac, and soon discovered that storing brandy in oak barrels improved the taste even more, but where to get these? Why from nearby Limousin forest, of course. Today the finest oak barrels still come from there." Alex gazes into Josephine's lovely golden glow. "The blends in this bottle aged in cellars close to Cognac's Charente River, where it was damp, and guess what? Damp-stored brandy added a *je ne sais quoi* quality to the flavours. Where you have dampness you also have mould, so the best cognac cellars had black walls and ceilings thanks to evaporation through the oak, called '*la part des anges*,' the angels' share. Cognac makers figure it amounts to millions of bottles a year, but do they begrudge the angels their share? Of course not. What's left in the barrels is richer, smoother, finer." Alex looks around, seemingly aware suddenly that he has been holding the floor, and smiles. "Nature, accidents and people smart enough to care, to watch and listen and add their ingenuity at every step are the creators of brandy." He turns to Salin. "This bottle will have cost you a small fortune, Leo. You don't keep it in its box?"

"No, she is too beautiful to keep shrouded. Instead I control the light, temperature, humidity of the room itself." He gestures towards the window. "When I am not using the room I keep blackout shades down, the heat mostly off. You're right, Alex, that we have nature to thank for cognac. And that mystery and miracle make each one unique, a work of art."

Too beautiful to keep shrouded. Dion shoots a glance towards AminaRose. Please God may the Russian's reference be coincidental. Listening, interested, her runaway friend shows no sign of disquiet.

"Nothing on Earth is more powerful, more creative than nature," Alex concludes. Setting the stage for their discussion about the winery? Good for you Dad, thinks Dion.

"Yes," says Salin, "nature is bountiful and clever, but she is also careless." He comes out from behind the bar. "Take, for example, a bottle of very, very old cognac. Not beautiful, not on display, not even valued as yet, therefore priceless."

"Oh!" AminaRose's face opens in wonder.

A small oak cabinet between the bar and the window has a set of dials mounted on its side. Salin takes plastic gloves and a white napkin from behind the bar, taps his phone screen. A quiet click releases the cabinet door. Extracting a bottle so old its shape is slightly asymmetrical, he lays it on the napkin in his other hand to show them.

"This cognac, made by a producer who no longer exists, lay at the bottom of the sea for a hundred years, until I liberated it last year. It was on its way to Saint Petersburg, part of a shipment of hundreds of bottles for the cellars of Czar Nicholas probably, when the Germans sank the ship during the First World War," says the Russian. "You can Google the story. This bottle I am holding is a lost fragment of my country's history." Dion leans close to look at the place where a wax seal is the only identification left.

"Where's the rest of the shipment?"

"Still at the bottom, alas, in a shipwreck too dangerous to salvage."

"So how did you get this bottle?" asks AminaRose. Salin tries to let a smile answer for him but all of them stare at him, waiting. He shrugs.

"A company of mine attempted the salvage."

"Can you hold the bottle up to the light?" asks Alex, hoping its glass is not too sea-worn to prevent his gauging the quality of the its contents. The seal looks intact.

"Who does it belong to," Theo asks, "if it was on its way to the Czar?" Salin moves his gaze from the bottle to the artist.

"Me. The ship went down in international waters and Czar Nicholas is long dead." Salin returns his prize to its cabinet.

"Not the Russian government?" Dion can't help herself. "Or, wouldn't Czar Nicholas have insured the shipment?"

Silence. Salin does not like her, that's been clear from the beginning. She's a late-date thorn in a Kokanakis Wines matrix he's been developing for five years.

"These are questions best left to lawyers," he says, "if ever anyone who thinks he has a claim cares to voice them." As if laws are obstacles not boundaries, easily circumvented. He turns to Alex. "The only point of owning anything — cognac, art, books — is to be in the company of immeasurable beauty. Speaking of which, look at this."

Beyond a fireplace in the study's outer wall opposite the door, at the front of the house, an antique desk with gracefully arched legs sits in front of a bay window. Its chair faces the room, its leather inlaid top bare except for a crystal ink pot. Gazing down on it, painted in black and white with a touch of sepia on the inside wall next to a row to bookcases, is a bearded, life-sized saint.

"St. John The Theologian," says Theo, moving close to examine the paintwork. St. John and many of his fellow Byzantine saints have lived on church walls all over Crete since the middle ages but this wall mural does not look like a copied reproduction.

"You've heard of *gicleé* printing?" Salin asks. "This is an adaptation. Amazing isn't it, what digitization can produce. And it's not a bad thing to have the writer of the Book of Revelations looking over your shoulder."

Theo steps back, looking up into the saint's sorrowful gaze.

"Depends what you're doing, I guess." He looks around for a computer. "Is this where you work?"

"No no. Well, some reading, thinking." Salin is standing close to AminaRose now, his arm out of sight. On her back again, Dion wonders? She looks perfectly comfortable. "Now, let us eat."

Salin's dining room opens onto a glass walled room at the back of the house. Outside they can see a pool. Purple red bougainvillea flowers tumbling across the villa's white back wall looks like a living painting. Balancing it, on the far side of the lawn under a wall made of cut boulders like the ones in Theo's castle's walls, is a garden full of blooming flowers that looks like a Manet painting in the fading light. Salin places Alex on his right at the head of the table, AminaRose on his left, where Dion should be sitting as *Yiayiá's* proxy. No matter, she is content here beside of her father, and thankful to have Theo in her sight-line across the table.

Salin's good humour feeds itself as Russian dishes follow one another, each accompanied by a matched wine. Alex takes time to taste each one before adding food to his palate, beginning with a chardonnay that comes with a bowl of borsch. Holding his wine goblet by its stem, he raises it to the light, then tips it to observe the wine's colour against the white tablecloth. Dion, AminaRose, Theo and Salin watch as he swirls his wine, then sniffs it.

"You must stop thinking," he tells them, finally raising his glass to his lips, "to free all your senses. Let the aroma linger in your nose as you sip. Your tongue has different taste buds, sweet, sour and so on. Run the wine over them all."

"These glasses are crystal," adds the Russian as they follow her father's instructions. "Holding their stems like so, at a forty-five degree angle, keeps your hands' heat away from the wine." His fingers are long, nails manicured. "This one comes from the Crimea." Which Russia insists that it owns, thinks Dion.

The sun sets, the flowers' colours fade, turning Salin's white-tablecloth-and-crystal-chandelier dining room into an oasis of light and tastes, wines and chat. By the time they reach the end of the beef stroganoff main course, served with a Georgian Mukuzani red wine, even Dion has relaxed enough to toss the occasional witticism into discussions that shimmy from good sailing trips through the Greek islands to conflicting merits of classical music versus rock 'n roll to the evolution of art through the ages. That she is Theo's model is revealed, Dion can't remember by whom. Salin turns his attention to her for what must be the first time, appraising her from the head of the table.

"I can see that. Beauty, in art and wine and food, we are all of us its servants, are we not, Alex?" He turns to AminaRose. "How do you and Dion know each other?"

AminaRose launches into her story of their summer on Cape Cod. By the time plum dumplings and a bottle of Alex's own Romeiko dessert wine arrive she is volleying beach anecdotes at her life-long girlfriend, laughing: "Remember, Dion?" A brilliant chameleon, you'd never guess where she really grew up, or where she's spent her entire adult life, or that she has a Masters of Business Administration or how many languages she can translate. Dion tries to match her, colouring in the verbal pictures AminaRose sketches at first then, feeling herself loosen up, she starts to improvise: "And remember Rose, that time when…?"

"It's a good thing *Yiayiá* didn't come," she whispers to Theo when the conversation swirls off into Alex's and Salin's differing appreciations of dessert wines. "She'd be a drunken heap on the floor by now."

"Salin's plan maybe?" Theo drains his glass.

Their host puts down his napkin and comes to his feet.

"Now Alex, you and I must excuse ourselves to sample some of those brandies. Please, the rest of you, enjoy some more coffee or a liqueur with Edgar Degas and the others in the living room. We will join you shortly."

Dion, her father and *Yiayiá* have gone over the tack her father will take in any discussion about the winery's future, the points the Russian will have difficulty refuting, but her father cannot be trusted alone with Salin. Especially not after dinner and wine, and while tasting samples of his favourite, highly alcoholic beverage. The Russian knows that, is playing his advantage. Dion comes to her feet.

"I'm here as my grandmother's proxy," she says, hopefully not combatively, "so I'll have to come too." Salin cannot refuse her, and she can ask questions, or maybe find some wiggle room or a way to buy some time. At least she will be able to deliver a clear report to *Yiayiá*.

St John The Theologian watches from the shadowed wall at the far end of the study as Salin retrieves three snifters from under the bar. Dion looks at the array of bottles behind him.

"So many choices, and beautiful bottles. How do you decide which ones to open?"

Salin considers his collection.

"Good brandy is like love. It does not necessarily live in a beautiful bottle. Once opened however, its flavours are released." He takes down three ordinary-looking vintages. A stout, macho-looking bottle of dark amber brandy has not yet been uncorked. "This lovely twenty-year old Georgian Ararat Nairi might accord with the brandy you hope to produce, Alex. And this is a lovely Hennessy cognac I got into just the other day." The third choice, also opened, is a round, squat, long-necked bottle of Armagnac. "A country cousin of the cognacs," says Salin, "less silky perhaps, but full of personality." To Dion: "Which may I offer you?"

"The Hennessy please."

"Alex?"

"I think you want me to try the Ararat."

The Russian joins him.

"It will be interesting to compare it with the Armagnac."

"And with the Hennessy?" Dion suggests, "to see what double distillation adds, because isn't that what you want to do, Dad?" Her father laughs.

"You're right, due diligence might necessitate the sampling of all three."

"Sit, please," says Salin, indicating the chairs. Depositing their drinks, he goes to his desk at the other end of the room and returns with a leather file folder like the one he brought to the winery.

Dion copies her father as he cradles the bowl of his brandy snifter in his palm, swirling, sniffing, tasting, smiling. Salin opens the folder on the coffee table.

"Due diligence, always necessary, Alex. But painful sometimes." He savours his Ararat, then skewers his guest with a look devoid of any of his dinner table bonhomie. "Now tell me, what is there to discuss in this new contract?"

Alex puts down his snifter and sighs.

"The root of the problem is who I am, Leo. You spoke of love just now, and that is a perfect metaphor for the kind of wine I produce. *Vin ordinaire*, or cheap plonk, is like sex. Given a few essential ingredients anybody can churn it out. But making love, that's a whole different story." Alex's large brown eyes fill with warmth. "Take your *Esprit de Joséphine*, one of only fourteen bottles produced. Her blends are literally the heart of the '*brouillis*' distilled from the original wines." He turns to Dion. "The first part of the condensed '*brouillis*,' called the 'head,' is too alcoholic. The 'tail' is just that. But the 'heart!' Further reduced, it becomes '*eau de vie*,' water of life. Delicate, nuanced, a perfect description of love." He looks at the Russian. "My wines too come from a careful, creative alignment of living vines and soil and sunlight, of moisture and aging and wood. Which can not be forced without suffering great sacrifices in quality. Just like love."

Salin savours his Ararat. Light from a chandelier set above the coffee table casts the room outside its glow into shadow as darkness deepens outside.

"What you produce is good, very good Alex, that's why we're sitting here tonight, but love is love, with or without out-dated methods," he says. "Also you can not afford to turn your back on technology. Or to romanticize what you do. It's time for you to join the 21st century. I think you have no idea what discernments, precision, finesses are possible using computers."

"You're right about that," Alex raises his glass, "but this Ararat Nairi took twenty years to reach its unique, exquisite flavour. And wouldn't you agree that whatever it cost you was worth it? It's not necessarily about old or new techniques, it's about natural growth which can not be hurried or stressed without harm."

"Oh? Tell that to the major wineries in Europe, Australia, South Africa, America." Salin runs his brandy around the inside of his mouth.

"Check the soil under those rows and rows of wire-grown vines. How healthy, vibrant, chemical-free is it? Soil is alive, I keep telling you that, Leo. Feed it with fungi and you literally heal the Earth while enriching your vines. Conversely, acres and acres of artificially fertilized vines, their grapes processed by computer programs, are simply not sustainable over the long-term. And how nuanced are the flavours of robotic clones?" Alex shakes his big head. "Bottom line: what you are proposing would sacrifice the quality of my grapes and wine and would murder my soil. Plant more vines, sure, we can do that. Our neighbour Irina is willing to sell and her fields are very much like ours. But as for 21st century approaches, the Earth needs us humans to listen to our environment more than ever now. To interact with it, not try to force our ambitions on it. If we don't make this change a few guys like you will go on getting super-rich in the short term, but then what?" Alex lets out a long breath, lifts his shoulders. "Nature always rights the balances between growth and destruction, Leo. Always. And in the grand scheme of life, humans haven't been around very long." He sips his Ararat, looking at the man who owns his future.

Tension ticks like a metronome. Salin puts down his snifter.

"You say you do not want to interfere with natural processes but do you not prune new shoots to keep your vines from tangling, or leaves that block the sun from your grapes, or cut early bunches of grapes to allow greater energy to reach those that remain? This is interference, to help nature produce more efficiently the product you want at the end. I simply want to do the same on a larger scale."

He took in nothing of what her father showed him at the winery, Dion knows that, and now Salin doesn't seem to feel the need to address any of her father's points. Still, shut the fuck up, she tells herself. Stirring the pot of rage that has been bubbling away out beyond her mind's control all evening will achieve zero, and when it comes to making wine, her father's passion can carry its own banner.

"You misunderstand me, Leo. My fault no doubt. I'm not against technology, or working with my vines to help them produce, in fact I thank God for the various tools I can use for measurements etc, but what I've been trying to tell you, what a lifetime of learning has taught me, is that what's most important in the growth of anything is relationship: a farmer with his or her chickens or goats or seeds, a vintner with his or her vines." Alex gazes at the golden liqueur in his glass. "Especially now." He lifts his eyes to Salin's. "Our climate is changing and heat variances, the amount of rain, bug populations, all of these, and everything else in a vine's surroundings affect the growth of its grapes and ultimately the taste of the wine that comes from them. Now more than ever a winemaker needs to tune into complexities as they arise and make adjustments with a kind of sensitivity no machine can produce. If you truly are interested in Kokanakis Wines, your best bet is to trust me."

"I would like very much to do that." Salin looks at his watch, closes his folder. "However, if you will not sign this contract you will leave me no choice but to take over Kokanakis Wines and replace you."

Dion stares at the Russian, who is finishing the last of his brandy.

"Wait a minute," she says, still in her seat. "Just so I understand: are you saying you will use a clause in your present contract with Kokanakis Wines to take ownership of our business when the contract expires on November 30th?"

"That's right," Salin gets to his feet. "Not just your business. Your land also."

"And you have no interest at all in the health of the land and its future. Climate change and its ramifications mean nothing to you."

"Your father and grandmother borrowed money from me they can not repay."

"And you must have known that when you lent it to them, but still you did. Why?" The least she can do now is call out the truth.

"Because my wine won the *Prix d'Or*," says Alex. "You funded us because you love quality, beauty, creativity, remember Leo?" The Russian affects a sorrowful smile.

"That kind of patronage can only go so far."

Dion gets up. She has no right to be surprised. *Yiayiá* knew what was going to happen, so did Theo. Her father would have known it too, if he'd been able to see past his hope. Salin has been planning this takeover all along. Because of a pathological need for ever increasing amounts of money? Or to use the winery as a money laundering venue, to keep the world from knowing that a Russian 'computer specialist' named Leonid Salin is becoming increasingly, insanely wealthy?

"Failure to pay a debt has consequences," Salin says in the doorway. "It's not personal."

"Wrong," Dion tells him. "Trying to maneuver my family out of our livelihood, our home and our ancestral land is intensely personal," she too affects a smile. "But we have until the contract runs out on November 30th to raise what we owe you. And we will." Her words sound like nonsense, she knows that. Still, for reasons she cannot fathom, a tiny piece of who she is believes them as, extending her hand, she tries to dredge up what she hopes looks like dignity. "In the meantime, thank you for a fascinating evening."

Robot saws advance through her father's vineyard, chopping limbs off his vines, forcing them into uniform rows. Just ahead of them Dion's foot is stuck in a hole, her hips sticking out, the whirring steel blade coming closer—

The antique clock in the hall chimes 2 am. Dion sits up, sticky with sweat. Gets up. Out on the patio candlelight flickering on one of the tables is the only source of light.

"Dad?" A half-empty bottle and one *raki* glass sit on the table in front of him. Cool air brushes against her nightie as she pulls on a jacket and joins him. Leaves shush above them. Her father pours a shot of *raki* into the glass she has brought then looks up, through the plane tree's silhouetted leaves, at a carpet of stars and a sliver of moon.

"Did you know that people were worshipping trees long before the Druids?" Dion says nothing. "Take this great old tree's trunk for example, how it leaned when it had to, then corrected itself to grow in the most advantageous way towards the light. Life unfolds in so many more ways than we can comprehend—"

"I know," says Dion, trying to forestall a lecture inside which he'll hide from what happened tonight.

"No chicken, I don't think you do know what I'm talking about." Plucking a wilting white bloom out of AminaRose's latest table centrepiece, he lifts it to his nose and inhales. "This heavenly scent comes alive in you when you smell it, see?" He holds the bloom out to her. She takes in its perfume, feels pleasure. Nothing to do with Russians, debt, fear. "Connections exist between us and all life, every cell of every living thing vibrating always to the tunes around it. Creating what we feel and think and do." Several petals fall off the rose as he replaces it. "So much of what our family is about lives here. When I was a boy in this vineyard—"

"You were here as a boy?" Dion tries to see him in the candle's tiny orb of light. "I didn't know that!"

"Just for a couple of months." He tells her about coming to Crete with his mother just before his grandmother, *Yiayiá's* mother died. He was twelve, and never forgot his *Pappoús*, a wizened little man with a bushy moustache who was fiercely proud of his tough, free-growing

Romeiko grape vines. "This soil is special," he told his grandson, rubbing a clump of earth between his fingers. "See? Sand gives it minerals, clay holds moisture so minerals can dissolve into living earth that gives its special flavours to Cretan vines. Not like those bastard European grapes!" Not until he returned here did Dad realize that his grandfather was referring to an historic *phylloxera* aphid devastation. Thought to have been brought to Europe on steamships from North America in the 1860s, *phylloxera* killed most of the grape vines on the continent. A few species survived, on the volcanic island of Santorini north of here, and on Crete. *Phylloxera* did not eat North American vines however, so European species taken originally to the colonies and grafted onto American vines were returned to the great vineyards of France, Italy, Spain — *Pappoús's* "bastard grapes." Ninety years later *phylloxera* aphids did find their way to Crete, but not to the Kokanakis vineyards.

"Your great-grandfather believed the oaks protected them," Dad tells her now. "There might not be science on that, but plenty of myths, other than the Druids, exist about the oak tree's powers. There's a reason they're used for the barrels in which our wines age."

Yiayiá's father made his wine using the winery's ancient oak press and aging barrels, experimenting with a recipe his father had followed. His results were so delicious that after the Germans invaded Crete in 1941 a German commandant stationed in Chania heard about Kokanakis wine, got his hands on a bottle of red Romeiko, and demanded more.

"Rather than give it to them *Pappoús* dismantled the wine press and hid the pieces, his bottles of wine and the vineyard's aging casks in an old root cellar under the pig pen, which is now our aging room," says Dad. "'Gone, all of it,'" he told the commandant who came to see for himself. 'Bombed by your planes.' Actually his wine was going to resistance leaders and the British commandoes."

"Really?"

"Oh yes," says Dad, "they were all of them involved in the resistance. Your *Yiayiá* joined up at sixteen. She met your *Pappoús* in a high mountain village where she delivered a load of food and penicillin, then stayed to teach the children to read."

Dion has never heard this family history. She thinks of her walks through the vines with her father, how his pleasure in communing with them was contagious. How far back did that kinship go, how much more would she know about who she is, how to be, what to do, if she had grown up knowing about her ancestry?

"Twenty years after the Second World War, when we came back here that time, I could see why my parents left," says her father. "I didn't know the cruelty of politics — I was only a kid — but your great-grandparents still lived in a one-room stone house, growing their own grain, grinding it into flour at a community mill. No wonder they left, I thought. Then, back in the U.S. in high school I forgot about all Crete. And next thing I knew I was in the middle of a Vietnamese jungle, eighteen years old, seeing peasant families gunned down, my friends blown up. By the time I got out of the army it seemed to me that the only thing that war produced was evil. In which I was complicit." He leaves a silence. She sees her father as a teenager raising his rifle, shooting at people.

"So how could I go home," his voice goes on, "work in my parents' restaurant as if nothing had changed? Instead when my tour was up I hitchhiked through Europe, slept on beaches in Greece, Italy, France, Spain, drank wine, discovered Moroccan weed."

Finally, in England he discovered solace by growing vegetables in the English commune where he met Dion's mother. Where, thinking, talking, playing guitar, singing, toking, loving under the stars, they produced Teddy and three years later her, their sweet Baby Dionysia. When they lost the commune and moved to Toronto, her father's knowledge of foods soon brought stellar reviews to a restaurant whose kitchen he worked in at a downtown hotel. From there it was a short leap into wines and a future as a sommelier.

"I used to meditate, you know," he goes on now, "a habit I picked up in the commune, and it's helped me off and on through the years. Until

Teddy and your Grandpa..." His voice catches. His head shakes. Dion reaches across the table for his hand.

She and her father have never shared more than their initial grief over their losses of a son, a brother, a father, a grandfather. Dion doubts her Dad and *Yiayiá* have ever gone there either. And after an initial outpouring of sympathy and casseroles, people in Canada move on from tragedies. Not like here, where cemeteries built as close as possible to the sky contain photos, keepsakes, oil lamps lit to keep the spirit of the departed with those who loved them. Tears stream down both their faces in the silence. Her Dad brushes his away.

"Then, going through your grandparents' papers I found the deed to this land and my commune days came back to me, the joy your mother and I found in tilling soil, integrating ourselves into our plant world, the same way my *Pappoús* did making wine. And I knew there was only one way to save your *Yiayiá's* life, and my own." A watery smile.

"When we arrived here fifteen years ago, I wanted to call the business we were reviving by your grandmother's family name, Aramenis Winery, to honour our ancestors who spent hundreds of years caring for vines on this soil. But 'No,' your *Yiayiá* was adamant. 'They lived the lives they were given, that's all. And my Gio and I, and my brothers, we all left. It is you, Alexander, and the future that must be honoured now.' So we used our present family name, Kokanakis Winery. And when I tend our vines I am touched by every breeze, every passing bird, every plant's line and shape." He stops talking.

Above them the moon begins its descent towards a new day.

"So I guess what I'm trying to tell you, chicken, is the only thing I know, that life is the sun's energy shaped into plants, animals, all nature, and this energy is ruthless. Can the rabbit escape or will it be torn to shreds so the wolf can have dinner? Also though, biology tells us that cell communities work together, collaborating. Your liver cells work with your gut cells which work with your brain cells, all of it miraculous when you think of the precision, timing, choice making required. And cells respond to their environment. Which is why what we tend with love makes our futures. Though I have to say, I'm not sure how." His voice dies away.

vii.

June heat raises a wake of dust behind the Vespa motor scooter Dion usually uses to take lunch to her father in his vineyards on the other side of the valley, or to pop into the village to buy beans or fish from the truck that brings them into the valley. Now though she slows to a crawl, searching shrubs on a roadside she doesn't know for signs of the goat path Theo uses to climb to his castle. She has only managed one painting session since Theo moved back up there and her knapsack is packed with dinner, a surprise to make up for how preoccupied she's been.

Credit institutions and loan agencies in the U.S. and Canada feel the same as her father's and *Yiayiá's* Rethymnon bank about giving them a loan using their Kokanakis home and winery as collateral, and Salin has stopped ordering Kokanakis wines for his north shore resort.

"Huh," grunted *Yiayiá* when Dion told her. "He wants to starve us into compliance? The Nazis already tried that and look where it got them."

Holiday couples do stop by for a winery tour and tasting but cash produced from this does not even cover their running costs.

"Come up to my castle," Theo has urged more than once. "Take a break. We'll catch the afternoon light, bring supper, stay over and talk, if that would help." And so many times she has pictured herself climbing the mountain, pushing her feet into the rock, using rough shrubbery to pull herself up, thinking of nothing but where her next footstep should land. Taking off her clothes to lie in grass bathed by cool afternoon air, her upper breast cupped in her hand, its nipple becoming erect as Theo's hand shifts her shoulder so that slanting rays of sunlight can paint her proffered body gold. So that his charcoal working with her body can relieve her of worry, if only for a little while.

Putt-putting around a bend, Dion comes upon a prickly gorse bush a little larger than its neighbours, glowing deep red-purple in the late day sun. Remembers it. Finds Theo's motorcycle hidden up a path behind it. Good, he's home. She parks her Vespa beside it.

Grass on the mountainside is dead now, flowers gone, dirt slippery dry under her running shoes as the slope steepens. Every other time she has come here, Theo has been with her, showing her which shrubs to hold onto, handing her up the last bit.

She misses him at the winery, watching him water *Yiayiá's* garden early in the morning, and the way he is with her grandmother, deferential but also teasing, making the old lady laugh. Dion doesn't even need all the fingers on one hand to count how many times in her life she's heard that sound. She misses Theo's helping her Dad in the vineyard, and their after-supper discussions on the patio.

Amina has decided to call herself Rose full time "to avoid making a mistake with Salin but also because I'm a new person now," she said. "And I like the name your father gave me." Dion wonders where she is this afternoon, hasn't seen her since midday. Maybe doing a chore for *Yiayiá*, whose energy seems to be flagging a little these days. Not with the Russian?

The first time Salin called to invite her to his resort, she declined.

"He wanted to show me his new yacht, which is moored there," she told the family over supper.

"And you said no because you didn't want to go?" Alex asked.

"That's right," said AminaRose. "You have taken me in, given me so much, how could I even consider it?" Alex contemplated his dinner plate, then:

"If you want to see Leonid Salin you should do so, Amina. Kokanakis Wines' business with him has nothing to do with you, and taking back your life isn't going to be easy. A beautiful woman claiming her freedom needs to learn to know what she herself wants, and then act on that." He ate a forkful of pasta, followed it with a mouthful of wine. "Why not practise that while you're here with us? Just be careful, Rose."

Dion watched Theo open his mouth, close it again. Not happy. *Yiayiá* lifted a slice of tomato into her mouth, occupied herself with chewing. The next time Salin called, AminaRose accepted his invitation.

"What if I want to stay the night?" she said, pulling on a pair of jeans she had ventured out to buy, with Dion, in Rethymnon.

"You like the guy that much?"

"I'm kidding." Amina buttoned a long mauve linen tunic she also bought and checked herself in the mirror on Dion's closet door. "Your father's right though, I can't hide here for the rest of my life. And who knows, maybe I'll find out something about him that you can use."

"No," Dion snapped, sorting through her top dresser drawer. "You mustn't involve yourself in our problems." She surveyed her companion. "You need a chunky necklace. I brought one from Canada, God only knows why. It's not as if I ever go anywhere. Ah, here." Blue and purple ceramic stones and glass threaded onto black cord. "I have matching earrings if you want them."

The jewelry looked perfect, of course it did. Dion felt a prick of jealousy. Amina turned away from the mirror to take hold of her hand.

"Thank you. For the shopping trip, the jewelry." Amina's brown eyes moistened. "For everything. For being my friend. I did not imagine the world had in it people like you and your family."

"Just remember, please, you are Rose, from New York."

She was also a forty-year old woman capable of escaping from Saudi Arabia on her own but still Dion, her father, and Theo played hearts late into that night. After Alex surrendered to sleep she and Theo raided the kitchen for midnight snacks. Theo filled two *raki* glasses.

"*Yamas*. Tomorrow I return to my castle to work."

AminaRose came home glowing.

Dion digs her runners into the ground, pulls herself up the steepening path. Stones rattle down the mountainside behind her. Rivulets of sweat tickle her forehead.

Do not stop. Do not look down. Two more footholds and she'll reach the stone wall at the top. She finds another scrub bush branch, pulls. It snaps. She teeters, bends forward, presses her body into the rocky dirt, her breath a furnace now.

Voices sound above her. More than one. Did she cry out? Theo's head appears above her, his hair a mess of curls.

"Dion!" Not happy. Reaching down he pulls her up over the wall into his castle. Where safely standing on terra firma, sweaty strands of hair glued to her face, she sees his mattress shaded by a tarpaulin strung up to one of the castle's turrets. On it, cool as a princess in a multi-coloured sundress she bought with the jeans, AminaRose has raised herself on an elbow. Her dark hair cascades over her shoulder.

"Hi." Her grin is a hundred per cent natural.

Theo's face is blank. Dion wants to disappear.

"Sorry—"

"No Dion," AminaRose springs to her feet. "It's okay."

"I didn't mean to intrude," Dion says to Theo, jealousy spiky as the dead grass assaulting her. Which is ridiculous. Theo is not her lover, he's not even a man she would look at twice. Also, 'I will never try to have sex with you,' he told her. His silence now asks why she doesn't bugger off. She turns back towards the path she has just climbed. "I'll leave you to it."

"No Dion!" AminaRose crosses the space between them. "I've just seen what a beautiful model you are!" Her bangled arm sweeps towards the castle's back wall, where Theo has glued new, textured paper to slats of wood.

On it is a nearly finished drawing of Dion lying on her side, power in her body's curving lines somehow coalescing just below her upper shoulder, in the nippled breast she is offering, then tapering down, the waiting gift in her pelvic shadows balanced by her lower legs' pent-up promise: Desire blowing intellect, criticism, vanity, everything but itself out of its viewer's mind. Embarrassment flushes through Dion: Who knew she was so transparent?

"Come," AminaRose pulls her back into the shade. "Have you got food in your knapsack? I'm famished."

Trapped like a bug in a jar, wings flapping frantically, how can she leave? Nor can she stay. She wipes the sweat off her forehead, leaving a brown streak.

"Here, let me." AminaRose takes Dion's knapsack, finds a napkin in it to wipe her friend's brow.

Sitting down with her on the mattress, Dion opens packets of food she brought for later tonight, does not dare to speak. Because once jealousy has slithered in, it doesn't care that it to has no business here. Theo looks morose.

"I'm sorry," she tells him again. "I was going to surprise you. I thought you might like to use the afternoon light." He has no choice but to nod.

"Let me take the Vespa back to the winery," says AminaRose through a mouthful of *Yiayiá's spanakopita*. Finishing it, she leans forward, her breasts almost but not quite visible inside the cleavage of her dress as she pats Theo's knee. "Thank you for showing me your work, Theo. And for being so sweet." Getting up to leave, she kisses each of them on a cheek and is gone.

The castle's energy feels depleted. Late June's setting sun slides down towards the western mountaintops, glowing gold on the rocks. Theo spreads his blanket for her. Dion takes off her clothes, lies down, assumes the pose. That's what she came for, and to do anything else would lay open confusions she has no idea how to untangle. Theo does not remove his cut-offs. Sitting with his back against the wall below his painting-in-progress, he looks, draws. Focusses on her foot, her leg, her breast. Does not adjust her limbs. Does not touch her at all. Throws down his charcoal.

"My hand is dead," he says. Dion flops onto her back. The setting sun kisses her breasts. A swallow traces loops on the sky.

"Your hand?" A giggle breaks loose. Theo looks away, scanning his art gallery then the castle turrets in the angled sunlight. A hawk is flying in circles above the valley now, hunting. Dion gets up, puts on her clothes, and crosses to the wall overlooking the valley. Because really what, beyond desire, frustration and his art, does she share with Theo?

The hawk soars on the updrafts. After awhile Theo joins her. The powerful bird's tawny wings flap into a quick series of backstrokes, hovering. Then, folding them, pointing its head towards the ground, it turns itself into a missile. Breaks just in time to pluck a vole or a mouse or a baby rabbit too small for the human eye to identify from up here off the valley floor. It writhes in talons that will not let it go as, pumping its mighty wings, the hawk takes off towards a copse of trees between here and the sea.

"Desire," she hears Theo's awe, "the most powerful force in the world."

The sun drops behind the White Mountains. Candy-red clouds sail across the evening sky. Remnants of her jealousy rot in the pit of Dion's stomach. Hopelessness, loneliness she thought she had left behind in Canada mix into it. She'd like to go back to the winery but climbing down through deepening shadows to the road by herself would be too dangerous. Anyway AminaRose has taken her Vespa. Theo makes his mattress into a bed for her.

"Not your plan," she says, and he must be able to hear that she means it because, lifting a shoulder, he gives her a scrap of a smile.

Lamb chops packed in ice courtesy of his Chania uncle, perogies made by his friend Kiri's mother, who is Ukrainian, and *horta* and wine, he must have assembled all of this for AminaRose. Dion has brought a bottle of her Dad's red Romeiko. "Take it," her father insisted last night. "Enjoy it on your mountaintop."

Theo has built up the stones around his fire pit to protect against a summertime threat of wildfires. Setting a metal grill across the top, he seasons the meat. By the time the coals are ready a languid half moon has taken over a darkening sky, and is there a finer meal than herb-seasoned

Cretan lamb grilled over a fire? They eat like cave people, tearing meat off the bones with their teeth, ripping pieces of bread from the loaf to mop up the juices. Her father's bottle of Romeiko wine mixes with the savours of lamb on Dion's tongue as they slide down her throat.

"You know your Dad's my hero, right?" Grease glistens on Theo's chin as he upends the bottle. Dion has told him what happened in Salin's study and about her father's reliance on nature as a solver of problems. "But he doesn't know what kind of bully he's up against. Leonid Salin thinks he can do whatever he wants because he can." Theo goes on talking about how easy it is for an experienced hacker to take over online interactions of any kind to control human thinking for governments or companies anywhere on the planet. "And every day they get more and more sophisticated."

Dion knows some of this, vaguely, from reading the BBC news.

"But what does this have to do with a little Cretan winery?"

Theo stares at the empty wine bottle.

"I actually have no idea. Except to say that your father's right – everything, vines, wine, computers, all of us – everything is nature. And nature is ruthless."

The night chill is making her teeth chatter. She wishes she was at home, in her own bed. Theo looks at her, his hair wild, his eyes full of firelight, his pointy face satyr-like.

"So maybe your father's right about trusting nature too, maybe there is some kind of move we can make. We just have to figure out what it is."

She wakens early. The sun, peeking out from behind Mt. Psiloritis, is just beginning to bathe the west side of the valley when she goes to sit on the wall overlooking the valley. Far below her the winery still lies in that shadow-filled place between yesterday and the day just opening. Memory and imagination line up in the pirate's castle, Teddy strapping himself into his hang-glider: "Come on, D!"

The Perfect Robbery was her older brother's idea. Teddy was fourteen, Dion eleven when, leaving their English commune, they landed in a tenth floor apartment in Toronto, Canada with their own bathroom, hot water whenever they wanted it, no dirt under their feet, no vegetables to dig up, no chickens, rabbits, goats. Teddy and Dion thought they were in heaven. Dad worked nights in a hotel kitchen and sometimes Mom would have to stay late at her bookkeeping job so they would take some of the paper route money Teddy was supposed to be saving for university and ride the subway to a downtown shopping mall. Where, eating pizza and drinking Coke on a bench outside a flossy jewelry store, they planned The Perfect Robbery.

Necklaces, bracelets, earrings, watches displayed in the window had no price tags because people who could afford them didn't care what they cost, Teddy said. And the store would be insured, so nobody would lose anything. And they would be able to buy a proper house with a garden, thought Dion. The Perfect Robbery must take place while the store was open, alarms switched off. Confusion is the best distraction, said Teddy, so they'd pretend to belong to someone going in. When lots of gold and silver and diamond jewelry was laid out on the counter, Dion was to burst into loud, tragic tears. Teddy would sweep whatever loot he could reach into his jacket pockets then slip away while everyone tried to figure out who the wailing child belonged to. Evasive action was the key to getting away with it. They'd meet at the pizza place and take a subway going one way, then jump off and go back the other way. Teddy worked out every detail and Dion was becoming frightened that they would actually do it, until a girl in his class highjacked Teddy's attention.

The sun breasts the top of Mt. Psiloritis. Soon the air up here will be too hot for climbers, for anyone. Fresh coffee scents come to her. Theo, still in his cutoffs, comes over with a mug for her.

"Come and look," he heads towards his drawing of her on the castle's back wall. "I like the pose, but the setting's not right." He considers his sketch. "I'm seeing sea light, waves."

"Didn't Botticelli already do that?"

"No, I'm not thinking mythically. But there's a beach on the south coast, off the road just west of Hora Sfakion, a small pebble beach, very private – you have to climb down to it – and there's a cave." He smiles, negating yesterday, everything but this. "We could camp there. If you want to, and can get away."

The sea, a wild, private beach, freedom, if only for a couple of days. "I'd like that."

AminaRose and Bowie are waiting in the kitchen when Theo brings her back to the winery. Alex took *Yiayiá* to Rethymnon hospital last night with chest pains. He'll call as soon as he has news.

Dion sags into a chair. Her grandmother is ninety-four and every bit as tuned in as the rest of them to losing her home, the winery and land that has been in her family for centuries. At night Dion often hears her discussing it with *Pappoús*.

Please God, she thinks now, don't let her have gone to join him, not just yet – though who could blame her if she has?

Theo and Bowie go out to the barnyard to feed Aretha and the chickens. Dion showers, changes, and returns to find AminaRose sitting on one of the chairs at the kitchen table, getting up, sitting down again. In the few weeks she's been here she's spent more time with *Yiayiá*, cooking, chatting, doing her hair, her nails, than either Dion or her father ever has. New light has come into her grandmother's faded eyes and Dion is mostly happy to see it. A tiny part of her doesn't understand though why *Yiayiá*, who refuses to discuss anything personal with Dion, accepts such intimacies from a near stranger.

Theo comes in with fresh milk and an armload of vegetables from the garden. He has to go into Chania to work in his uncle's *taverna* tonight but will be back tomorrow to help in the vineyard and the garden. As soon as he leaves, AminaRose takes hold of her friend's upper arms, looks into her face.

"Dion! All night I've been worrying, about your *Yiayiá*, but also I need to tell you I am so sorry, I should never have gone to Theo's castle—"

"No no—"

"Yes yes, you have feelings for him." Her brown eyes are full of sympathy. "You have saved my life and me? I'm a spoiled brat. I didn't think—"

"Stop it, Amina! Theo and I are not involved."

"But the picture he's painting, and the way you were when you saw me?" AminaRose scrutinizes Dion's face.

"Honestly, I have no idea what any of that was about." Pulling a carrot out of a bunch on the table, Dion turns away to run it under the kitchen tap, to hide the ridiculous, totally uncalled for flush spreading up her neck. Finding a knife, she starts chopping. AminaRose picks up some potatoes, scrubs them at the sink and finds a peeler. And suddenly Dion hears herself telling her friend about Theo's art project on desire and how they found the pose he's painting, and it's the first time she has put his exploration of her body into words. Detailed, explicit, her descriptions keep on coming, as carefully calibrated as a runaway train.

"No wonder the poor boy was bursting with need!" AminaRose says when finally she finds some brakes.

"With desire you mean. Which you ruined, by the way." She tells AminaRose about Theo's failing hand yesterday, laughs. Her friend looks down at the potato she is holding.

"I am so ashamed. When I went with him it was just to see his castle and his paintings. Then we started talking and he listened while I told him a little about my life and it felt so good, you know? So I started playing around, pretending he was the pirate and I was his captive and suddenly that did not feel good." She looks up. "Too close to home maybe. I didn't for one minute think about what Theo would take from it. Anyway, nothing happened Dion, nothing at all, before you came along. But since I came back here, all night I have been trying to figure out why I did that. He was hoping to make love, I knew that. So why did I give him hope?

"All I can think is that when you have lived more than half your life in a man's harem, given whatever you want but still servicing a man sexually, and closely chaperoned anytime you leave the walls around your shut-in life, you never learn how to behave freely, you know? How to make good choices. And you, Dion, are the last person in this world that I want to hurt." Sadness deepens lines radiating out from her eyes. "I don't think I should stay—"

"Don't even go there, Amina! You're safe here and all of us love having you." It's true, her own petty jealousy an irritation, transient as a virus, nothing more. Except if her grandmother survives today, losing the winery will surely kill her. And then what?

Dion takes a bite of the carrot she's just peeled. Its crunchy sweetness takes her back, past all the years in Toronto, to an early memory of her and Teddy eating carrots their mother had just pulled out of the ground at the English commune. "Stop it!" she cried, laughing. In another life. Here, now, birds chirruping outside the kitchen window don't care about wine and love and bank balances. An enormous blue bumblebee comes in, buzzing. And quickly flies out again.

"My father's right," Dion goes on. "Life happens here, now. So keep exploring what you feel and want and think as a free woman here with us. As for Theo, he's a puppy, he'll recover."

Dion doesn't mention Salin, and AminaRose has said very little about their dinner. Remembering his hands on her at the villa though, and her cleavage leaning over Theo at his castle yesterday, Dion's mind wants to obsess about what will come next. But her brain doesn't have the bandwidth, not today.

Yiayiá and Dad return in time for dinner at midday. Her father is all smiles.

"A panic attack," he tells them. "The doctor ran every test known to medicine and concluded that the old girl's probably going to outlive all of us."

"God forbid," says *Yiayiá.*

viii.

Theo's motorbike, its panniers loaded with camping and art gear, labours up into mountains Dion has only ever seen from the valley. Their lower skirts are covered with olive trees and tufts of green where grasses are protected by their shade.

Summer heat is becoming intense so they waited a few days to make sure *Yiayiá* had recovered before they left. AminaRose and her father will keep a close eye on her and everyone agreed that getting away for a break will be good for Dion. She has exhausted every source of financial aid she can think of for the winery. There's nothing left to do but try to make ends meet while waiting for a stroke of benevolent magic. Or for the inevitable.

"So go," said AminaRose, "sightsee, swim, lie in the sun, pose for Theo."

Now though, her arms locked around Theo's chest, her breasts against his back, a new jitteriness has come into Dion's stomach. Anticipation? No, more like the feeling you get waiting in the dentist's chair. Which is totally unhinged, backed by no logic. Theo's fingers touch her only to create what he wants to paint, and she never touches him, other than when riding behind him like this. How will it be on a remote beach though? Desire needs to attach itself to something: Girl meets boy, hawk sees prey. And when hawk is hungry, it doesn't care what kind of edible it finds.

The motorbike thrums beneath her. Her arms feel Theo's sinewy strength, like a vine that, leaning with the weather, will not break. Stopping for flocks of sheep and their shepherds blocking the road, she smells wood-fired outdoor ovens in villages nestled into the White Mountains' folds. *Yiayiás* dressed head to toe in black even in the mid-summer heat carry bags bulky with vegetables bought from a truck whose rooftop loudspeaker, ahead of them, has been broadcasting fresh tomatoes, courgettes, artichokes, aubergines. High above them, in cliffs broken by slides of scree seemingly impassable to anything but wild goats, caves are black holes.

British commandoes and Crete's Resistance hid radio equipment and fugitive Allied soldiers in these mountain heights, Theo tells her. Some of the old *yiayiás* they've seen will still remember.

Like her own *Yiayiá*! Was one of these mountain villages where her grandparents met? Shame on her for not knowing, thinks Dion.

Theo is full of World War II stories: Here is the church where British commandoes hid in the crypt while, feigning innocence, its priest lied to a German patrol someone must have alerted. Here is the mountain birthplace of Crete's most famous Resistance runner, who ran barefoot across all these mountains carrying messages.

He stops the bike outside a village *taverna* and here now is his mother's cousin, an aged woman with swollen legs engulfing him in a hug then sitting them on a terrace overlooking a valley thousands of feet below. Feeding them a steady stream of dishes. "*Raki*!" cries her husband, who has been playing cards with a couple of other old men at a table in the corner. And Dion watches Cretan Theo come to life, his fine-boned face expressing rapid up-and-down Greek that sounds like invective until suddenly everyone bursts out laughing.

By the time they cross the mountains' barren high plateaus the sun has begun its descent over a sparkling blue Libyan Sea far below. Theo stops at the top of a switchback road down to Hora Sfakion, the last south coast village accessible by road. A ferry leaving the village's harbour looks like a toy. Her bum numb, Dion gets off the motorbike, finds a little clump of bushes and squats behind it to pee.

"Picture this bay full of row boats and fishing boats seventy-four years ago." Theo is standing beside the bike when she returns. "Taking several thousand Allied soldiers trapped after the German invasion out to British destroyers sent over from Egypt. There was no road down the mountain then and after making their way up here from the north shore the men had to get down to the sea in the dead of night — the ships couldn't risk waiting very long — so they made a chain, each man holding onto the shoulder of the one in front of him. To keep from losing their footing or getting lost, but also to stop anyone breaking into the chain because there were only so many spots on the ships and if someone stole their place they'd be left behind. As hundreds were."

Standing right where they are now. She sees it, her stomach queasy with their fear. Where were *Yiayiá* and her Gio during all this?

"Or," Theo goes on, "you can dial back further and picture Turkish or Venetian or medieval pirates' or Roman or Mycenean ships on the horizon, all coming to take over this jewel of an island in the middle of the Mediterranean." He kickstarts the bike's engine, turns to shout over its growl. "There's a reason we Cretans don't take kindly to bullies."

She hangs onto him, trying not to look as he leans into hairpin bends cut into the mountainside. Near the bottom a small road snakes away from Hora Sfakion to a mountain village west of it. Theo turns onto it, slowing to find a landmark she can't see, and parks his bike. His beach, at the bottom of a near vertical drop below the road, is invisible from above.

Late sunshine is still scorching pebbles that have gathered in a wrinkle of the coastal cliff face. They drop their packs, sleeping bags, water bottles in the blessed shade of a single tamarisk tree between the cliff and the sea. Behind it seas from some bygone era have scooped out a cave — their shelter for the next three nights.

Theo tears off his t-shirt and jeans and hot foots it over the pebbles into the blue green waves. Dion scans the empty clifftop above.

Nobody lives within several kilometres, Theo has told her. Still. Nude as a model, she takes off her t-shirt, jeans and panties, bra easily now. Real-life naked though?

Theo is thrashing around in the water, swimming out to sea. Her t-shirt under-arms, the crotch of her jeans are sweat-soaked and the air is hot. She strips, tiptoes quickly down to the water, splashes through foaming waves to hide her body in the water's coolness.

She has swum in the sea exactly once since arriving in Crete. Early in April the weather was warm enough on a day she and her father made a trip to a little library started by British ex-pats near the Plakias Bay beach. Now she flips onto her back, closes her eyes to the sun's late afternoon light, feels her breasts bobbing on the surface, her arms and legs weightless, her torso rocking in a saltwater embrace. Some say Crete was the setting for the bible writers' Garden of Eden. Saint Paul stayed on Cretan beaches during his travels. She can see why: If there is a heaven on Earth this golden moment must surely be it.

Theo has arrived at her side. Standing chest-deep in the water, his curly hair pasted to his head by the sea, he looks older, ageless even, like a character out of a Greek myth. Not Eros.

"I need you to come and pose. Right now." She hears his excitement. Does not want to leave her water cradle. "Please, before we lose this light!" He reaches for her hand to pull her upright, then wades towards shore. Seawater swirls between her legs as she lowers them. "There," he points at the waves foaming across the pebbles, "where the sea meets the shore. This is exactly what I'm looking for!"

She arranges her body's pose at the water's edge while he runs up the beach, hurries back, penis jigging, arms full of a sketchpad, pencils, paintbrushes, watercolours.

Rays of light are coming low across the sea from the west now, touching with gold whatever lies in their path — wavelets at the shore, wood grain in a driftwood log thrown up onto the beach by some bygone storm, Theo's curls, springing back to life already, her body lying on its side for him. Sea foam breaks against her back, laps at her legs. He kneels beside her to position her shoulders as she offers him her breast, and beneath his dripping sea saltiness she picks up the musky, sweet-sharp scent of desire as he gets up to step back, observing the play of light on her body, then bends again to tilt her shoulder slightly so that her proffered breast is bathed in gold.

Sunlight warms her as he draws. Cool sea foam sneaks down between the pebbles to tickle her lower armpit. It fondles her bum, finds its way between her legs into places no one but she has touched in recent history. Her nipples tighten. Muscles inside her belly want her body to buck, her legs to open as, sticking up out of his lap, Theo's penis watches while he draws.

Darkness comes late in July but when it does on this wild scrap of south coast beach it is absolute. She lies beside Theo on still warm pebbles, looking past a crescent moon at the Milky Way's millions of stars. Inside her sweat pants and hoody – no need for underwear – her skin is tingling as if it, and she, were brand new. She thinks, for the second time today, of the Greek gods, to whom anything was possible. Whoever dreamed them up must have felt like this.

A sucking, breaking roar wakes her in the cave. Theo's sleeping bag is already empty. Outside a south-west wind is tossing the blue-grey dawn sea into white caps. Waves high as her shoulders crash onto their beach. The sun is not yet high enough to reach them but the wind is not cold. Theo hands her a mug of coffee brewed on his propane ring.

She spends the morning in the shelter of the cliff on the west side of the beach with one of *Yiayiá's* cheese pastries and her Kobo reader. Theo drops down beside her, picks up a book she has brought in case her reader runs out of juice, as there is no internet or cell phone service here.

"A geological history of Crete," he reads.

"Surprisingly riveting," she tells him. "I found it in the Plakias library."

"Cool." Spreading his towel, he lies on his stomach and opens its pages.

The climbing sun glitters on the busy sea, reflects light blue on the undersides of waves breaking on the beach, heats the wind whipping the tamarisk's bright green froth of leaves. Dion marvels at the way its roots hold fast to this rocky ground, its limbs shooting out branchlets for needle-thin leaves, the only kind that can survive here. Their shadows dance on the pebbles. Until, reaching its zenith, the sun reduces the wind to fitful gusts. The waves die down. Theo glances up from his book.

"I love how Crete's rocky underlay, and its location as a meeting point for Europe and Africa and the Middle East explain so much about humans. There were people here more than a hundred thousand years ago! Which means humans must have known how to build boats, sail, navigate. Then came the Minoans, who were incredibly advanced, much more so than their Greek conquerors a couple of thousand years later."

"I wonder if any of them lived here, in this cave," Dion sheds her sweats — after less than a day! — then hands Theo her waterproof sunscreen. "Can you rub some of this on my back?" Sitting she turns away from him.

He moves her hair, which has grown down to her shoulders, and drips cold lotion between her shoulder blades. Swirling it with the palm of his hand, he works his way up around her neck then down over her back, her sides, squirts lotion into the small of her back and spreads it down over the top of her bum, and suddenly nerve endings all over her body want her to lie down on the pebbles, for him to rub lotion over her breasts and belly and thighs. Then to forget the sunscreen and be like the people in erotic prehistoric pictographs she has seen, the woman bending over, the man coming into her from behind.

Did those men take time first to touch their women in all the right places, Dion wonders, to make her want him so much she would do whatever he asked—

Theo's hand stops.

"Thanks." She gets up. "Coming for a swim?"

Skipping across the hot pebbles, splashing out through the waves, she strokes away from shore, dives down, arms pulling, legs scissoring the water, her hair streaming behind her, down, down into delicious currents of cold. Coming up, gulping air, she descends again into a sun-shot blue that has nothing to do with humans or money or sex or desire, her every cell thrilling to an energy that cannot belong to air-breathing humans.

When Theo wakes her from an afternoon siesta in the shade of the tamarisk, the wind has become a breeze. Gentle waves spread a lace of white foam along the water's edge. She swims out to find the cold underwater currents again, to go deeper this time into their blue silence. Where mermaids live.

Hair flowing, her body sleek in the water, she strokes towards the water blue light then, squeezing her thighs together, flips her feet into a dive. Smiles into the deep. Theo will be waiting, sitting crosslegged just above the water line with his sketchpad and paints but down here sensuality has no strings attached.

Who dreamed up mermaids, she wonders? Who would want to encase the lower half of alluring seawomen in fish scales? Or were the spiny scales there to repel intruders until magical mermaids made their choice and slipped them off?

The golden light doesn't stay long. She swims the path it is laying back to shore, her mermaid breath whooshing in, bubbling out, her body gliding through the sea. Flowing light-gold patterns gleam on pebbles in the shallows. She pulls herself through them, her hair floating in the foaming lace between sea and land until, flipping onto her side, facing Theo, she cups her upper breast and lifts it out of the water as if her body, being mostly made of salt water, belonged to this moment, this place.

"Stay exactly like that!" Theo's hand moves across his page.

A mermaid's self-possessed laughter sounds like song as, tweaking her lifted nipple, which is already erect, she watches his arousal intensify. Raises her upper thigh just enough to let the wavelets' cool fingers steal into her vagina. Wants to open fully to them, to unfurl like a flower, so her man, whoever and wherever he is, can find his way into her deep blue sea self.

Theo draws page after page.

The wind does not return. Their days take on a pattern. Morning brings a glare to light and sound energies. Dion reads or daydreams, Theo experiments with paint colours, then they swim for fun, racing each other, or diving down to pick up treasures glinting indistinctly on the sea bottom, or exploring little caves and rocky outcroppings at the end of the beach. Theo is a strong but messy swimmer who taught himself at an Iraklio beach long before he morphed into a computer-hacking art student. Dion, who learned the front crawl and elementary backstroke in British swimming lessons, teaches him how to economize on movement, how to use his breath. Afternoons are for eating, slathering sunscreen all over her scorched skin, then sleeping in the tamarisk's shade. Waking, she swims alone, out into what she thinks of now as her own mermaid depths. There's no use trying to tame her hair, which the sea has styled into sun-bleached ringlets.

"It looks great," says Theo.

Light inching towards its golden threshold tells them it's time for posing, drawing, painting. After it fades they eat food brought from home before darkness drops like a curtain, then drink wine or *raki* and, lying on their sleeping bags under the stars, talk into the night. About the world, the climate crisis, Earth's future. About why AminaRose is consorting with a cybercriminal and what could happen to her. About their own futures. Theo's wiry frame contains not a single grasping or malevolent bone. He wants only to paint. Dion envies his goodness, his knowing what he wants.

On their last night, underneath her tingling skin, inside the exhilarated energy of her sea self, in the freedom of a darkness so complete nothing exists but the planets and Milky Way stars and possibilities beyond judgement or censure or ridicule, an idea dribbles, random as a pebble, into Dion's mind.

"What if I took something valuable of Salin's and hid it somewhere on his property, and then ransomed it back to him for enough money to clear our debt?" Voiced aloud, the idea steals her breath. Waves break and recede in the darkness. Lying beside her, Theo does not laugh or call the idea dumb.

"What would you take?"

"Something small enough to bury. So not a painting." The pebble begins to roll. "How 'bout his two million-dollar bottle of Henri IV Dudogne cognac!"

Theo hoots with laughter.

"Right, from a locked study guarded by cameras controlled by computers—"

"All of which must run on power. Which can be switched off."

"Uh uh. All his systems will be backed up, probably by solar batteries. And even if you did manage to liberate Henri IV, why would Salin pay a ransom to get it back? He'd just laugh, then find a way to screw you, and buy another one."

"A two hundred thousand-dollar ransom would be a lot cheaper than the two million-dollar cost of a new Henri IV." Such a beautiful pebble. It picks up speed.

"Two hundred thousand, two million, both are peanuts to Salin, and guys like him don't like losing. Stealing the bottle and selling it would be a whole lot simpler, and safer."

"No. Stealing it would make me a thief."

Theo laughs again.

"As opposed to?"

Dion stares up at the heavens.

"As opposed to, if I'm caught: 'Officer, can I help it if this man can't find his stupid bottle of booze right here in his own garden?' Not stealing, not even a lie." But.

A brain teaser, wishful dreaming under a sky full of galaxies and a moon that's filling out more every night, that's all this is.

Pebbles sometimes find their way into a pocket though. Rolling up her sleeping bag the next morning, Dion is hardly even aware that she's thinking out loud:

"If desire's at the root of everything what's the best way, I wonder, to use Salin's?" Theo looks up from the coffee he's making on his propane hot ring, frowning.

"His desire for Amina?"

"No! Amina must have no part in this. His desire for power," Dion shoves her sleeping bag down into its bag. "And the beautiful stuff it brings him, like our winery."

Theo gazes out at a sea that has brought power-seeking invaders to his home island since the beginning of recorded history.

"Desire's dynamite, you have to be really careful how you deal with it."

They take the coastal route home, east from Hora Sfakion through low hills and gently rolling plains between the mountains and the sea, stopping at Frangokastello, where a ramparted eight-hundred year old Venetian castle still guards a sandy beach. Above it pink-skinned holiday makers are sipping drinks at *taverna* tables set on a promenade. Theo walks past them, down to postcard blue water and strips to swim. She can not do the same. Her bikini feels cumbersome as a raincoat against her skin but watched by prying tourist eyes, she can not take it off.

Dressed again, they sit on a brick wall beside the bike to eat ice cream cones.

"I've been thinking," says Theo, "stealing the cognac bottle might be doable."

"No, I told you, I'm not a thief. And if I got caught what use would

I be to my Dad and *Yiayiá* inside a Greek jail?" She takes too big a mouthful of ice cream, winces with brain freeze. Anyway where would a trussed-up middle-aged chicken like her find the guts to steal or kidnap anything?

"If we planned it right we wouldn't get caught."

"Not 'we,' Theo. Salin lent money to Kokanakis Wines—"

"Right, and where did that money come from, D?"

No one but Teddy has ever called her D. Dion busies herself running her tongue around her ice cream cone, catching drips before they fall.

"Leonid Salin makes his money by hacking into the world's computer systems," Theo goes on, "by staging cyberattacks, and finding more and more ways to destabilize countries Russia wants to mess with." He takes a bite of his ice cream. "And it has to be 'we' who do the stealing because I bet I'm the only one of us who's ever been a thief."

Dion stares at him. He shrugs.

"Petty stuff, as a boy on the docks when the cruise ships came in, thousands of tourists pouring out to gawp at my city for five minutes, handbags hanging from shoulders, often open. And me and my Mom with no breakfast. This was before I discovered drawing for money."

Dion crunches her cone, says nothing. Because once a pebble is in your pocket you can't help taking it out, running your fingers over its polished smoothness, licking it to brighten its mauve and green and the white line running through them. Mineral art, it sits in your hand. Unnoticed until you look at it. Like so many things in her life. Dion finishes her ice cream, wipes her mouth.

"You may be a thief," she says, "but I can read Leonid Salin."

"Oh?" Theo too is finished.

"Yeah, because I'm just like him: I want what I want. Some examples: my deodorant contains dementia-causing aluminum and its container, like my body wash bottle, is made of plastic that probably winds up in an ocean somewhere, but still I buy them, use them. Which has to mean that what I want for me matters more to me than polluting our planet."

Theo puts on his helmet, digs into his pocket for his bike keys.

"Both Salin and I put ourselves first, never mind the consequences," Dion realizes. "The difference between us is that I don't cross the line—"

"What line?" Theo throws his leg over his motorbike. "You think buying plastic containers of chemical crap isn't a crime? Those who live on oceans where your garbage washes up might have some opinions about that."

Dion pulls her helmet down over her head but she can still hear him.

"If we stole Henri IV all we'd be guilty of is taking from a soulless slime bag who's trying to screw your family out of everything you own, including the only home you have."

"Not 'we,' Theo!"

"Yes 'we!' You can't pull this off by yourself and do you have any idea how much I'd like to take that guy down? Especially if it was for your family."

Fitting herself onto the bike here in the mermaidless, clothes-wearing world, Dion has no idea what to say. Everything she has always thought or felt or been suddenly seems irrelevant. So many pebbles make a beach, every one of them uniquely shaped and coloured, all of them millions of years older than any lacework of laws made by humans.

Mountains come right down to the sea between Frangokastello and Plakias on Crete's south coast, some of its beaches Allied landing and rescue sites during World War II, according to Theo. Watching the sun-blue sea, Dion revisits herself swimming naked and free into its depths. Where a new pebble-idea flashes suddenly, bright as a jewel on the seafloor:

Salin's world runs on fear, on long black sinews of worry — usually about what could happen to us next — that wind themselves around our spines and nerves and muscles, robbing us of critical thought.

Fertilizing this fear, then feeding people what you want them to think/do in order to feel safe is how manipulation works. That's what the Russian is trying to do to her family. But what if she could somehow stop her fear? Where would that take her?

ix.

They've been gone four days. It feels like weeks. *Yiayiá* is sitting on the patio in dappled shade cast by the plane tree's broad branches, wearing a pair of tan capris that belong to Dion and a peach coloured silk blouse she must have brought with her from the U.S. The only clues to her usual Cretan self are a pile of tough-looking green beans lying on the table beside a paring knife and a homemade frapuccino in her favourite froth-ringed glass. Dion drops into the chair opposite her.

"Where's Amina?"

"Gone to the north shore with Salin," says her grandmother, "to visit his new sailing yacht."

"You look great."

"Well," says *Yiayiá*, "I was lying in that hospital bed thinking about my Gio and how we left here, left the past behind to make a new life of our own. And we succeeded. I was a successful American business-woman. 'So why don't you start acting like one?' Gio told me."

Never before has Dion heard her grandmother lay out any feelings, preferring to deflect or deny or dress them in wit, or censure where her son is concerned. Now however fatigue is radiating out of her shoulders in the heat. And her eyes must be going. A sheen of fine clay dust covers the tabletop. If she could see it she would have wiped it away before sitting down.

"And before you were a business woman you were a Resistance

fighter," Dion reminds her. "We've just been through the mountains and I'd love to hear about that."

"And you also raised three beautiful children," adds her father, stopping to wink at Dion on his way from barnyard to kitchen. Bowie leaves his side to run yipping circles around Theo, his tail wagging his entire back end.

"Pfff," says *Yiayiá*. "The point is, since apparently I'm not going to give up the ghost just yet, I let your pants out a little at the waist to fit me, I hope you don't mind?"

"No no, of course not." Dion would like to lean over to hug her grandmother but doesn't dare.

"Anyway it doesn't matter," *Yiayiá* goes on. "Whatever clothes I put on, still I can see the bottom of the flour sack in the kitchen and where will we get money to buy more?" Her faded blue eyes do not meet Dion's. "All this trouble is because of me, you know that don't you? I allowed a single investor—"

"Shsh," Dion covers her grandmother's hand on the table. Theo offers her one of his smiles.

"Don't you worry about flour, *Yiayiá*. Dion and I are going to take care of that."

Dion flashes him a 'Shut up!' look. Her father appears with three more frappuccinos (ice, milk, Néscafe and sugar shaken in a tumbler with a screw-top lid.) And now Dion notices two waist-high terracotta amphorae outside the fermenting room door.

"Oh Dad—" What did he use to buy them?

"They were museum pieces, one of the big wineries was getting rid of them," he says. "They've never stored anything as far as anyone can tell, and I thought Minoans, Greeks, Romans all fermented their wine in amphorae, so why not try a storage method that's 4,000 years old? As long as we still have a vineyard. They cost me a case of last year's wine."

Theo downs his coffee and gets up.

"I have to go to Chania. My uncle needs me in the *taverna* tonight and then I'll pick up supplies to make the paper for my painting. Could

I borrow one of your tarps and make it here, Alex?' he asks. "It won't take long."

"Sure," Dion's father looks pleased, "and afterwards you can help me put out jars of a sticky goo and meat mixture I make to keep the hornets from feasting on my grapes." Which are growing fat now in summer's oven-like heat, he tells them, each Romeiko bunch its own mix of red, purple, green grapes.

He goes off to clip vine leaves, gauging how to block just enough but not too much sunlight from this year's grapes. As if he and his family were not nearly destitute. As if all that mattered was weeding and watching and waiting for his crop's right harvest moment: just before the sun shrivels the grapes or fall winds and rain beat them to death. Inside the fermenting room baskets are washed and piled, waiting for a team of harvesters.

Who will be paid how, Dion wonders?

A summer breeze plays through the plane tree's shade. A gecko scoots across the patio stones. *Yiayiá* picks up a green bean, rubs dirt off it then lops off its stem end with her knife and drops it into a colander. Dion picks up a bean, rubs it clean and hands it to *Yiayiá*, then another one, and tells her about their trip up through the White Mountains, then down to Theo's beach tucked under a cliff west of Hora Sfakion.

"Where were you during the war, *Yiayiá*, in the Resistance?" And why, she wonders, hasn't she ever asked about this before.

"Pfff," *Yiayiá* bats her questions away, "that was a long time ago, another life."

"A brave life if you ask me," Dion counters, handing her another green bean.

"Pfff," her grandmother expels her breath again, looking up at the plane tree's leaves rustling above them. "What else was I going to do? One day life is normal, I'm washing clothes, weeding the garden, doing what my mother tells me. Next day German soldiers are dropping thick as a rain storm out of the sky, and the killing begins." She too sips her coffee. "Well, my friends and I, here in the village, we had to do something. Our fathers were not happy about our leaving but they were never happy about anything we did outside our houses anyway and in the high mountain villages people were cut off, starving." *Yiayiá* and her friends Irina and Katerina joined a group of girls carrying flour and medical supplies and whatever else they could scavenge up goat paths German patrols didn't know about. Before they came down for the next load they ran classes to teach anyone who wanted to learn how to read and write. "It was not dangerous, most of the time, not really," she says more than seven decades later, "as long as you were careful—"

"Not dangerous! You could have been shot, or worse—!"

"I was seventeen and everybody, children, mothers, grandparents, everybody was risking everything, down to protecting their chickens with pitchforks." She fixes faded blue eyes on her granddaughter. "Now why don't you tell me what this is really about?"

Fatigued or not, *Yiayiá's* brain doesn't miss much apparently. Dion inspects the tabletop.

"It's just, Theo told me about the war and the Allied rescue at Hora Sfakion but all I know about you and *Pappoús* is that you met up in the mountains. And I wondered," suddenly Dion finds herself close to tears, for her grandmother as a girl in war and for her now, an old lady about to lose everything. "How did you do it, fight in the Resistance?"

Yiayiá gazes into the morning sunlight.

"We did what was necessary, that's all. Many died." The old lady turns back to her beans. "And then after the war Greece started arresting our own Resistance fighters, who just a year or two earlier were heroes."

"No! Why?"

"Many Resistance groups were led by Communists and the British, our allies during the war, were terrified of communism and Stalin. That's why your *Pappoús* and I left for America." Her eyes return to Dion. "Sometimes we have to make difficult choices, Dionysia, if we don't want to be destroyed by powers that have regard for nothing but their own designs."

Dion gets up, plants a sudden kiss in the old lady's hair. "Thank you, *Yiayiá*."

Theo moves back into the fermenting room with most of his painting materials. July breezes cannot blow away heat pounding even the scraps of shade he has made in his castle and everyone here is glad to have him back, especially *Yiayiá* who treats him like a Cretan grandson. He takes over her garden, sketches her bending over her herb pots outside the kitchen door, and Amina hanging laundry, and Melodious munching weeds among the olive trees, cats hunting in the barnyard and Alex sitting on the patio with a bottle of wine and Bowie under the table. Dion turns the kitchen's back wall into an art gallery.

Leonid Salin invites Rose for lunch and a swim at his villa. Several swims later he invites her for dinner. She spends the night. Dion is preparing supper while *Yiayiá* naps and Dad and Theo are out tending the vines when a car stops on the road outside the front of the winery. AminaRose floats into the kitchen, pours herself a glass of water. Her olive skin doesn't beam emotions the way Dion's does but as she pulls out a chair and sits down at the table, her movements are languorous, physically satiated.

Salin has asked her to go with him on a week-long sailing trip to Santorini. They'll detour to several islands along the way.

"And oh Dion, such a lover he is!"

"You're going to play Rose for a whole week?" Dion picks up a tomato, chops it into quarters. 'Such a lover,' what does that mean? What exactly does he do? She can not ask, doesn't know how. Discussing sexual intimacies never happened with her mother or school friends or buddies at work. As for Teddy, even bring up the subject when they were kids and he'd snap your head off — anyway what would he know about how it is for women? — And then he was dead.

"What if you've let something slip," she says now, "and he's found out who you are and this trip is a ruse to get you away, to sell you back to your husband?" Salin must be wondering why Rose is still here.

She picks up another tomato. Sees the Russian in his designer polo shirts and jeans and gold watch: a man who couldn't care less about Kokanakis Wines yet wants it. Will take everything they own, if necessary, to make that happen. She sees him in his living room full of paintings the night of his dinner, a guiding hand in the small of Amina's back. Then again in his study with her and her father after dinner. Cold, heartless. Glancing across the table, she catches her friend smiling at her glass of water. After twenty-plus years in her husband's harem is power in a man all she knows?

Or is she a match for Salin, an open-cleavage vampire woman sucking the richest blood? Would she or Theo or her father or her ancient, possibly dying grandmother be capable of spotting a blood-sucking vampire woman?

Not in gentle, good natured, compassionate Amina who is still smiling at last night's memory. Dion scoops the tomato pieces into a bowl where a sliced cucumber lies waiting.

"A man like Salin can get into anybody's computer. He could easily have read everything there is to know about your disappearance, even internal memos your husband thinks are private."

AminaRose shakes her head, picks up a red onion, as if to weigh it in her hand.

"Look Dion, I hear your fear for me, and I appreciate it. And if you want me to turn my back on Leo while I'm here I'll totally understand that, I've said so from the beginning. But please don't think that because I've spent half my life locked in a palace I'm ignorant. I know that anybody who has as much money as Leo is not innocent, I've sat in those boardrooms." She puts the onion down again. "But the world'll keep spinning no matter what I do or don't do, so if it's all right with you I'd like to do what your father advised: enjoy my life a little bit while I figure out where it should go from here."

Dion's sex questions mushroom: How did Amina become her husband's favourite wife? What exactly does she do in bed with a man? What does she like, what tips her desire over the edge? How long does it take? She takes the red onion, strips off its outer, deep purple peel. Can't ask any of them.

"And if, worse case scenario, Leo does eventually guess who I am," AminaRose goes on, raising an eyebrow, "by then I'll have seen to it that he doesn't want to lose me."

Dion cuts into the onion.

"That doesn't sound like love."

AminaRose sighs. Dion chops. Another sigh.

"I think maybe love is not in the cards for me."

"Or me it seems," Dion's eyes have started to smart. She wipes them on a tea towel.

"Not true for you, dear Dion!" AminaRose sounds shocked. "You are a rare woman!"

"Rare?" Dion tries to laugh. "I don't think so."

"Yes rare. A *Joséphine*, that's what you are," says AminaRose, "like that brandy we saw at Leo's house, destined for only the best. Beside you I am plonk." She plucks the knife out of Dion's hand, picks up the onion. "Here, let me do that before you cut yourself." Starts chopping. "Sex for me is play, you know? A bargain made with a man for a few moments' pleasure, nothing to do with love."

"Oh?" Dion's tsunami of unasked questions still hangs in the air. "What about your Australian, that sounded like something more than just play."

AminaRose's knife pauses.

"Maybe. And look where it's landed me — in fake Rose's life."

"Well look where my supposed *Joséphine* life has landed me," says Dion. "The truth is, Amina, if you're plonk I'm just plain old grape juice. I've never even had an orgasm during sex!" As soon as the words meet the air she wants to snatch them back. But. Like a car accident or murder, once it's done nothing can reverse it.

"But Theo's painting—?" AminaRose sounds puzzled.

"Is about desire."

"And you've never... not even by yourself?" The damning flush she can do nothing about spreads up Dion's neck.

"Yes, I've done that."

"So things work down there."

"Right but..." Dion risks a glance at her friend. "Theo says I'm a trussed up chicken."

Tossing onion pieces into the salad bowl, AminaRose tries to strangle a laugh. Adds olive oil, a splash of vinegar, sprinkles salt, grinds pepper into the bowl until laughter she can't contain bubbles out warm, the farthest thing from judgemental. The sound, let loose, ripples through Dion's nervous system until finally, gasping, AminaRose wipes her eyes on the dish towel. Picks up two forks and tosses the salad.

"Oh Dion, what a sorry pair of old hens we are!"

Harvest

Sunlight scorches parched earth.
Grapes bunched
under vine leaves broad as hands
are ready,
their juices concentrated,
their skins translucent.
Winemakers judge
heat, light, wind, rain,
waiting to divine
a perfect harvest moment.

i.

Returning from his night in Chania, Theo dumps a bag of flour from one shoulder, and a bag of rice from the other onto the kitchen table.

"Tips were good last night and my friend Kiri gave me a ride here in his truck on his way to Iraklio."

Yiayiá is making coffee. She looks at the bags and shakes her head.

"No no Theo, we can't—"

"You don't think it's free, do you?' A pretend scowl. "No no no, this is payment for a job I need you and Dion to do for me."

Half an hour later *Yiayiá*, who is wearing a long pink and purple wrap-around skirt from Dion's cupboard this morning, starts cutting a pile of reject white t-shirts from a Chania printer into ribbons as fine as she can make them and tossing them back into their box. At the table beside her Dion is ripping up white paper scraps from a printer Theo knows and returning them to their box. The work continues the next day, Alex asking *Yiayiá* whether she prefers the company of music or Greek television or neither, until Theo's paper materials are ready for three heavy-duty blenders he has borrowed from his uncle. Dion loads them with a mixture of paper and cloth bits and water. *Yiayiá* is in charge of running the blenders, stopping to mix the mush then, when it's fine enough, announcing that they're ready to be emptied into a plastic vat a local wine co-operative gave to Alex when he first arrived, that he has never used.

Meanwhile, on a flat piece of ground outside the fermentation room, Theo hoses dust and cobwebs out of one of Kokanakis Wines' tarpaulins that, after harvest about a month from now, will dry a load of sun-shrunk green, pink and red Romieko grapes carefully watched by Alex until they are ready to go into their own fermentation tank.

The tarp is old and stained but if traces of grape colour leach into the paper Theo is about to make, that's all part of the organic creation of this painting.

He loves making paper. Choosing its contents, textures, colours allows him to enter his art sensually before his paintings come into being. When the tarp is clean he lays a frame he has made out of a pile of boards brought down from his castle over it. Going down on his hands and knees, he smooths the tarp against the inside of the boards, then folds it over their tops, creating a shallow one-by-two metre trough. A layer of felt he has cut fits snugly above the tarp in the bottom of the trough.

Dion watches him through the kitchen window. What Godgiven power has parachuted this small artistic dynamo into their midst? Beside her, tending the three blenders on the kitchen table, *Yiayiá's* hands are busy, which is when she is happiest. Theo has noticed that.

When the frame is ready Dion helps him manoeuvre the vat full of mush out the kitchen door. Her father comes out of the fermenting room.

"What's the right music for your paper, Theo? Debussy? The Doors? What do you like?"

Theo is stirring the slurry of white paper and cloth mush in his vat with a large wooden paddle. He stops to listen.

"Maybe the birds are enough for now." He takes a small cloth pouch Dion recognizes out of the pocket of his cut-offs and pulls out seaweed and driftwood fibres he has saved from the Hora Sfakion beach. The seaweed has dried into a brittle, light green film. Theo crushes it between his fingers then lifts the filaments to his nose.

Does the smell awaken thoughts of her lying in the sea foam, turn his insides into live energy, Dion wonders? He drops the seaweed and wood fibres into the vat, stirs it into his mush. Next out of the pouch comes a handful of sand. He pours it into the vat and stirs, then looks at Dion:

"Can you help me?" He wants to tip the vat over a couple of concrete blocks he has laid outside his frame, to pour his mush into the frame. "Not too quickly," he says, and she watches thin streaks of green, brown-grey, and multicoloured specks so subtle they are hardly visible pour out in a white flow that will become a one by two-metre sheet of paper.

Theo wipes the bottoms of his bare feet with his hands then steps into the trough, stirring the mush with his paddle, using his feet to push it into the corners of the frame. Her Dad has gone off to his vines and *Yiayiá* has stayed inside, out of the heat, to rest in front of the sitting room television. Amina is not back yet from her sailing trip with Salin. Dion kicks off her flip-flops and joins him. The felt feels soft under her feet. She squishes mush between her toes, lifts a foot to watch it drip. Overbalances.

"Oh!" She bumps against Theo as she falls. He steps out of the frame to catch his balance. She lands on her side inside it, mush cool on her thigh through her cut-offs, soaking the side of her black Romeiko Grapes t-shirt. Under which she is wearing nothing because why would she, it's so hot. And so, "Oh," she cries again, turning to lie on her stomach in the cool mush, kick-stirring it to cover her legs. Not worrying about what Theo will think or what if her grandmother comes out or her father comes back to see his soon-to-be-forty-year old daughter making like a nearly-naked mush-wrestler. Not worrying about anything.

She pulled life-choking fear out of herself one day last week. Theo wanted another beach session to study seaside textures, paint tones and perspectives before drawing on the new life-size paper he is making, so they drove down to Plakias, forty minutes away on the south coast. A turquoise sea was sparkling under an oven-hot August sky. Theo thought the beach's nudist section, at the far end of the bay where a cliff of shorn rock protects sunbathers from leering onlookers, would be empty first thing in the morning. No such luck. Dion had barely struck her pose in wavelets washing onto the sand when nudists started padding down from their seaside hotels to lie like well-oiled walruses too close to Theo's easel.

What must they think of her lying there in the sea foam, offering her breast? That she was an over-the-hill porn star? Get up, said Fear. Cover yourself.

But no. She took a good look at their blank-faced staring – as if her lying like that gave them the right to decide who she was and judge her, find her wanting – and then yanked out her fear by its roots.

What we tend with love makes our future, her father had said. And new thoughts lead to new choices. Next thing she knew she was breaking her pose, standing up. Striding out through the surf towards the horizon, early sunshine bathing her bare back. Theo would have to settle for beach and sea and sky colours today. Turning, she waved to him and the walruses as if she were a goddess, or a mermaid returning home, then dove down into sea blue, people-free silence.

Returning to shore, she found a cluster of grinning nudists gathered around Theo, watching him sketch a lumpy, tanned-all-over woman standing knee-deep in the water, one arm raised in a facsimile of Dion's over-her-shoulder goddess wave. A moment later Theo tore off his drawing, gave it to a pear-shaped man who opened his wallet. By mid-morning Theo had enough cash for fresh cheese pies and hot coffee from a local bakery.

Now, writhing in Theo's papery white mush, the absence of fear shows Dion what a grip it has held over her life since Teddy died. Without it she can see clearly, sense Theo's shock as he watches her. Can laugh freely, delighted. Her face streaked, hair matted with white mush now, she turns onto her side, strikes her seaside pose, her t-shirt sticking to her breasts, nipples clearly outlined as this new fear-free self locks eyes with Theo, slides a mush-slimed hand under her upper breast and squeezes, making mush drip off her nipple. The crotch of his cut-offs comes alive.

AminaRose comes around the corner, on the driveway. Slim and tanned in a floral dress and new gold hoop earrings Dion hasn't seen before, she would look like a supermodel except for the surprise on her face.

"What are you doing?"

Theo's face reddens. Dion sits up, still laughing.

"We're making paper for Theo's painting. But," coming to her feet, her t-shirt sticking to her like paint, Dion wipes stretched-out hands down her head and hair, pushing the mush downwards, down her shoulders and arms so it can drip off her hands, down her chest, stomach, thighs. "Clumsy me."

"Here," Theo gestures for her to turn so that he can scrape his hands down her back. She wants him to move them down further, to press them up between her legs. But he's not painting and she's not modelling right now.

AminaRose watches, saying nothing. Thinking—?

Dion doesn't care and, marvelling at that, she lifts a leg so Theo can scrape mush covering her ankle back into the trough. Then, extending a dripping hand regally, as if she were a gluey goddess, so Theo can steady her as she steps out of the frame, she raises her back foot for him to wipe.

"Shall we pour in some more mush?"

By the time she has showered Theo is satisfied that the mush is thick and flat and even over the felt. He unfolds the edges of the tarp outside the frame and gets her to help him yank it out from under the felt, so the mush's excess water can seep away into the ground, leaving what will become paper. Smaller frames with screens and felts, which will make a batch of trial papers with what's left of the mush, look like chicks gathered around their mother.

By sunset the paper for his painting is congealing nicely. Theo removes its wooden frame and spreads a second piece of felt over it, then Dion and AminaRose, who has changed into shorts and one of Dion's t-shirts, help him bring more concrete blocks from Alex's drive shed to lay side by side over the felt, to press as much water as possible out of the new paper.

His painting, which hopefully will hang on a gallery wall someday, will be called 'Dionysia,' he says.

A flush AminaRose and Theo are coming to know makes Dion duck her head. Beyond one drawing on Theo's castle wall, she has never actually pictured a finished painting of her fully exposed body. And freedom from fear doesn't automatically dissolve trussed-upness apparently. Is it with her for life, she wonders, like a birthmark?

She is about to turn out her bedside reading light when AminaRose, wearing a new lace-edged silk nightie that leaves very little to the imagination, knocks and comes into her bedroom with two cups of herbal tea.

"I've missed this," she says, curling herself into the armchair. "*Yiayiá* looks tired."

Dion too has missed their tea times.

"She is tired, she's ninety-four." And every time her grandmother looks into her kitchen cupboards and sees the bean and rice and sugar bins emptying, she worries.

AminaRose nods as if she has heard the thought.

"When we came into the harbour this morning," she says, "Leo asked me to come and live at his villa."

"You mean permanently?"

"Yes. Why go back to the States, he said? With him I'd have everything I could possibly want, he'd see to that, and he can do a lot of his work here."

"Doesn't he have a wife and kids in Moscow?"

"Yes, but his kids are in their twenties and his wife leads her own life. He does have business in Moscow and also has to travel, but he would love to know I'd be at the villa when he gets back." Light from Dion's bedside lamp burnishes AminaRose's cheeks as she looks at her friend. "I can't go on sponging off you and your family forever, Dion. And I do like Leo."

"Like?" It comes out short, sharp as a golfer's chip shot. She takes a long slow breath. "Why would you want to live all alone in Salin's house doing nothing but waiting for him? Isn't that what you just ran away from? And how many times do we have to tell you, having you here with us is a wonderful boost for *Yiayiá* and for Dad and for me. Also, I wouldn't be surprised if Salin knows who you really are. We've done some research on him, Amina, and he has ties with a government that poisons and jails and shoots its adversaries."

"I know that." AminaRose's face becomes a shell, a wisp of contradiction in her eyes the only sign of what might lie behind them as she sips her tea. "Look, I understand why you would think the worst of Leo. And I love you all here, feel so lucky to know you, but I cannot go on mooching off you and honestly, the prospect of returning to the U.S., to my parents, or trying to make a life there by myself..." She shakes her head.

Another woman with no idea which way to turn, Dion thinks. How many of us live there: different bodies, different stories but just as lost in a world that seems to be spinning further and further into hatred, destruction. How is it that one man can own a multi-million dollar yacht while here in her valley households are struggling to support unemployed relatives? Like Irina's granddaughter Georgina who, abandoned by her husband, is expecting her baby any day now. How will Irina, who is in her nineties, feed and clothe them? And if Leonid Salin succeeds in taking Kokanakis Wines, how will *Yiayia* and her father—

She can not go there. Dion concentrates on her tea. Who is she to judge what Amina wants or thinks or does?

"Okay then, tell me why you like this man so much you might live with him."

"Because he's adventurous and fun and smart! You know why we went to Santorini? Wine. Vine snobs can keep their Cabernets, Chardonnays and all the other aristocratic French grape varieties. Growing up in Georgia, he's always known there's a wider, richer, more complex wine world out there. Give me an unbleached Santorini Assyrtiko over a Chablis any day, he says." Amina wriggles deeper into her chair. "And he's so sexy! You see a cut-throat Russian, I know a lover who likes to feel and touch and smell and taste—"

"And possess?" Dion can't help herself.

"Well, yes, but that's the spice, don't you see? On Leo's boat sailing was easy – to trim the sails, you pushed a button; to come about, another button – you just stood at the helm steering. So he bought me a bikini and this see-through shirt and before our first day was out the bikini top was in the sea and in the evenings I would stand beside him, holding a drink while he steered with one hand and fondled me inside the shirt with the other, and oh God! I'd hold the drink up to his lips, then mine, until we dropped anchor in some deserted island cove and moved to this cushioned platform in the stern where he would make love to me on and on, over and over until the moon was high in the sky above us. When we got to Santorini he bought me an evening gown and those earrings and we sat out on a terrace overlooking the sea at the top of the town, drinking wine and eating grilled sea bass, and he said: 'Would you like this to be your life?'

"But no, I told him. I want my life to be about more than dressing for dinner. So on the way back sometimes I'd break out of his arms, throw off the shirt and dive into the sea. Or get up at daybreak and row myself in to walk onshore. Or when he was on his phone I might start kissing his neck, rubbing against him, and he didn't like that and I liked that he didn't. Because I do like sleeping with Leo, and waking up in his bed, but never again will I be caged." She pauses, then: "And I'm also thinking maybe there's some way his wanting me could help you—"

"No."

"I might be able to come up with some kind of business plan he would agree to—"

"No Amina, please! What you do with Salin can't have anything to do with us."

"I only want to help."

"I know, but we're fine."

AminaRose looks at her across the room.

"Yes, but for how much longer?"

Dion puts her cup down on the bedside table and slides down under her covers.

"I need to go to sleep."

By the end of August Dion and Theo have visited all the beaches popular with nudists, in small coves hidden behind coastal ridges just east of Plakias, where patches of white, long-petaled flowers Dion has never seen before are delicate dancers amongst the sun-scorched tufts of grass at the top of the sand.

"Sea daffodils," Theo tells her. "Aren't they beautiful? They only grow in sand."

He sets up his easel, charcoal and paints then positions Dion in the surf and draws. Bathers coming down through the rocks as the sun climbs higher see Theo beckoning her when he is finished and tearing off the new sketch. Watching couples approach, boyfriends ask if he will draw their girlfriends. Parents want pictures of their adorable toddlers. Theo and Dion arrive back at the winery with flour, rice, beans, a lamb roast, a beer for Alexander the Grape, a package of *Yiayiá's* favourite Turkish delight.

Eating take-out *gyros* on a promenade bench in Plakias after their nudist sketching sessions, she and Theo roll her Henri IV pebble-idea back and forth. She runs kidnap scenarios. He shoots them full of holes, favours theft. They discuss Operation Henri IV with no one but each other. Her Dad would either nix the idea or accidentally give it away and *Yiayiá's* nerves have already landed her in hospital once this summer. Amina must know nothing.

"Salin could be sucking her into his orbit to use against you somehow," Theo suggests. "For sure he's checked into this Rose Williams by now, and found no trace of her in America." Fear clutches Dion's spine. Where Salin is concerned, she can not control it.

Theo is pretty sure his Boston friends could find a way to bypass the Russian's alarms.

"Any system can be hacked if you know what you're doing," he says. "The problem with that is Salin will identify any hacker anywhere. And then punish them."

"Which is why I have to carry out Operation Henri IV alone." Somehow.

"No, D! This is a man who fabricates violent uprisings!" A vein in Theo's temple throbs visibly. "Against him alone you can not win." A gust of wind off the sea flattens his curls against his head, making him look like an ageless pixie. "Together though we can find a way. Leonid Salin may hide behind a locked door doing computer dirty work all day but in the end, like you said, he is just a man ruled by desire."

An armament-loaded destroyer of a man, Dion thinks, compared to their leaky dinghy of need. And what might be sheer madness.

"Your father wants to take me to Elafonisi, to my cousin's guest house." *Yiayiá* is staring at a pile of clothes beside an open suitcase on her bed, pretended irritation struggling to hide a shoot of pleasure edging into her eyes. "We used to stay there when I was a girl."

Alex the Grape is leaning on a shovel behind the olive grove at the back of the property, outside the tumble-down shed built into the stone wall, with Theo.

"I'm thinking we can convert this into a studio for you," he says. Fumes in the fermenting room will make Theo ill when the doors are closed in the fall, and this shed was once a one-room hut. "We can clear it out then use some bricks and mortar and wood left over from our renovation to turn it into a combination bedroom and studio, get you one of those solar-powered heaters so you can paint uninterrupted without fear of freezing up in your castle this winter." He watches confusions chase each other around Theo's face. "No pressure man, but

Yiayiá and Dion and I could really use your help, if you feel like staying here for awhile."

Dion hears about it at supper. Is this her father's way of telling them he has decided to cave into Salin's demands, she wonders? Because if he doesn't they will not be living here this winter. Or has her father somehow divined what she and Theo are trying to plan? Neither seems likely.

"You could start on the studio right away," Alex tells Theo, "if I can talk you into looking after the winery and barnyard for a few days while I take *Yiayiá* to Elafonisi. She needs a break from this heat." He turns to Dion. "Can you come, to help me with her?"

The night before the trip AminaRose, who has just returned from a couple of days at Salin's villa, brings Dion another late-night cup of tea.

"I'm not going to move in with him," she says. "I told him I'll stay overnight with him sometimes while we're both here but that's it. And it felt good, for me and for him not to always have what he wants. I wanted to let you know that." Her smile is a plum, full of juice. "So thanks, Dion, for your kind ear and advice."

AminaRose will be at the winery, alone with Theo, or at Salin's villa, or both while she is gone.

None of that is your business, Dion tells herself.

ii.

Yiayiá's cousin's guest house is a blue concrete block on a hill above the famous Elafonisi beach at the western tip of Crete. When Dion goes to her grandmother's room the morning after their arrival, *Yiayiá* is not there. Nor is she on the patio or in the vegetable garden or in the kitchen with her cousin's son and his wife, who have inherited the house.

A path winds down from the guest house, through rocky scrub, to an aquamarine sea so shallow patterns of sunlight play across the bottom. Protected by a spit of sand that arcs out to a small island, the beach at Elafonisi draws tourists from all over the world with their towels and floaties, drinks and picnics and umbrellas as late summer temperatures climb higher. This early in the morning though only one gym-fit swimmer in a leave-nothing-to-the-imagination Speedo is wading out through knee-deep water still as glass. *Yiayiá's* beach wrap and sandals are a neat pile beside a nearby shrub.

The old lady is sitting in water up to her waist wearing an ancient black bathing suit and her wide-brimmed canvas gardening hat. Sunshine is warming shoulders that have not seen daylight for as long as Dion has been in Crete. Loose, wrinkled paper-thin skin sagging on her arms as she trails a leisurely hand through the water speaks of a vulnerability her granddaughter has never seen.

Dion is wearing shorts and a halter top, didn't know swimming was on the early morning agenda.

"*Kali mera* (good morning.)"

"Oh!" *Yiayiá* looks around, did not hear her coming.

Dion sensed her grandmother's fatigue beginning to lift as soon as they turned off the main road yesterday. She used to travel here with her family in a donkey cart or in the back of someone's truck, she told them. Eighty years later weather and sun have peeled off much of the house's exterior paint. Inside, mould has etched a black design on the living room wall. Welcoming them with *raki*, her cousin's son smiled but his eyes did not look comfortable. Alex slid an envelope across the table.

"For our room and board."

"*Ochi, ochi,*" (No, no,) said both the cousin and his wife but then *Yiayiá* weighed in, her Greek cadences, volume, intonations, inflections strong as a Cretan wind. Telling them where the money had come from? 'Consider it an advance on my rent,' Theo had told them, insisting they take it, 'for my new studio/home.' Whatever her grandmother was saying appeared to solve the problem: '*Yamas!*' cried the cousin, refilling their glasses.

"I was just thinking," *Yiayiá* says now, lifting her hand, watching early sunlight turn dripping seawater into prisms, "the sea here is just like a lover." Aged mischief peeks out from under her hat as she looks up at her granddaughter.

Alluding to what? Dion sits down in the sea beside her. Is a storage of memories about to open?

"Water can be so many things," her grandmother goes on, "roaring seas crashing in on the North shore, or plumes of white spray plucked up by *meltemi* winds down in the south, or like this, smooth as glass." She chuckles. "People are the same. Some are waterfalls, some babbling brooks, some flowing rivers." Pause. "Some stagnant marshes." *Yiayiá* turns her gaze out to an unbroken horizon. "Always changing though, just like this sea, always making new life under the surface." Her hand drops back into the water, its refracted fingers wiggling now, dancing new patterns of light onto the sand beneath it.

Dion's shorts are clinging to her in the water, the material bunching in her crotch, the sea finding its way inside it, triggering another possibility, that her grandmother is commenting on her orgasm problem. Thanks Amina.

"You've seen a lot of life," she says, to shift her grandmother's focus, then waits. Has been trying to find a way to get her grandmother to talk about her past. "And there must have been times during the war when you and *Pappoús* had to step outside the law?"

Yiayiá darts a look at her. This is not the conversation she had in mind. After what seems to Dion like eons, her grandmother's body begins to tremble. Terror seizes Dion by the throat.

"*Yiayiá?*"

Hiccoughs of laughter erupt.

"Outside the law? Me?" *Yiayiá* wipes her eyes with her hand, grinning for the first time her granddaughter can ever remember.

"Seventy-five years ago your *Pappoús* and I helped kidnap Major General Werner Kreipe, the Nazi in charge of the occupation of Crete."

"What! How?"

"The actual kidnapping wasn't that hard," says *Yiayiá* as if they were talking about planting vegetables. "Two British commandoes and our Resistance cell hijacked his car on his way to work. But then they had to hike through the mountains with him for nearly three weeks, waiting for a boat to take them off Crete while every German on the island was looking for them." The old lady's gaze goes back to the horizon. "Your *Pappoús* scouted for them up in the mountains above Asi Gonia, where they hid in caves Gio and the others had known since they were boys. My job was to bring food, until a British boat finally managed to pick up the general at Rodakino."

Dion knows Rodakino, a narrow, hair-raising bridge over a wrinkle in the mountains' coastal skirts that she and Theo had driven over on their way home from Hora Sfakion. She imagines her grandmother climbing towards high mountain caves with baskets of food no excuse could explain, should a German patrol catch sight of her.

"Sounds like something out of a spy thriller!"

"Where do you think the ideas for those thrillers came from?"

They gaze together at Elafonisi's light blue sea.

"Where did you find the courage?" asks Dion.

A breeze brings them the chirruping of birds in some bushes on the other side of the beach, then shivers away, out to sea. Dion begins to think her grandmother doesn't have an answer, but digging through seven decades of memory takes time.

"Life happens Dionysia, this minute then this minute then this one," she says at last, her dripping hand coming out of the sea to gesture at a flotilla of white clouds sailing into the morning sky from the west. "We tell each other stories to try and make sense of it all but no one can predict what is to come next, war soon teaches you that." She turns to her granddaughter. "So you have faith."

"Faith, in what? You've never been a church person."

"In yourself!" snaps *Yiayiá*. "Because where else is God?" Another pause, her grandmother's fingers playing with the water again. Her voice, when it comes, has been recalibrated into uncharacteristic softness. "Think of your body, Dion, what makes its nerves, brain, blood, bones, muscles, organs, all work together in perfect harmony? Or think of an onion, a carrot, a juicy red tomato. The same is true. The power that makes that happen is the God I listen to."

Dion stares at the water, disappointed. Did not expect *Yiayiá's* guidance to come in the form of God platitudes. Her body feels chilled, needs to release Operation Henri IV, to hear it out loud here, where it's safe to see if it could fly.

"So," her grandmother's usual brusqueness has returned. "Why do you keep asking about your grandfather's and my war? What is it you want?"

Dion's teeth start to chatter. Because once out who knows what the idea might unleash. Shocking ninety-four-year old *Yiayiá* might kill her. If, on the other hand, it resurrects her grandmother's Resistance self, Dion will have to unpack Operation Henri IV, turn it into reality. Her grandmother is scrutinizing her face.

"Tell me, Dionysia."

She listens without interrupting. Then does not tear a strip off her granddaughter, tell her to forget such dangerous, illegal foolishness.

"What makes you think you can outsmart a predator like Salin?" she asks instead.

"His ego. He's an alpha-wolf, ego big as a skyscraper."

"And you believe this ego that thinks he can go on taking and taking does not understand that in the end it can not be allowed?" *Yiayiá's* fingers, lifting out of the water, are puckered by seawater.

"Exactly!" Thankfulness washes through Dion.

"Something like this has to be planned down to the finest detail, if it's doable," says her grandmother. "And the simpler a plan, the better, your *Pappoús* always used to say that. So we will think about it. Now, help me get to my feet and take me out a little way so I can float."

Dion's sea-soaked shorts stick to her thighs as she stands. She should take them off. She looks around. The early morning swimmer is still doing his laps. A trussed-up chicken, is that how you want to live out your life, ask her inner thighs? Or, she pictures herself waving like a goddess to the beach nudists on the south coast. Her grandmother's bird-bone hand holds onto Dion's as she takes a step out into the sea. Such courage.

"Wait." Dion pulls off her shorts, her thong, shrugs out of her halter top.

"No tan lines," *Yiayiá* remarks.

They go out far enough to lie down, their bodies rocking in an aquamarine sea so dense they can float in it without moving at all.

Same time and place, weather and water are still sunlit blue as Dion, wearing a bathing suit, sits with her grandmother in the next morning's early peace. Some of her nerves hope *Yiayiá* will veto Operation Henri IV. Most know she won't.

"Circumstances must be perfectly aligned for love or wine or heists to work," *Yiayiá* begins, "because they're all patterns unfolding." Yesterday's mischief sneaks back into her grandmother's voice. "A gentle touch in the right place at the right moment is all it takes to make every one of them succeed." Pause. Dion has no reply.

"Yesterday you told me Leonid Salin's weakness is his ego."

"That's right."

"Well ego would rather lose a bottle than pay ransom."

"That's what Theo thinks," says Dion. "He also says kidnapping Henri IV is too risky."

"He's right. Straight theft is the only sure, safe way to make this work."

"But that would make me a thief, *Yiayiá*, a criminal. No better than Salin."

"If you feel that way, don't do it. Crime is crime, Dionysia. As to the right or wrong of it," she sighs. "What I see on this Earth are beetles and butterflies, dogs and cats, plants and presidents, lovers and thieves and starving children all trying to take what we need — and giving too, one way or another, whether we know it or not. Leo Salin's been pouring money into Kokanakis Wines for five years, and he wants to go on doing so. What we'd be doing is controlling how he does that."

Brilliant. Dion's whole body opens into a smile that includes the sun's underwater light patterns on the sand, its sparkle on a sea too bright almost to look at. But.

"Not 'we,' *Yiayiá*! Because what if we got caught?" Dion sees them in handcuffs then in a jail cell full of the stink of failure, her father turfed out into the street, alone.

"Yes 'we.' Operation Henri IV can not be done alone." Her grandmother waits for argument. Dion can't find one. "So," the old warrior raises a dripping index finger. "Three points to consider:

"One: Every eventuality, every security system has at least one weak link. You just have to find it. In the kidnapping of General Kreipe it was a turn in the road between his house and his office, where his car had to slow down, and the general's known impatience with checkpoints on the roads." Her middle finger rises.

"Two: Timing has to be precise. The British commandoes dressed in German army uniforms. Resistance look-outs watched the general's house until he left it at night. When his car approached the turn the commandoes stepped into the road, stopped the car as if it was a check point, opened the door, asking for the general's identity papers, and shoved a gun into his chest. The Resistance took the driver away, one of the British took over driving, and the general was bundled into the back seat with two other Resistance fighters. The other commando put on the general's hat and they drove on, through Iraklio then west towards Rethymnon on the north shore, speeding through twenty two checkpoints before abandoning the car on a dirt track leading up to Anogeia, a Resistance centre high on the slopes of Mount Psiloritis."

"And then what? How did they get the general to walk?"

"They put him on a donkey. A plan to take him off the island at Limni Beach, which was south of Anogeia had to be scuppered because of radio problems. So they spent the next three weeks on the move, my girlfriend and me finding and delivering food while they tried to establish radio contact with Egypt."

"You should have told us about this long ago, *Yiayiá* – Teddy would have loved it – You and *Pappoús* were heroes!" Her grandmother's hand returns to the sea.

"No Dionysia. Violence between the Resistance and the Germans escalated after General Kreipe's kidnapping. And the reprisals that followed killed many, many innocent Cretans. But," *Yiayiá* sighs, "should we not have carried out this mission? Morale across Crete was boosted: If we could do this we were not helpless victims of the Nazis. And reprisals were going on all over the island anyway. So you did what felt right at that particular moment, and history advanced." *Yiayiá* raises her ring finger.

"Finally, point three: Trust nothing, especially technology, and have contingency plans for every step of the way. If those fail, be ready to improvise."

A breeze is rippling the sea. Dion turns her head to look up at the rocks behind this stunningly beautiful beach, and the path winding up between them. Every Cretan who wasn't a collaborator risked their lives, their futures. And every mountain, every tree, every family living here – and everywhere on this planet for that matter – is enmeshed in scary symphonies too complex to parse or judge or make right.

"Now," her grandmother goes on, "describe the inside of Salin's house to me."

History will advance, thinks Dion, there's no stopping that, and she has the blessing of a woman who helped kidnap a Nazi general. And what's the simple removal of a bottle beside that? She describes the villa's grounds and main floor.

"The windows in his study, where the bottle is, are they latched?"

"Yes but closed when we were there, the light, temperature, humidity carefully controlled."

"So this Russian computer genius lives in a locked mausoleum. What about the kitchen? Everybody needs to open a window there."

"And a door," says Dion, following her thinking, "while cooking, cleaning up, putting out garbage."

Later in the evening, after Alex and the cousins have excused themselves from the supper table, the light has not left *Yiayiá's* eyes when she leans across the table to Dion.

"When we get home we will call on Mr. Salin. If I am to be a signatory of this new contract, there are one or two clauses I would like him to clarify."

Yiayiá is sitting forward in the Fiat's front passenger seat, craning her neck to the left as Dad drives up through a mountain gorge southwest of Chania on their way home.

"There!" she cries. "Pull over, Alex." A sign points to stairs leading up to a cave, high on the mountainside, devoted to *Aghia Sofia*. A small taverna watches the entrance. *Yiayiá* turns to Dion in the backseat. "If you would take me to the washroom, your father and I will then have a coffee while you climb up to visit a cave where humans have been worshipping since the Neanderthals lived here."

The stairs go on forever, heat bouncing off the rocky mountainside as she climbs higher and higher above the highway. To do what?

An enormous cave in the mountainside, higher even than the flight path of birds, opens at the top of the stairs and standing there, a breeze cooling the sweat she has worked up, Dion looks out beyond the White Mountains' westside peaks into a sky that, untrammelled by goings-on far below, stretches as far as forever. Behind her a few stalagmites and stalactites speak to the age of a cavern where human remains date back several thousand years.

Tucked into a corner beside the cave entrance is a whitewashed Greek Orthodox votive spot devoted to the saint named for the great goddess of wisdom, Sofia. A painting of her, attended by three women

– Faith, Hope and Charity – is mounted on the cave's stone wall behind a simple altar table. Dion looks closely at them. Is this what her grandmother wanted her to see?

Faith: In the execution of a criminal act? Faith's face is too vacuous to be convincing.

Hope: Please, Dion tells her picture, even a particle will help!

Charity's do-gooder face wears a beatific smile.

"You're already with us," Dion tells her, "because everyone in our valley would benefit from Operation Henri IV."

Wisdom, Faith, Hope, Charity are all female saints. Worshipped way up here while down on the ground war and greed rule, and the religion the saints belong to is a strict patriarchy. Dion returns to the cave mouth, to look out at birds gliding above forests, rivers, the road far below.

A new, and very old perspective, revealing what lies behind, around and beyond laws people like Leonid Salin leave in their dust, that's what *Yiayiá* wanted her to find up here.

"I'll do it," she tells Theo. They are sitting with *Yiayiá* on the patio under the plane tree. Her father is in the barnyard saying hello to everybody. "I'll steal Henri IV, become a thief."

Theo glances towards her grandmother.

"It's all right, *Yiayiá's* in on it."

"What made you change your mind?"

Leaves rustle high in the plane tree as a large bird that must have been perched up there takes off. It's a kestrel. They watch it hover over the vineyard, preparing to swoop. To kill something.

"Desire," says Dion. Never mind rationalizations about right and wrong and whether laws can distinguish between the two. "I want what I want. Like Salin."

"Yeah right," Theo says sarcastically. "You want to eat, keep a roof over your grandmother's head. What does he want?" He looks to *Yiayiá* for corroboration.

The old lady says nothing, her smile enigmatic.

iii.

Research is the key to any successful venture, in war or business, *Yiayiá* tells them.

Two yellow birds of paradise plants in the pots outside the Russian's front gate point at the winery's Fiat, their thin, sword-like leaves rising straight as guards in the morning sunshine. Theo, who has moved into his new studio/shed, is driving. Stopping outside the villa's front door, he and Dion each take one of *Yiayiá's* arms to help her out of the car.

"Park around the side by the kitchen, like last time?" Theo asks when Salin's man answers the door. Curt nod. Salin is nowhere to be seen — a very different welcome from last time.

St. John the Theologian watches as the Russian, wearing a crisp white shirt with a thin gold chain inside its collar and khaki slacks, comes to his feet behind his desk when his guests are shown into the study. Light coming through the window behind him is muted, it being a western exposure. The room feels cool even though the sun is already high enough to reach the side window across from Henri IV Dudognon's plinth. Salin must be running his air conditioning, that's why the windows are closed, thinks Dion. Blackout blinds above both windows are also pulled down when the room is not occupied probably, to preserve his precious brandies.

"Please," Salin indicates two chairs across the desk from him. "Sit."

Dion settles her grandmother into one of them, then plops a large black handbag *Yiayiá* has carried for as long as Dion can remember down on the floor beside it. Teddy used to tease his grandmother about her bag: "Why don't you take up bowling? You could fit your shoes, ball and a full course lunch for your whole team in there!" Always though, whatever was needed – scissors, a bandaid, gum, a tin cup, now a spare adult diaper, baby wipes – could be found in that bag. *Yiayiá* looks up at St. John, tilting her head towards their host.

"Keeping him honest, are you?" Returning to Salin: "As a child I was afraid of St. John the Theologian. So judgmental with that long beard, and unforgiving. Do you have him in Russia too?" Salin's businessman's smile does not waver as he shrugs.

"Byzantine art, that's all St. John is to me. Communist Russia, where I was raised, did not concern itself with church saints."

Yiayiá raises her eyebrows and looks up at the saint again, as in 'And yet here you are.'

"Will you have coffee?" Salin asks.

Yiayiá looks over her shoulder at his servant/bodyguard hovering in the doorway.

"*Paracalo* (please,) with milk, though we needn't take much of your time."

Dion leans down to take a notebook out of *Yiayiá's* black bag, opens it to a list of questions her grandmother has prepared, and pulls out her phone.

"You don't mind if I record this?" Playing the same pain-in-the-ass stickler for details and legality she was last time, with her father.

Salin barely bothers to raise his shoulders. A tray with three tiny white china cups full of traditional, straight-to-the jugular Greek coffee arrives. They sip in silence while *Yiayiá* raises glasses she wears on a chain around her neck and refers to the notebook.

"It's not so much the contract's wording I wish to discuss, as how you mean to apply it," she looks at Salin. "Last time we set up a contract with you I made a mistake. Now I must do all I can to safeguard the futures of my son and granddaughter, I'm sure you can understand that."

"Of course." Salin glances at his watch. *Yiayiá* reads a clause she instructed Dion to write down before they came and begins to talk about what exactly is encompassed by it, and listening, Dion can hardly imagine this aged businesswoman is the same grandmother who just last week was sitting in the sea laughing at her naked granddaughter, who just last month could hardly find enough energy to get out of her chair.

The casement window behind the Russian looks out on shrubs under a garden wall and an oak tree that, moving with the wind, cannot be heard. The window at the other end of the room, near the plinth, has flowers outside it, Dion remembers. Who ever looks at them?

Yiayiá is describing Alex now, in words Dion would never have put into her mouth, telling the Russian her son's genius with grapevines is responsible for his creation of Kokanakis Wines and its prize-winning wine out of a vineyard that was nothing more than a tangle of long abandoned vines. How she must be assured that any new contract she signs has written into it safeguards against their wines' dilution into mediocrity.

Salin soothes the old lady with words while also making clear that he is mouthing pleasantries, and will do as he pleases. A look of horror suddenly deepens wrinkles on *Yiayiá's* face.

"Please, is there a washroom?" she asks, clutching her granddaughter's hand. Salin looks at Dion.

"Down the hall, second door on your right." *Yiayiá* looks as if she is trying not to panic.

"Will you bring my bag?" Dion picks it up and takes her grandmother's arm.

"I've got you, *Yiayiá*. Take your time." So that as they move, at the pace of snails, towards the door, she can try to judge the reach of the room's two cameras and the angles they cover, and review furniture placement, distances, the way the light plays across the other end of the room.

A camera in the hallway outside is trained on the study door and another door next to it, that has a number panel combination lock beside it. Must be his computer room and camera monitoring station. Another camera above the washroom doorway looks into the dining room where they had dinner. Beyond it, through the glassed-in garden room, there is no sign of Rose in the pool this morning. She's not at the winery either, and Theo says she spent a lot of time at Salin's villa while they were at Elafonisi. She must be upstairs, in her silk nightie. Having breakfast in bed?

The washroom is also a change room for the pool, complete with showers and towel shelves. *Yiayiá* uses the toilet, washes up, needs no help. Neither of them speaks.

"I'm sorry," *Yiayiá* tells the Russian on their return. "Old age has a nasty way of interfering with even the best laid plans. Now," she turns her attention back to the notebook, asks a few more questions. Listens. Nods. Closes the notebook, hands it to Dion. "I have all I need for now." Salin stands, smiles as if her signing is a done deal.

"You may rest assured, Mrs. Kokanakis, that my wish too is that Kokanakis Wines should prosper." Meaningless words bland as pudding *Yiayiá* would never eat. Dion's mouth starts to open. Her grandmother's bird-thin hand grips her knee as she levers herself up.

"Thank you, Leo."

He comes around the desk to take her elbow, guide her towards the door, leaving Dion to pack away the notebook. St John's camera will see her turn off her phone's recorder but not her activation of its camera, her tapping the telephoto option. Still, she needs to be closer to Henri IV to pick up enough detail. *Yiayiá* shuffles across the study. Picking up her bag, Dion holds it in her arms, sidestepping awkwardly towards the other end of the room, as if trying to avoid colliding with Salin and her grandmother while fumbling with her load. So neither St. John nor the bar camera will notice her snapping diamond-studded Henri IV Dordogne on his pedestal and the window behind him. *Yiayiá* and the Russian reach the door. Any second now they will look to see where she is. Outside the window delicate white flowers are blooming in a bed of sand. Dion moves closer to them, camera snapping.

"Are those sea daffodils?"

"Yes." Salin turns back to her grandmother, to shepherd her out of the room. Leaving Dion free to hover for a moment, looking out at the flowers while taking a close-up of Henri IV.

No one speaks as Theo drives down Salin's road. He likely has audio as well as a visual surveillance set up, says Theo. Not until they turn onto the road to the winery does Theo let out a "Phew!" Dion leans forward in the back seat to check on *Yiayiá* beside him. Her grandmother's wrinkled lips are pursed but twitching, amused.

"There's a camera on a pole above the gardener's side gate, another one above the kitchen door," Theo goes on. "The cook, the gardener, Salin's man all came in and out of the back door while I was there so the alarm must be off during the day. And there are two sheds against the property wall just down from the kitchen. One's made of concrete blocks with vents but no windows, padlocked. Probably where batteries to store power from solar panels on his roof are, and his generator. No wires though, they must be buried underground. The other shed is the gardener's. There's also a greenhouse down beyond the pool at the back of the property, where it looks like there are flower and vegetable gardens."

"I got bottle, room and window shots," adds Dion. "And there's a bed of sand outside the study window, where the sea daffodils are. In case we want to bury the bottle there in the dead of night."

"No," say both her grandmother and Theo. As if they were children elated in the grip of play.

Except that this elation, like in children's play, sparks only briefly. *Yiayiá* spends the rest of the day in bed.

Dion and Theo hike up to a little church nestled into the cleft between the low mountains at the top of the valley, where Theo's pirate's brother, the abbot, once had his abbey. From there they'll be able to make their way down through rocks and scrub, olive groves and oak trees to a wrought iron gate in a six-foot concrete wall at the back of Salin's property, behind his pool and garden.

Late summer air, hotter than any Dion has ever known, makes her legs heavy. Sweat glues her hair to her scalp, her heartbeat quickens, but a spring in the church's garden runs out through a pipe in a rock wall into a pool below it. A tin cup attached to a chain invites wayfarers to drink in peace. Dion feels the cool water course through her body, splashes some on her face, her neck.

An enormous tree beside the spring, whose trunk is as wide as a small car, must be hundreds, maybe even a thousand years old. Part of its canopy has been sheared off by lightning but what's left offers blessed shade. Dion sits down, resting her back against its bark. Who else has sat here? The abbot, his brother the pirate whose ruined towers are almost indistinguishable from the rocky top of the nearest mountain? Ancient Minoans did for sure. Three metres away from the tree a libation basin her father says predates the Greeks has been carved into a boulder at the top of stone steps still visible in a little knoll.

Theo spreads their picnic on the ground. They eat, drink lemonade then rest their heads against the tree's swollen roots to watch its leaves flutter against a sky too blue to belong to this ravaged ground. Dion closes her eyes. Feels one of Theo's fingertips — no 'May I?' — stroking the inside of her wrist, up to her elbow, down again. Lovely.

A frisson of breeze wakes her. She has no idea where she is until, turning her head, she sees Theo lying beside her under the ancient tree. Sleep has wiped care, ambition from his fine-boned face, turning him back, almost, into an innocent boy. Who is willing to steal for her.

Theo picks up the knapsack. They step back out into the heat. Picking his way down through a steep outcropping of rocks below the church's garden, Theo turns back to take her hand, steadying her as she follows.

No cameras appear to guard a gate at the back of Salin's property.

"There are some inside it for sure though," says Theo.

On another day they hide the Vespa behind some bushes and watch from across Salin's road as his man leaves in the car. To run errands? Theo waits while, wearing one of *Yiayiá's* black cotton dresses, her hair tucked under a purple and white kerchief (to distract attention from her face) Dion carries a basket of cheeses to a side gate outside the villa's kitchen door. To explore this entry point. And to see if she is physically capable of turning Operation Henri IV into anything more than a summer dream, a distraction on the road to ruin.

The gate is unlocked at this time of day for the gardener and tradespeople coming and going, but if the camera mounted on a pole inside it picks up anything recognizable about her, Operation Henri IV will fail before it starts. And God only knows what will happen then, to her, also to Amina if she's here now, inside Salin's house. Dion's heart beats a tattoo against her ribs as she opens the gate. Forces herself not to look up at the camera. Knocks on the kitchen door. She has practised all the Greek words for her cheeses but will not pretend to be a vendor, her Greek isn't good enough. All she needs to say, in English, is "I live up the road and thought you might like these." As if it were a good turn by an ex-pat neighbour.

No one answers her knock. Dion's hand shakes as she tries the latch. It lifts. A camera monitors the entryway to the kitchen. Head down, she calls a faint "hello?" Two female voices – the cook and the maid probably – are haranguing each other and laughing in the kitchen. They do not hear her, which is good, but this entryway feels too risky.

Is their plan too risky too?

Have faith, says *Yiayiá*. But faith is not something you can order up, like a brand of beer at a bar, before committing an act from which there is no return.

On their next outing Dion waits while Theo watches the gardener leave, then goes in through the kitchen gate to the garden shed, collects a wheelbarrow and takes it down to examine the massive flower garden at the back end of the grounds, where fall flowers are blooming now, then around to the protected side of the house where the sea daffodils are under Salin's study window. To see if he can do it without attracting attention, a story ready if he's caught, about needing to peek at the Salin's paintings through a window and at his fabulous flowers. Nobody stops him. To think this means they are not watching would be a mistake.

Yiayiá drinks frapuccinos on the patio, harvesting impressions, sensations, information they bring home. A plan develops. They must feel as close to it as Theo feels to his paintings, as Alex feels to his grapes, *Yiayiá* says.

They will not sell Henri IV anonymously on the Dark Net.

"Computers, the internet, they are Salin's world," says *Yiayiá,* "so we must have nothing to do with them."

Dion hears Theo's voice objecting, her grandmother's clipped rejoinder, but not their words. She is thinking about The Perfect Robbery, how when Teddy's new girlfriend put paid to it relief washed through her eleven-year old self.

Teddy would pull off Operation Henri IV. Teddy was an adventurer. And he's not here, reality saw to that.

iv.

Every corner of Theo's new studio shed is crammed with painting paraphernalia now and his new paper is dry and pressed, its texture and shade of white exactly as he hoped. Something about the painting he is preparing is not right though. He spends every spare minute examining studies he has hung on his newly whitewashed walls. Neither understanding nor solutions arrive. Maybe they need to go back to their wild beach, maybe Crete's autumn light will tell him what is missing.

Alex offers them the winery's Fiat.

"Harvest is a week away," he says, "and I can use the truck for what I need to do." A jalopy that looks older than Dion, that's used only to transport baskets and grapes from vineyards to the winery, is oiled and ready in the drive shed behind the plane tree. "And your grandmother promises to stay healthy, right *Yiayiá?*"

His mother pays no attention. Sitting in her favourite chair under the plane tree on the patio, wearing a white Kokanakis Wines t-shirt with a tilting glass of red wine on it and her print skirt, she is also ignoring a pile of zucchinis waiting on the table in front of her to have the dirt rubbed off them. Instead one of her hands rises in front of her, turning this way and that as if she has only just realized it belongs to her. Her fingers wiggle.

Alex looks concerned. Dion pulls up a chair. Is her grandmother away with the fairies?

Surely not. Her eyes have been clearer, her mind ten years younger ever since their trip to Elafonisi.

"Is your hand bothering you, *Yiayiá?*" Dion picks up a zucchini.

"No no," The old lady lets her wrist drop. "I was just thinking about gravity."

"Oh?" Dion whispers, glancing towards her father.

"Yes," *Yiayiá's* hands swoop, rise, swoop. "How every movement uses it, some muscles working against it while others give in, all of it so graceful, fine-tuned, precise." She flicks a look at her granddaughter. "If only you will let it be so."

Dion recalls her grandmother in the sea at Elafonisi and she's heard Theo's concern about something missing in his project. And is clearly fixated still on Dion's sex life.

A discarded soft drink bottle, a few cigarette butts speak of others having used their wild beach west of Hora Sfakion during summer's scorching heat, but today the rest of the world feels far away as, dropping their gear under the tamarisk tree, peeling off sweaty motorcycle jeans and hoodies they race into froth-capped waves.

Dion swims away from shore, looking for her cold underwater mermaid sea currents.

They're gone, warm water everywhere, no matter how deep she dives.

Later in the afternoon she stretches out on her side, wavelets breaking over her shins then foaming up over the pebbles as September's descending sun's rich gold luminescence touches the side of a passing container ship and the rocky cliff behind their beach and the tamarisk tree, and her body. Water sucks at her downside breast, her thigh, then recedes.

Theo clips one of his new small papers to his easel.

"The sea and light are exactly right." Still naked, he comes to squat in front of her – "May I?" – and angles her body so that sunlight pours over her shoulder to burnish her upper breast with gold. He pulls her upper leg forward, bends it so the light can play over her knee, then runs a finger light as a lover's down her side, over her hip bone, along her golden thigh, his penis coming to life. Her nipples respond but only a little, as if 'been here, done this and for what?'

Theo pads back to his easel. A wave swarms into her vagina, rattles the pebbles, titillating. But Aphrodite must be occupied elsewhere. No current rushes, no waterfall is imminent. And this autumn energy is starker, less willing to linger. A wave spanks her butt cheeks.

Amina's description of making love with Leo Salin on his yacht comes to Dion, her bikini top thrown into the sea, his hand fondling her breasts under a see-through shirt as she feeds him his drink: 'You see a cut-throat Russian, I see a lover who likes to feel and touch and smell and taste.' Their bodies playing off each other into a crescendo of surrender without which there is no real music.

That's it! She sits up, her back blocking the golden sunlight.

"Sorry, sorry."

Theo stares, his pencil paused in mid-air. But.

Desire, the essence of his project, needs a goal, that's what's missing. Her desire and Theo's are attached to no outcome.

So many memories curl up of lying beside men she thought she could climax with. Who were aroused, then ready, some of them holding themselves as long as they could for her sake. Not understanding that her desire's eddying, shifting, many coloured currents needed to flood onto an intimate plain of trust on the other side of surrender. No trust, no flood.

"Sorry," she says again. How to put all this into words?

He drops his pencil, sits back on the ground.

"It's okay. You've got a lot on your mind."

There must be a way to salvage this, she thinks later, lying in her sleeping bag under the stars. Wind sweeps a night chill in off the sea. How can a woman about to turn forty take a twenty eight-year old man into the urgent volatility of female desire, she asks the wind? How can Theo feel the power of female ripeness closing around him if it has no destination? Watching her desire from six metres away on the beach will never produce what his project requires.

Morning light is harsh. Where late afternoon sunshine invites you into its embrace, the sun's early rays care for nothing but their strengthening selves. Dion swims out, looking again for her mermaid sea. But no, it's migrated to somewhere else. Anyway, she needs talk to Theo.

Try to make him understand how her desire's source of power lies in its goal, somehow stumble through what she would need in order to surrender to that power. But words are like boats, floating on the surface only, not connected to what lies beneath them, and bound to capsize.

Golden afternoon light lasts only last a few minutes on their last afternoon. Little waves wash over her lower leg, into the small of her back. Theo mixes colours.

Help him, she thinks. Crawl out of the sea foam and across the pebbles. Take his erection into your mouth, flick your tongue against it, hear him groan, his hands holding your head in place, your body undulating against his legs in time with your sucking until desire, his, yours, jumps the skin between you–

So that, teetering at the brink of the waterfall, you pull away and hand him his paintbrush?

Good luck with that. Anyway she wouldn't get that far. Her wet knees would stick to the pebbles as she crawled. Her breasts would swing under her like udders, dripping seawater, and seeing her scrabble up the beach like a crab, he'd throw down his paint brush before she got anywhere near him, thinking something was horribly wrong–

Something about what she's thinking must be reaching him. His paintbrush has stopped. He stares at her gold-tinged body lying in a lapping sea, takes the paper off his easel, drops it into the sand.

She starts to come out of her pose, to go to him.

"No!" His hand comes up. "Wait." He picks up his sketch pad, looks at her lying at the edge of a sea that is green-blue calm behind her now as the golden moment dims. He draws a few lines, turns to a new page, stares at her, sketches for less than a minute, turns the page. "Can you kneel now?" The sun is painting a few scraps of cloud candy red when finally he stops.

"Come and look." He sounds awed. She sits down beside him.

Her kneeling body is little more than the line of her back, its tilt above her haunches speaking of a vulnerability her shoulders, a little hunched, try to offset. Her face and breasts point forwards, towards what must be faced. So much spoken – the depth of her need, the smell of the sea, the power of its waves – by what is not there.

Theo spends the rest of the day exploring his new way of drawing by rendering her standing, packing, squatting over his hot ring in her hoody. Candy red clouds turn indigo then purple then grey before disappearing into the night. They eat, pass the wine bottle back and forth, discuss the magic that lies just beyond what is seen. The moon rises over the sea.

"Speaking of magic," he says as they lie in their sleeping bags under the stars, "now let's think about how to get into Salin's study, take Henri

IV Dudognon off his plinth and out of the house unseen, then turn a diamond studded bottle of hundred-year old cognac into cash. 'Keep it simple,' *Yiayiá* said — like my lines! — and 'timing is everything.'"

"And 'there must be no technology involved,'" adds Dion. "She doesn't want me to wind up in prison because the power went out or the internet collapsed."

Above them the stars watch until silence finally takes Dion into dislocated dreams that miraculously do not wake a nearly-forty-year old body sweating through a chilly night.

V.

They pull into the driveway to find AminaRose trying to hang laundry. One arm of Alex's shirt has tugged out of its peg though and is flapping in a north wind funnelling up the valley. Brassieres and panties, each secured by a single peg, look as if they're about to take flight. And something in AminaRose's shoulders looks jerky.

In the kitchen drawings by Theo now cover the entire back wall: *Yiayiá* washing vegetables at the sink; Alexander the Grape bending over one of his vines, feeling a bunch of grapes; Amina gazing out a window; Melodious plodding along, branch cuttings from the olive grove piled high in his side panniers; chickens scratching in the barnyard; Dion brushing her hair on the patio.

Her father is rarely anywhere but in the vineyards or in his little lab off the fermenting room crushing sample grapes, measuring and recording sugar levels, watching weather reports during these last pre-harvest days. Drought conditions, wind warnings, unpredicted rain all affect his grapes and picking them too soon or too late can have cataclysmic consequences to the juices they produce. Today though, Dion finds him sitting in the kitchen, unshaven, wearing a frayed sweatshirt stained with prior years' grape juice. One hand is lost in his hair, the other fidgeting with a pen and a mess of invoices on the table in front of him. Hearing them come in, he looks up.

"How are we going to pay for this harvest?" His eyes flick back and forth as if new scenarios, all of them horrific, are invading his peripheral vision. "Power, bottles, corks, labels. Where's the money?"

Yiayiá, coming through the kitchen from the tv room, on her way to the bathroom, says nothing. Theo retreats to the vegetable garden.

"I'm working on that, Dad," says Dion. Keeping her father out of the Operation Henri IV loop has been easy. He usually takes no interest in finances, doesn't even know that Theo's beach sketches have been supplying their kitchen cupboards with beans, flour, rice all summer, would be mortified if he did. All of which is good because the deeper they go into planning Operation Henri IV, the more crucial his not knowing about it becomes. Because not only must he not scupper the plan by ruling against it, his reactions in the weeks ahead must be one hundred percent genuine, guileless and innocent.

"I thought you said the bank won't give us credit," he persists.

"That's right." She is trying to dream up what to say next when *Yiayiá* returns, goes to the stove where a pot of lentil soup is simmering. Theo comes in with two tomatoes, an onion and a zucchini. Dion takes them to the sink. With feta they will make a salad to go with the soup and bread *Yiayiá* made yesterday. Bowie leaves his place under the table to follow Theo back outside to call AminaRose. Her father sweeps his papers into a pile and picks them up, making way for their midday dinner.

Bread breaks, soup spoons click, salad crunches in a pall dense as a raincloud over the table. Under it, Bowie rests his snout on the floor between his paws. AminaRose finally gives up any pretence of eating and begins to weep.

"Dear girl," says Dad, who is sitting beside her at one end of the table. "*Yiayiá's* soup is not that bad, surely?" AminaRose tries to laugh, wipes her eyes.

"I'm sorry," She looks at Dion's grandmother at the other end of the table. "I love your soup, *Yiayiá*. I love you all, and am so thankful. It's just..." Her eyes retreat to her lap. "I don't know what to do. I would go home to the U.S. but my husband will be having my house watched, and anyway my parents would make me go back to him. Well my father would, and my mother wouldn't stand against him." Tears course down her cheeks. She wipes them away. "Why did I not think about any of this sooner? Because now Leo wants me to accompany him to an event in Iraklio—"

"You can't go," Theo breaks in. "If someone takes a picture there and your husband sees it—"

"What if he does?" *Yiayiá's* eyes are steel-hard. "At some point the man has to accept that she does not want to live with him."

"No he doesn't," Dion counters, "if he kidnaps her and then locks her up in the dark. But I agree with Theo," she tells AminaRose. "You can't risk going to Iraklio, getting photographed."

"But if I say no, Leo will ask me to do something else another time, and is bound to wonder why I keep refusing." AminaRose's voice quavers. "I think I have been very naive, and taking advantage of you all." She gives into her tears. "I'm so sorry. I'm just so afraid of what lies ahead as well as behind." Alex hands her his napkin — hers is soaked — and waits, soup forgotten, while she blots her eyes. Then:

"You're in good company, Amina. We too have to think now about what to do next, and how and where." Bleakness leaches the energy out of her father's voice. "And when it comes to making life altering choices, each of us has to do it alone."

Yiayiá takes a last spoonful of soup, dabs her mouth with her napkin. Dion gazes at the clutter of dirty dishes and glasses, crumbs and a chunky crust all that's left of her grandmother's loaf. Theo gets up to clear the table. AminaRose pushes back her chair and leaves the room. In despair, they think.

But no, returning, she deposits a heavily loaded, flesh-coloured nylon travel purse, the kind you strap around your waist next to your skin, on the table in front of Alex.

"Take it, please," she says, "so only one of us has a difficult choice to make right now."

"Nonono," Dion's father recoils from the purse. "This is your nest egg and you're going to need it, whatever you decide to do."

"You just said each of us has to make our choices alone. Well this one is mine." Unzipping the purse, AminaRose pulls out a wad of American bills, some of them worth a thousand dollars, and then spreads a three-layered diamond necklace on the table's scrubbed wood. "My husband wanted me to wear this on our final night in Istanbul, to celebrate our twentieth anniversary."

Where, Dion wonders? In their hotel room, where only he would see it, neck candy to be worn in bed, a symbol of what her husband thought he owned? Theo reaches for one of the thousand-dollar bills.

"I've never seen one of these before." He passes it across the table to Dion, who runs her fingers over a slip of paper worth more than the winery has generated in months.

"I took it from the hotel safe," AminaRose tells them. "I call it my salary for twenty years of service. The necklace is insured though so I'm not sure how to sell it."

"I can take it apart for you, if you want, so you can sell the diamonds," says Theo. "My mother has a jewelry workshop in Iraklio with acetylene torches." A small smile, like a patch of sunlight after rain, lightens AminaRose's face.

"Thank you." She turns to Alex. "I'd like to invest the cash in Kokanakis Wines."

Alex shakes his head, tears rolling down his cheeks.

"That'd be a very poor investment, my dear," he says. "You'd never get it back. And it's about time for me to stop hiding like a snail in my vines."

"No Dad." "No Alex." Dion and Theo say at the same time.

Hands flat on the table, *Yiayiá* starts levering herself to her feet. "Enough."

"Please *Yiayiá*, wait just a minute," AminaRose looks around the table. "You all tell me to make my own way, that it's for me to decide. Well, this is my first step. It won't save Kokanakis Wines but it will get this year's harvest into production, so at least you won't lose that." *Yiayiá* opens her mouth to object but apparently AminaRose too owns a steel-plated will. "Please," she says again, "this is my choice." And now the patch of sunlight spreads, taking in all of them. "And maybe my future, whatever it is to be, will flow from this choice."

Dion looks around the table. These, her most precious people, are all dancing on the head of a pin. So many ways for them to fall. Unless they can keep balancing each other.

"We're all of us energy interacting, Dad, creating whatever comes next," she says to her father. "You keep telling me that. So now don't you have to let Amina do what feels right to her?"

In the end though the next dance step on the head of the pin has to be her grandmother's. This vineyard is her birthright. They all sense this and wait, until once again *Yiayiá* spreads her arthritis-knobbed hands on the table top.

"Thank you, Amina dear." She comes to her feet. "We will accept your generosity, but only if you agree to let us pay you back at the end of November."

By pulling off a two million-dollar heist. If her grandmother thinks they can really, actually do it, it must be possible, thinks Dion.

Please, she asks whatever deities might be overseeing this kitchen, give me even one small grain of AminaRose's and *Yiayiá's* courage.

vi.

Willow baskets older than *Yiayiá's* memory and wooden crates and a few lighter plastic ones Alex is forced to use are repaired, cleaned, delivered to his vineyards. Canvas tarps need hosing down with a special solution. Alex and Theo have already scoured and rinsed out the inside of the wine presses and fermenting tanks, also a steel, generator-run crusher and de-stemmer a vintner friend has talked him into trying this year. Oak aging barrels, some newly purchased, some inherited, which Alex the Grape credits for 'the nose and mouth' that won his wine a world-respected *Prix d'Or*, are made ready.

Dion and *Yiayiá* spend their days moving between the garden and kitchen, drying oregano, sage, rosemary and thyme, turning zucchinis, eggplants, tomatoes into stews. Also adding and subtracting strategic ingredients to and from a heist plan, sifting ideas, running through them moment by moment over coffee on the patio, probing for weaknesses, adapting, transforming, creating together. Dion tells *Yiayiá* about Teddy's Perfect Robbery and hears her laugh, really laugh for the first time since Teddy's death. And realizes that she too has not felt the thrill of this kind of energy since then.

There is no danger of AminaRose overhearing their plans. Crete's weather has stayed sunny and warm and she spends most of her time now at Salin's villa. Decides to leave with him for a weekend sailing trip to Elafonisi.

"And I think I might tell him who I really am," she announces to Dion, packing the night before they are due to leave. A jam jar full of late roses on the windowsill, a sketch of Bowie by Theo tacked on the wall over the bed, a multi-coloured quilt from a Rethymnon market stall, a slight scent of a cologne Salin probably bought her have turned the storage room into AminaRose's own sanctuary. Which she seems determined not to inhabit. "That my name is not Rose."

"Why?" Dion drops onto the end of Amina's bed.

"Because," Amina folds a silk negligee and puts it into a hold-all she has bought. "Maybe I trust him."

"*Maybe* you trust him?" Her voice sounds like a hyena. Dion sucks in a breath, expels it. "You have to be sure, Amina. How do you know it's not just wishful thinking, when he won't even tell you what he does for a living, how he got so wealthy?" Amina picks up a handful of thongs, her shoulders lifting dismissively as she stuffs them into her hold-all.

"Wealthy people do business and I've told you, I know what that means." She turns to an array of lotions on a beat-up dresser Alex found in a friend's barn.

"But what if you don't? Anyway what will you gain by telling him your real name?"

Amina's dark eyes fix on Dion.

"A real relationship, that's what, something more than servitude or playacting. You say I can't trust him but how can he trust me if I won't even tell him my name?"

Dion has no answer to this.

"I just can't stand the idea of you winding up right back where you started," says Dion. That's not exactly true. What she really can't stomach is the thought of what Salin will do to Amina when he discovers his Henri IV cognac is missing. "Why don't you at least think about it a bit more?" Amina zips up the hold-all, smiles her response.

She returns from Elafonisi glowing. Finds Dion in the pigpen, dusk slowly bleeding light out of clouds above the barnyard, and perches on a low wall around it. Salin now knows that she has run away from her marriage.

"I had to tell him, how could I not? Lying out on the deck after making love in what must surely be one of Earth's most magical places, we got talking about our lives. He wants me in his, he said, whatever it takes to make that happen. And I, well I think I might want that too, D." She has picked up the nickname from Theo. "But not under false pretences. So I told him the whole truth, my real name, who I was married to, all of it."

"Wow." She sounds so happy, thinks Dion. Freely happy. "What did he say?"

"That it made no difference to him!" Laughing lightly, Amina looks younger than she is in the softening light.

Behind Dion chickens are clucking, looking for grains she has just spread on the dusty ground. A pig named Pat (for no one in particular because he'll be slaughtered soon) snorts around her boots, looking for the load of kitchen scraps in her bucket.

"So what now?" Dion tips her bucket-load onto the ground.

"'I don't care where you've come from,' he said, nuzzling me, 'as long as you're here with me,'" says Amina. "He doesn't need to go back to Moscow very often. He says he can work better here with no intrusions, no sitting through endless meetings with people who understand zero about the computers running their lives. Here in his villa, surrounded by his art and music and wines and brandies, when he's not working he can read and swim and sail and make love with me. 'Sound good?' he said."

"You're not allowing yourself to be owned again? I mean he takes you out on his boat, throws your bikini top into the sea," Dion says. And thinks but doesn't mention that when people cross Russians like Salin they tend to wind up poisoned or falling off balconies or mysteriously disappearing.

"He didn't throw my bikini top into the sea, I did." Amina jumps down off the wall.

vii.

Yiayiá is stuffing forkfuls of spinach and feta filling into half-moon breakfast pastries Alex will deliver to his pickers, along with their harvest baskets, as soon as they come out of the oven.

"Theo, can you dig out as many potatoes and leeks and onions as you can find?"

Dion is charged with getting out the tablecloths, napkins, glasses, cutlery, plates for tonight's harvest dinner – her first. Last year her father had moved his wines out of the fermentation tanks by the time she arrived in November. His red Romeiko wine was aging in oak barrels for a carefully calibrated number of months (or years,) his white wine and dessert rosés settling in steel tanks. Dion knew nothing of this. Wine was for drinking, in her experience, a glass with dinner, large quantities at parties. Later in the winter, while she helped her father bottle and label some of his vintages, he gave her a crash course in blending the past – five thousand years of wine making experience in this part of the world – with close listening to today's environment, climate and viticultural discoveries.

"Scientific art," he told her, "that's what winemaking is." And tuning into life on this land, in this sun and wind and rain, working with his family's vines to create his wines, he looked happier than she had seen him since she was a child on the English commune.

This morning Alex is dragging wooden crates from the fermenting room into the yard beyond the end of the patio, ready for pickers in his closest vineyard. His much lighter willow baskets and plastic crates are stacked in the bed of his ancient jalopy. Once *Yiayiá's* pastries are ready he will drive them, a canister of thick Greek coffee and a carton of miniature china cups to pickers gathering at the rest of the vineyards.

Theo, silhouetted against the rising sun, looks like some kind of mythical sprite as he leads Melodious, the donkey, around from the barnyard. Last night he invited the family to see his new studio shack and have a *raki* around a new fire pit he has made outside it. Today he and Melodious, who is to be fitted with a special carrying frame, will transport full crates from the vineyard behind the patio to the fermenting room, and keep pickers supplied with fresh ones.

Dion's job is to record the number of crates or baskets arriving from each vineyard, which press they go into and which fermentation tank receives them at what time, so that bunches grown together stay together until Alexander The Grape decides how to marry flavours waiting inside each lush, ripe-to-bursting grape. Amina will spend the day helping *Yiayiá* in the kitchen.

Returning from the barnyard with eggs and a pail of goat milk for their coffees, Dion finds Irina's granddaughter Georgina on the patio, rubbing her arms against the early morning chill. Her brother Iannis and one of her cousins, who are with her, will help Theo. Irina will arrive when Georgina's baby wakes up and needs nursing.

"Come in," Dion tells them in newly learned Greek. "Have coffee and breakfast while the day warms up." Fresh out of the oven, *Yiayiá's* pastries are flavouring the air.

The sun clears the shoulder of Mount Psiloritis, touching the closest vineyard as Dad leaves. Theo and his pickers disappear into it. *Yiayiá* dispatches Amina to the garden with a basket and verbal list of the vegetables she wants and sits down with a cup of coffee. Peace, like the pregnant pause before a storm, descends on the kitchen.

SuperHeavy's "Miracle Worker" breaks it as her Dad's truck clatters into the driveway, Bowie sitting proudly in the passenger seat. Climbing into the truck bed, Alex lifts a great bunch of translucent, heavily ripe, red, green, light purple Romeiko grapes to show Dion. Then together they tip the laden baskets into a steel grape press.

From here these grapes' juices will go into Dad's stainless steel fermenting tanks. Grapes from Theo's vineyard are to go from Melodious's back into the round wooden wine press, motor-run now, that *Yiayiá's* father had hidden from the Nazis in World War Two. From there they will travel, bucket by bucket, up a ladder into the barrel-shaped, ceiling-high wooden fermenting tank to make her Dad's "heritage red wine." Another vineyard's harvest, destined for Kokanakis Winery's prize-winning dessert wine, will be laid out on the tarps to dry out in the sun.

"Back in your great-grandfather's day homegrown Romeiko wine was rotgut, glorified vinegar," her Dad tells her as they lift and tip and record. "But he believed better care of the vines and grapes and the right timing could change that. And he was right. Now, mixing Romeiko with complimentary or contrasting grape varieties also makes for whole new ballgames." His friend Costa's grapes will arrive later today.

Clouds roll in to cover the sun. Trucks pull in, Alex inspects their basket loads, directs like an orchestra maestro where each will go. *Yiayiá*, Amina, and later Irina chop, mix and look after Georgina's baby in the kitchen. Dion watches, counts, records. By the end of the afternoon two of their three fermentation tanks are full. Irina, Georgina and some of the others have gone home. Melodious is munching under his favourite olive tree. Dad and Theo, their faces, arms and shirts splashed with grape juice, look like creatures out of a Lord Of The Rings movie. Casseroles for tonight's harvest feast cover the kitchen table.

A low autumn sun is leaving the sky when the pickers and their significant others trickle onto the patio. Dad and Theo have plugged in the plane tree's fairy lights and lit the wall lanterns though, and candles flicker on two long tables laid with finger foods and pitchers of last year's wine. Standing in the kitchen doorway, wearing an embroidered off-the-shoulder peasant blouse and flowing skirt Amina has lent her, Dion watches her father welcome those who have made his dream real for what might be the last time. And listening to their staccato Greek rising and falling, their explosions of laughter, she finds herself close to tears.

"Give me those," Amina takes two plates of *dolmades* (stuffed grape leaves) out of her hands and heads for the tables. At the drive shed end of the patio Dad has charcoal burning in his grill. Beside him Bowie, watching closely, lifts his nose as smells of roasting chicken, lamb and pork billow on smoke curling up into the plane tree's yellowing leaves.

Yiayiá is sitting on her favourite chair wearing a navy blue dinner dress Dion has not seen before. Amina must have bought it for her while she and Theo were away at the beach. Her grandmother looks ten years younger in it, and a perfect fusion of her American restauranteur and her Cretan selves. A tear drops onto Dion's cheek. She bats it away. *Yiayiá*, who knew Teddy, who shaped her father's early life and now, at ninety-four, is the lynchpin in all of their lives here, does not approve of tears.

Plates empty. Voices rise. Geysers of laughter erupt. *Yiayiá* signals to Amina and Dion to bring out the next round of food, to refill jugs, until Dad stands, calls for quiet, then raises his glass:

"To my mother, Dionysia, for once again providing this harvest feast. Without you Kokanakis Winery would not exist, *Mamá*. And to all of you, *Efkaristo poli* (thank you so much) for helping me bring in this year's joy. *Yamas*!"

A nearly full moon peeks through the clouds, David Bowie's voice calls out "Let's dance!" and Dad helps *Yiayiá* to her feet. Dion is surprised by how graceful she is waltzing with him under the patio's fairy lights. Theo and Amina follow their example, Theo in a new white tee-shirt, Amina's long dark hair shining above an A-line dress that looks perfect, both of their bodies free of cares as Theo propels her into a twirl. Amina's chest expands into the music, her hips cradle it. People stop drinking, eating, talking to watch, clapping out the beat, then getting up to join them, everyone so free in themselves, as if the world were healthy, sane, full of loving life.

Theo's friend Kiri, tall, muscular, everything that Theo is not, offers her a glass of *raki*, wants to dance. Dion knocks back the drink, has no idea how much wine she has put away as she takes his hand. But it's no good, she is not Amina, not fluid, not sexy, not even graceful. Amina jettisoned twenty years of imprisonment inside a black abaya and *niqāp* the minute she arrived here. Eleven months after her own arrival Dion feels like a withering grape left behind on the vine. She cannot put aside what lies ahead, cannot feel in her body a family tradition that has existed on this land for as long as *Yiayiá* can remember.

"I'm sorry," she tells Kiri, miming a stomach upset.

It's not entirely fake, her head is ringing just this side of an ache. Lying on her bed in the dark, she hears her father's playlist end. A live

Greek mandolin replaces it, a tambourine, maracas, bongo drum join in. Someone starts singing mournful Greek. Dion's tears wet the pillow.

She is not open, not free. So how on earth did she imagine she could pit herself against a ruthless Russian hacker? Pie in the sky, that's all these last months of planning have been, a very old lady's and her loser granddaughter's useless dream. Her father and *Yiayiá* are going to lose everything and there is nothing in this real world she can do to stop that.

Out on the patio someone calls out. The beat picks up. Feet start to stamp. Someone knocks on Dion's door. She wipes her hand across her face, holds her breath. Maybe they'll think she's asleep. More knocking.

"D?" The door cracks open. Amina comes into the darkness. The bed joggles as she sits on it. "What's wrong?"

Self-conscious reserve stands no chance against sympathy. Dion sobs, can't help herself as a hopelessly tangled mess of unvoiceable worries soaks the pillow.

"It's everything I guess, the winery..." Amina must not get even a whiff of Operation Henri IV. "And I've had a lot to drink." Amina gets up, switches on the bedside lamp and brings her the box of tissues on the dresser.

"Come on, get up."

Dion shakes her head, more tears.

"I can't." She put on mascara for the party. God only knows what it looks like now.

Amina stays where she is. And self pity, full-fledged now, revolts Dion. What would *Yiayiá* think?

"Please?" says Amina. "The party's not the same without you. Come and dance with Theo and your Dad and me. I'm not leaving 'til you do."

"I can't do it, Amina," she says again. "You're beautiful and brave enough to run from your life with nothing more than a pocketful of money and a necklace, then to give those to us. To risk what your husband will do if Salin gives you up."

The clock in the hall begins to chime midnight. Amina waits until it finishes. Then:

"Not brave," she says, "just desperate. Until you found me."

"And now you're with Salin." Caged by another tyrant, says her tone.

"For now, yes. But I keep telling you, D, do not worry about me with Leo. If or when it ends I'll do whatever is necessary. Now please, let me fix your face and come back out." Amina's hand squeezes Dion's. "No good will come from your lying here crying."

A group is standing shoulder to shoulder on the patio, stepping Zorba-style into a traditional dance, to music that must be as old, surely, as Dionysus, god of wine. More people get up, join in. Amina takes her to Theo at the far end of the dancing line. He smiles, puts his arm on her shoulder, attaching her to the line. Amina joins her other side and looking around, Dion sees that regardless of what else is happening in their lives and how they feel, everyone she knows in Crete is dancing.

Clouds sail across the night sky, the moon popping out between them. Pitchers and bottles empty. The mandolin slows into a resonant, yearning song that seems to have a hundred verses. People dance to it in couples. Kiri finds Dion, asks if she's well enough now to resume their dance. Dion feels the warmth in muscled shoulders designed for work. He smells like wet grass mixed with cologne. Her body relaxes. The moon begins to descend behind the plane tree. Alex starts a playlist of slow dance tunes. Kiri's arms hold her against him, guiding their movement but not transgressing, not exploring.

Yiayiá, watching, sees Theo tap Kiri on the shoulder and cut in. Smiling, she signals to Amina, who is standing at the edge of the patio talking on her phone, to come and help her get to bed. The song ends. Theo draws Dion to one of the tables where a candle is still burning in its glass globe beside a half-empty bottle of *raki*. He hands the bottle to Dion with his free hand, then picks up the candle.

"Come to my shack, there's something I want to give you." She hears his smile. A new painting, a small preparatory piece using his new technique?

A pre-dawn glow is beginning to backlight Mount Psiloritis as he leads her into the vineyard behind the patio. Vine shadows jig in the candle globe's flickering light. Theo's hand feels familiar around hers. Outside his front door a freshly laid fire waits in the stone circle. Oak trees above his shack, outlined against the moon, shiver in a night breeze as he lights it. His sleeping bag is laid out beside it.

"Sit with me."

She sits cross-legged inside her skirt. He sits close beside her, his heat mixing with the fire-warmth on her face, arms, legs as he pokes the logs, unscrews the top of the *raki* bottle.

"May I?" He waits for her nod then fits the bottle into her mouth, tilting her head back just enough to give her a sip. The liquid trickles into her throat, warms her chest. "May I?" he says again, whispering this time, and now his hands are up inside the back of her blouse, feeling for the hooks of the strapless brassiere she is wearing.

"What did you want to give me?" she breathes as the brassiere clasps give, freeing her breasts.

"You'll see," his breath is hot inside her earlobe.

Her nipples graze her blouse's fabric. His hand comes around to cup one of her breasts, something he has never done before, and now here is his mouth, taking in her nipple through the cloth. The fire crackles, sends up sparks as, looking up, he leaves a transparent circle of wet on her blouse. Desire jolts through her. He finds the other nipple, gives it the same treatment, two patches of wet now, her nipples clearly visible. He licks them through the cloth, desire pushing her way out into a white water current now.

"May I?" He lifts her blouse over her head, finds a freshly aroused nipple and sucks. A bolts shoots down into the white water. Her hand comes up, finds his springy soft hair. Gently he pushes her to lie down. She does not want to resist. But.

"Theo?" He doesn't want to make love.

"Shsh," he says. "Let me give you a gift."

The ground through the sleeping bag is hard, cold on the side away from the fire, the moon high as a bright coin above her as his fingers come up inside her skirt, tug at her underpants. She lifts her pelvis. He pulls them off then circles his fingers lightly, pressing gently. She hears a gasp and now his lips are covering hers, wetness pulsing into her vagina, his palm circling, a finger probing up inside her and there is only this white water rush now. Until he sits up, runs his wet finger down her thigh, her lower leg, raises it to kiss her foot's instep then her ankle, her calf, the back of her knee, her foot pointing up at the moon as he kisses the inside of her thigh, his lips light as a butterfly. Her body arches, juices pulsing, heart pounding. He stops, looks at her. Lies down again, takes a breast into his mouth, suckling her while his fingers circle, circle and, clinging to him now, she will do anything, anything—

It doesn't take long, on this harvest night, for the rushing current to overflow.

"Please!" Her pulsing body wants him inside her. "Please!"

Out at the edge of her consciousness a tiny tag of reason trying to ask – does he have a condom? – is no match for his knees pushing her thighs apart now, her legs wrapping themselves around him, his thrusting them both into ecstasy.

Her eyes open to morning sunlight playing hide and seek with a curtain Theo has strung across a window in his shack. His sleeping bag, covering her in his bed, is full of the smell of them together, but he is not in it. She remembers their moving in here, making love again, then again, pulsing pleasure reaching into her toes, her fingertips, her every cell, his mop of hair tickling her nose as he kissed her. Finally, as the first of the valley's roosters crowed, he tucked his hand between her thighs and they went to sleep. She stretches into a new, grace-filled languorousness.

Where is he? She looks at his drawings and small painting studies tacked to the shack's walls. Has he gone out to pee in the forest? She stretches again. Her nipples feel tender, her vagina sticky wet.

They used no contraception! He probably thinks she takes the pill but they have never discussed this – why would they? – and she stopped taking it over a year ago when her body ceased to be a playground.

She tries to think how many weeks have passed since her last period. Is too old to be making this kind of mistake. Can only hope whatever almost forty-year old eggs she has left were not home for his swarming sperm, because where in liberated but still Greek Orthodox Crete will she find a morning after pill?

Theo is not outside. Maybe at the house then, preparing a breakfast tray? She imagines *Yiayiá* and her father trying not to smile. Closes her eyes.

Sits up. His knapsack, his brushes, sketchbook, paints, the cardboard tube that holds his new papers are all gone.

viii.

"Oh my love, how thin is the line between me here and you. One small step, if only I knew how to take it." Sitting on the side of her bed, *Yiayiá* looks up at Gio in their wedding picture beside the cross on her bedroom wall. "But no Dionysia, Irina would say, that's for God to decide. And she's right." A November wind rattles *Yiayiá's* bedroom shutters. "I can't come to you, my beloved, until I right the balance I upset. Plotting, with our granddaughter, to break the law upsets me a little because what if it all goes wrong? It won't, she tells me, if we do it right and between us we will have solved our problem.

"No thanks to that no-good deadbeat artist of hers. Oh Gio, why did I let myself think so much of him? Was it out of hope for our dear Dion?" *Yiayiá's* voice quavers. "If you could have seen her during these last months with him, gradually coming out of her shell. The morning after harvest night, before she realized he had left for good, her smile, her whole body was carrying a joy I recognized from all those years ago with you, my dearest." The old lady's face softens in the light of the bedside lamp but only for an instant. "Three weeks he's been gone now. I thought he was better than that but," her shoulders lift, "a rolling stone, that's what he is. He got what he wanted from Dion, gave her a gift of thanks and that's all.

"Dion says he'll come back in time to help us, she's dead sure he will, and if he doesn't she says we can manage without him. I don't know."

You have no other choice, says Gio. Our son is American but what kind of future would he find at seventy in the United States? This where he and you and Dion too, poor mongrel that she is, belong. So much emotion in his voice.

"Yes. We were so lucky, weren't we my love, to know always that Crete is where we came from, that this land and sea and sky are part of us – even though we had to leave it." She listens for Gio's acquiescence. "And you're right, Alex has never had that, until now.

"You should have seen him yesterday morning, Gio, with Salin. Dion and I were in the kitchen when we heard a car stop outside the winery. The bell outside the street-side showroom door jingled, which was odd because there are never any bookings this late in the year. Dion went to answer it."

The Russian looked at bottles of last year's wines gathering dust on the showroom shelves, at dust motes dancing in light from its floor-to-ceiling windows, then asked to see her father.

Dion didn't want to let him any further into the winery. The week's news had been full of internet viciousness and the poisoning of another Russian dissident. But turning Salin away would create tension they can not afford right now and her father, who still knows nothing about Operation Henri IV, would have nothing to give away.

Since the harvest, when he is not poring over recipes and sugar charts on the computer and past years' winemaking notes spread all over the office, which Dion has vacated since there is no money to manage,

Alex spends every second taking samples from his fermentation tanks and barrels, measuring sugar content, acidity, noting viscosity, sediment deposits, scents, tastes, in his little lab behind the fermenting room. Decisions on further fermentation and how to experiment with blending grape yields are born there.

"Dion and Salin found him peering into a hand-held refractometer thing he uses," *Yiayiá* tells Gio.

"Hello," said Alex, none too happy to be disturbed. Then, focussing on Salin: "The personality of a wine is complex and, just like in people, when you blend various characteristics together new unforeseen behaviours sometimes burst out. So you have to be open to new ideas, and ready to adapt. A critically timed marriage of science with art is what makes the difference between inspired uniqueness and mediocrity in a wine." He allowed himself a smile. "Sometimes nature herself whispers what must be blended in, but only if you're listening." He put down his tool. "Look at me, rattling on. Come." Ushering them out of his inner sanctum, he took Salin back to the showroom, brought our crystal glasses out from under the counter.

"*Raki?*"

Salin shook his head.

"It's a little early for me, sport."

"Our present contract is up at the end of the month," *Yiayiá* goes on, "and Salin came to make sure Alex understands the consequences of his refusing to sign the new contract. It could be argued that I am just too old to be competent, he said! Alex, bless his sweet heart, dropped any semblance of cordiality then."

"You mean do I understand that if I don't agree to steer the new profit-mongering, soil-depleting winemaking behemoth you're proposing you'll kick my family and me out of our home?" he said.

"Alex listen—" said the Russian.

"No, the person who needs to listen is you," Alex told him. "Much as you'd like to ignore the fact that more and more species are becoming extinct on Earth every day, that fact still exists. Cadavers are mounting everywhere in the world, thanks to your blind and deaf profiteering. I keep trying to tell you, Leo, that everything alive is connected, and you're not a stupid man. Surely you understand by now that every grape I harvest is a product of its relationship with everything else growing and living with it, including you, me. A little winery is not the only thing you are about to destroy. Automate another parcel of the world's land and you'll kill far more than you are capable of knowing.'

"Dion was so proud of her father," *Yiayiá* tells Gio. "'Look,' she said to them both, 'why don't I make some coffee and maybe you two can find some kind of mutually beneficial way forward?'

"Salin had no time for that but Dion hopes her fruitless attempt at peacemaking will steer blame for Operation Henri IV away from us, especially from her father, who has not signed up to become a criminal."

Gio fills the air with silent curses.

"So now Dion and I spend every spare minute sitting by our Aga in the kitchen." *Yiayiá* smiles at the way wood fire heat wraps itself around you. "Remember, dearest, how we'd huddle together by a fire, trying to read a map of your next guerrilla target by the light of its flames? I'd watch your finger tracing paths that did not exist on any Nazi map, my seventeen-year old self yearning for the feel of that same finger raising my chin to kiss me, or brushing against my breast as if by accident." *Yiayiá* puts a hand to her breast, chuckling. "These sad little sacks might not raise a stir now but if I imagine us lying together behind some bushes on a mountainside, I can feel my own fire flickering. Can you not find a way to reach out for me, hold me in your arms the way you used to after you returned from blowing up or stealing something?"

After, Gio reminds her, not before. Now tell me what you and our granddaughter have dreamed up so we can review every detail, see if it can be done.

A few birds are roosting in the bushes outside her bedroom window. Inside, the house is quiet. Dion must be in her room reading, Alex is either doing the same or still tinkering with his barrels and tanks, making his magic. Amina spends most of her time at Salin's villa now. No one will hear her whispered words.

"We have three objectives." She puts up an arthritic left index finger. "One: Relieve Leo Salin of his Henri IV Dudognon bottle of cognac; two," her middle finger goes up. "Use its diamonds to raise the money we need to pay off our debt to him by November 30, thereby negating his right to take over our home and winery and land, and three," her ring finger's swollen knuckles, which keep gold engagement and wedding rings that once belonged to Gio's mother safe, joins the other two. "Do this without violence, without failing, without getting caught, and without implicating Alex or Amina." *Yiayiá* stops. "I only wish it could be without dear Dion too." She listens, nods.

"Yes, simple is best. Steal the two million-dollar bottle of cognac, remove and sell its diamonds. Pay off our debt with cash. Receive a signed receipt from Salin releasing us from any further obligation." *Yiayiá* listens again.

"Yes, I know I'm tired. And my legs are weak. And I'm a little forgetful, I know. And now that there are only the two of us timing is going to be even more crucial. And Dion is shaky, but she is also determined—"

Gentle laughter from Gio.

I wonder where she got that.

"—And what happened with Theo seems to have hardened her resolve. But oh Gio, if she gets caught it will mean police, a trial, a Greek prison. If anyone is to be caught it should be me, because," *Yiayiá's* voice flutters: "'Oh dear, officer, I'm so sorry, what was I thinking?' And if they don't believe me, throw me in jail. Kill me please."

Gio is not amused.

Just do your part. Do not ruin the whole mission by having a panic or a heart attack. You've already been in hospital once this year and the last thing Alex and Dion need is for you to drop dead—

"I won't, I promise." *Yiayiá's* hand reaches out to touch a Bible she keeps on her bedside table just because it's always been there.

Okay then, take off your slippers and lie down now, so I can whisper in your ear, come into your dreams. Help you remember that evil exists for us to collide with, my darling, to break old patterns so something new can take their place.

Wine

Fermentation, transmutation
occur unseen,
grapes' juices
co-creating with time
in dark silence
an elixir, a gift
from vineyard angels
who know exactly
what they want.

i.

"Happy birthday D," Dion tells herself, sitting in her hoody and jeans in a patch of November sunshine outside her gully. She hugs her knees.

Forty.

The gully she thought was a home for her soul seven months ago is a gash of shadow in the stream bank now, a home for spiders, not for her. Brittle oak leaves still attached to their branches at the top of the stream bank clatter like bones in a gust of wind.

No one knows it's her birthday. Her father, immersed in wine tasting, timing, temperatures, hardly knows what day it is, let alone which one marks her birth nearly half a century ago in another life, and when *Yiayiá* is not resting her old bones by the kitchen Aga or the television, chores and cooking and whispered conversations with Dion's dead grandfather leave no brain-space for birthdays. Amina drops by, looking completely at home in designer jeans and cashmere sweaters now, but cringe-worthy birthdays have never been a subject between them. Theo knows, she told him she came to Crete a year ago right after her last birthday. So what?

Good riddance to him, *Yiayiá* said when it was clear, several days after the harvest, that he had left them without even saying goodbye. Six weeks later Dion rocks back and forth on her haunches.

She knows why Theo left. His gift to her on harvest night, his thank you for six months' access to her body, was probably supposed to be a hand-administered orgasm. He did not realize any more than she did that unleashing the full-out, body/mind/soul-consuming power of what he himself called the greatest force on Earth would consume him too. And, shocked by having lost himself inside exactly what he did not want to do, he will now consider himself a failure. Recycled desire, luscious anticipation of what is already known, lacks the primal urgency he set his heart on painting. To make matters worse he will think that, having finally experienced orgasms – more than one! – she'll want more. Another gust of wind chases itself through dead grasses in the stream bed.

He's right. Her body/mind keeps skipping back to that night by the fire, his touch so gentle, sensing her body, exploring, giving. Until – "Please, please!" – she shattered the carapace inside which she had spent her whole sexual life.

She told *Yiayiá* that Theo would come back for Operation Henri IV because she was sure he would, but its appointed day is tomorrow. Maybe Theo now thinks the fake Henri IV he created – finding a bottle the right size and shape, using her pictures to cover it with papier-mâché painstakingly shaped to match the hideous knobs marching up the sides of the real Henri, painting its contours gold and platinum then studding them with costume diamonds crushed to the right size, filling the bottle with water to give it weight – has been enough of a contribution. Because why on Earth would an up-and-coming artist in his twenties want to commit daylight robbery in some God forsaken valley with a needy, frumpy-dumpy forty-year-old?

She has packed herself a birthday party: a half bottle of *raki*, some rusks and a plastic container full of *Yiayiá's* homemade sun-dried tomato and olive pesto. She digs the bottle out of her knapsack, unscrews its cap and raises it to the sinking sun.

"*Yamas* Dionysia." *Raki* sliding down her throat brings heat. And memory: His fitting the bottle into her mouth. How can she not be thankful for what happened next? Another swig.

Forty. And look at me, Teddy: No more pencil skirts and heels, pant suits worn like shields, no more yoga spandex or slinky dresses or clubbing. She misses not a second of that life.

What she does miss is Theo's friendship, the buffer they created between now and ruination by discussing, questioning, arguing, planning, and then practising for Operation Henri IV.

She and *Yiayiá* have spent the last weeks going over every detail, in the garden or out on the road, ostensibly walking up to visit Irina, her granddaughter Georgina and the baby, in case Salin has bugged their house. Now, right now, she has to make a final decision about whether she and her grandmother can pull off Operation Henri IV alone, without it killing *Yiayiá*.

"You're ninety-four," Dion has pointed out more than once, "and subject to panic attacks!"

"That's right," her grandmother answered, "and we can use that."

Is Operation Henri IV an exit strategy, Dion wonders, a way for *Yiayiá* to finally fall into *Pappoús's* waiting arms, or is resistance simply in the old warhorse's blood? When she called Salin to set up a contract signing session for tomorrow, a day when sunshine is forecast, Dion couldn't help asking why he was forcing her father to destroy everything he believes in. The Russian let silence speak for him: He wants what he wants. Myceneans, Dorians, pirates, Venetians, Turks, Germans thought the same, and again and again Cretans stood against them.

Staring into the failing light in the stream bed, Dion tries to run through Operation Henri IV's unfolding with only *Yiayiá* and herself. No diversions, no perfectly timed distractions behind which to hide. Their execution and their luck will have to be perfect. And in Athens, turning the bottle into dollars, she will have to act alone.

Alone. What's new about that, people going about their lives, eating together behind their dining room curtains, nothing to do with her? There was a community baseball park beside her subway stop back in Toronto and sometimes, on her way home from work on a warm spring evening, she'd stop to watch pint-sized girls and boys wearing team t-shirts try to hit the ball, run the bases, parents laughing, cheering. Sometimes she'd sit in the rickety bleacher to watch, as if she belonged to someone. Dion takes another swig of *raki*. The sun's rays, almost horizontal now, turn luminous for a moment before the shadows begin to darken. Alone is where she lives.

'So you have faith,' *Yiayiá's* voice. 'Faith in yourself, your nerves, brain, blood, bones...'

In her mind which dreamed up this heist. In her spirit which sold her meaningless Toronto life to come here, which spent her life savings with no idea what would come next, which has refused over and over during the last seven months to give up or give in.

Have faith in herself or do nothing. Those are her only choices and this forty-year old self can not do nothing. Because of some kind of certainty that has always been with her, she just didn't know it.

Is that what faith is, she asks the shadows?

Better pack her knapsack, heave this aging body to its feet and go home while she can still see. Dead leaves clacking in the grove of oaks sound like witches. Dion stops to look up at them.

"Could you come with us do you think, to help?"

ii.

Late morning sun is shining right on schedule when Dion and Alex help *Yiayiá* into the front passenger seat of the Fiat. Dion's grandmother has turned herself back into the Cretan widow she was when Leo Salin saw her at dinner here in the spring: shapeless black wool skirt, cardigan, coat, shoes. Her back is rigid, her jaw set. Alex is wearing what he calls his funeral suit, fitting garb for a man about to sign himself into indentured servitude, he says, knowing nothing even now about Operation Henri IV. Dion has felt guilty keeping him in the dark but they need his guilelessness. Also, if she winds up on trial for grand theft he must not be implicated. She is wearing jeans and her hoody, as if refusing to mark the occasion.

Amina has been staying at Salin's villa. That she won't join them is crucial, but also likely. Salin won't want her to see him in action.

Nobody speaks, the Fiat's engine the only sound as Alex turns onto the road that leads to Salin's villa. Dion, riding beside *Yiayiá* in the back seat, reaches out to take her hand, hoping her grandmother's stomach does not feel as nauseated as her own. In the ornamental urns outside Salin's front gate the birds of paradise have been replaced by small blue flowers.

"Prospero they're called," says *Yiayiá*, "probably because only magic can make a plant bloom this late in the year."

Please witches or God or any other kind of energy that is watching, please lend us just a little bit of that magic, thinks Dion, taking back her hand so *Yiayiá* will not feel its sweat.

Salin's gate opens – his man must have been watching for them – and Alex pulls up to the villa's front door. He helps his mother out of the car while Dion shoulders her blue leather knapsack/briefcase, and picks up *Yiayiá's* voluminous handbag. In it today are an extra diaper, clean underpants, baby wipes, smelling salts, and Theo's Henri IV replica. Salin meets them in the foyer.

Dion looks past him into the inner reaches of his house as if this were an ordinary day, as if her nerves were not twanging so loudly in her chest, her arms, her legs she feels sure everyone must hear them.

"Is Amina around?" she asks. "I've hardly seen her in weeks."

"She might join us later," says Salin, ushering them into his study, making clear that the choice is his.

Sunlight is angling through the study's side window. Good, thinks Dion. It sparks off Henri IV Dudognon's thousands of diamonds on its way across the hardwood floor and carpet towards the four chairs and coffee table, where Salin has a bottle of water, four glasses, two copies of his new contract and two ballpoint pens waiting. Down at the other end of the room St. John the Theologian and the camera mounted in the corner of the ceiling watch from the shadows.

Salin pulls out the closest chair, facing the bar and the camera mounted above it, for *Yiayiá*. Dad sits down next to her, facing Henri IV Dudognon on his plinth. Dion is on her other side, her back to Henri. Parking her grandmother's bag at her feet, she slips off her knapsack, takes out her phone, lays it on the table to record the meeting just as she did last time she was here, looks at the time and takes long silent breaths to calm her nerves, slow her heart beat, like she and *Yiayiá* have practised. Salin moves around Dad to take the last chair, his back to the bar. The air in the room is cool, a bit stuffy, as if it has been closed up until now. *Yiayiá* draws her cardigan closer around her, raising one of its sleeves so she can see her watch as Salin hands one copy of the new contract and a pen to Alex, and slides the other across the table to *Yiayiá*. Dion picks it up, riffles through its enumerated sections.

"Is this the same as the copy we have at home?"

"Of course." Bonhomie gone, impatience barely suppressed.

You are not intimidated, Dion tells her nerves. Reaching down, she rummages in her grandmother's bag, takes out *Yiayiá's* reading glasses. Tries to keep her hand steady as she passes them to her grandmother.

"Remember, you told me you want to reread everything one last time."

"You did that last time you were here," Salin reminds her.

"Yes," *Yiayiá* looks at him over the top of her glasses. "And you'll recall that I told you I cannot sign without being absolutely certain that my son and granddaughter will retain their stewardship of our land."

"And I told you that will depend on Alex's performance," says Salin. "Nothing in the contract has changed since then."

"Still, you will allow me not to make a mistake I made once before." Said as brusquely as a Detroit business woman, as if what idiot would sign something without carefully scrutinizing it? And it strikes Dion suddenly that her grandmother's irascibility is, and probably always has been an impenetrable cloak inside which she can take shelter from any kind of emotional weather. Taking up the contract, she sits reading as if she were alone, as if these minutes were not carefully measured. Alex follows her lead, reading.

Dion watches the mantle of Salin's politeness begin to wear thin. His eyes flick down to the paper trembling in *Yiayiá's* hands. Good. She takes a marked up copy out of her knapsack and, laying it on the table so as not to give away her own hands' shakiness, pretends to review it. Exactly in line with her grandmother's and father's intention, stated by Dion over the phone when she set up this meeting to sign their way into a future dictated by the Russian.

Minutes tick by on Gio's big watch, strapped to *Yiayiá's* wrist. Salin consults his phone. *Yiayiá* moves her pen along each line as she reads one page, the next. She has just turned the third page when the pen begins to tap against the paper. Alex looks up.

"Mom?" *Yiayiá* does not reply. Salin, Alex and Dion watch the pen continue its spasmodic passage across the page. "Are you okay, Mom?"

"What?" Annoyed at the interruption. But does her face have a drained, greyish look, or is it a trick of the light? Dion's heart hammers as she picks up the bottle of water. It wobbles in her hand. Alex takes it from her, unscrews the top and pours his mother a glass.

"Here, Mom. Take a break."

Salin watches. Dion breathes.

"Oh." *Yiayiá* puts the contract down. The pen slides out of her hand onto the floor. Dion leans down to retrieve it. Alex helps *Yiayiá* hold the glass to drink. The old lady looks at Salin. "I'm sorry."

"Please, take your time, Mrs. Kokanakis."

Yiayiá sips some more water, picks up her pen again. Puts it down. Raises a shaking hand to her heart. "Oh dear—"

And here now is the line they have to cross. Under the cold-eyed scrutiny of a seasoned predator. Without help. Salin's man hovers in the study's open doorway.

"Oh," *Yiayiá* says again, the word light as an exhale.

And then a miracle, an alarm bell ringing somewhere in the house, just as it was supposed to! Salin gets up. Fires guttural Russian at his man in the doorway, excuses himself and leaves the room.

Yiayiá betrays no sign of surprise before her body crumples forward and slips out of her chair into a patch of sunlight on the floor.

"Mom!" Alex shoves his chair back, kneels beside her.

"*Yiayiá*!" Dion too slides down onto the floor and there's no time to wonder, no need to pretend her terror because if this is playacting her grandmother is a star. Dion's instinct is to hold her, help her father wake some sign of life. But no. After all the weeks of strategizing and rehearsing, arguing and worrying, here is her life's sharp turn. That once taken will be irreversible, choice no longer offering an escape. Because here, vibrating with fear beside her, is her dear father who, if she does not do her part in this moment, will become a helpless participant in the rape and pillage of vineyards into which he has poured his life.

"Mom?" he cries again. *Yiayiá* is lying motionless on the floor. Alex pushes his mother's chair out of the way. Pulling off his sweater, he makes a pillow for her head.

Get Up Dion! Now! If she does not, neither *Yiayiá* nor she herself will ever forgive her.

"Mom?" her father says again. Then to Dion: "She needs to go to the hospital."

"First let me get her some air," Dion springs to her feet. "And get the sun out of her eyes."

How many times have she and *Yiayiá* practised Dion's wedging her foot under her grandmother's bag, pretending to stumble in her haste to get to the window while lifting it just enough to kick it six feet across the floor to the base of Henri IV's plinth? The camera behind the bar will not be able to see the floor this close to the bar and hopefully the table and chairs will block the view of the one beyond St. John the Theologian, in the far corner. Both will record her rush past the plinth to the study's casement window, her opening it, then pulling down the blackout blind, reducing this end of the room to deep shadow. These floor tiles are more textured than the ones in the winery's kitchen though, less worn. *Yiayiá's* bag does not slide as Dion stumbles forward. She has to repeat tripping accidentally, and how many seconds have passed since Salin left the room? How long before he comes back? The alarm bell's shrill feels like it's coming from inside her bloodstream.

'Improvise,' orders *Yiayiá's* voice inside her head, 'NOW!'

She's still in a crouch, as if regaining her balance, her back towards the St. John camera. Sliding her hand into the bag, she feels for Theo's replica Henri IV bottle. Tucks it under her hoody, holding it there with one arm while she darts past the plinth to lower the window blind with her free hand and pulls up her hood. All this happens on automatic, her brain schooled by practice. Her lunge back towards the plinth, through shadows it will take the cameras a few moments to adjust to, stops time the way trusting your body to a man-made hang-glider wing does. The way a leaping ballet dancer, front leg flexed, back leg long, does. The way a breath, exhaled, pauses in that no-time space where every possibility exists except the reversal of time.

Her back to the bar, the plinth between her and St. John, she brings fake Henri IV out from under her hoody. Raising it with both hands between her body and the plinth, she slides it onto the plinth behind the original Henri IV. Realizes she has not breathed in. 'You must keep your breathing even, slow.' How many times has *Yiayiá* told her that? She takes a breath but can't help holding it, has to trust that if an alarm she doesn't know about will be triggered by her touching real Henri IV, it will sound the same as the one still ringing. Which will be switched off any second now.

No sound announces her lifting real seventeen-pound Henri IV past Theo's bottle then lowering it between the plinth and her body until she can cover it with her hoody. Cradling it there with one hand, her other one moves Theo's replica into its place in the centre of the plinth. Hopefully, in the chaos about to unfold, no one will notice it. Later, when Salin reviews the St. John camera footage from the far corner of the study, she can only hope low light and her hood will blur its focus enough to make it impossible for police to identify her conclusively. Doubled over to manage the bottle's weight, she tries to look as if she's in a hurry to get back down to the floor, to her ailing grandma.

"Is she breathing, Dad?" Alex is stroking *Yiayiá's* forehead in the semi-darkness.

"I think so, she has a pulse—"

The alarm stops ringing. The air goes on vibrating. Or is it Dion's breath expelling great jags of fear as she extracts Henri IV from under her hoody and slides the two-million dollar gold and platinum coated, diamond-studded bottle into *Yiayiá's* bag. Then pushes her hood back. Glances at her father, who appears to have noticed nothing. Voices explode somewhere down the hallway outside the study.

"Look I'm sorry," Theo! "I was supposed to drive but got back late from Chania, so thought I'd wait in your back garden. Didn't realize that's a crime, that you have the place wired like a prison camp—"

Relief crowds every other feeling out of Dion.

Two voices, Salin and his man, speak Russian. Then, further away, on the staircase probably, a third one joins them.

"Theo!" It's Amina. "What are you doing here?"

"We need to get your grandmother out of this madhouse," Alex tells Dion.

Marched into the room by Salin's man, Theo sees *Yiayiá* on the floor.

"*Yiayiá*!" He struggles against his captor. "What happened? Let go! Can't you see—?"

Gratitude wells up inside Dion.

Salin turns on the ceiling light and suddenly the room is too bright. All he has to do is look towards the plinth.

"Salin, for Christ sake," cries Theo, "can you tell your thug to lay off me? I was only strolling around—"

Thank you thank you thank you Theo because, ignoring him, Salin is crossing the room towards them, leaning down beside Alex to put two fingers on *Yiayiá's* neck.

"Could we borrow a blanket?" Dion asks him. Please may she have concealed Henri IV well enough. *Yiayiá's* bag is less than a foot from his shoes. Amina comes into the room.

"What's going on?"

Right on cue a sour smell (produced by certain vegetables eaten for breakfast) rises from her grandmother. A puddle of pee leaks out from under her onto the tiles. The Russian steps back. Alex gets up.

"Theo, help me get her into the car. We need to take her to the hospital. Now."

"Wait Dad, let me change her first."

Here comes the tricky part: how to keep Salin's gaze, averted now, from wandering to the plinth or too close to *Yiayiá* and her bag. Dion looks up at the Russian. "Could I also trouble you for a warm cloth and a towel?" Salin speaks to his man. "And could you also turn off the overhead light please, to get it out of her eyes?" And render cut glass shards less distinguishable from diamonds in shadow, hopefully.

But now a worried Amina is squatting beside her.

"What can I do?"

Amina, who has helped naked *Yiayiá* bathe, has seen her most intimate self, must be removed. Now. For Christ's sake Theo, Dion's anger chases her gratitude, if you're going to bloody show up out of the blue at the last minute, do something!

He is shaking out arms still smarting from being gripped, knows what has to come next.

"You need to move back, Amina." He reaches down to draw her away. "If *Yiayiá* wakes up and sees you here it might disorient her."

Salin's man hands Dion wet and dry towels. She reaches past Amina to pull *Yiayiá's* bag closer and looks up at the men.

"And can we have a moment of privacy please?" She leans close to her grandmother. "*Yiayiá?* I'm just going to change you, okay?"

Her grandmother does not respond. She did pee at just the right moment though, which must mean she's fine. Now neither Salin, who is standing a couple of meters away with her father, nor Amina nor the cameras must pick up Dion's hand bringing her grandmother's bag still closer so she can rummage inside it for her old lady diaper and wrap it around Henri IV, so many different dangers ticking through every second. Amina is still kneeling too close. Because she loves *Yiayiá*. Dion hears her friend's freewheeling laughter in the winery's kitchen, sees her tenderness in doing *Yiayiá's* nails, her generosity in giving Dad all her money. Not a threat.

Salin is watching them surreptitiously, Dion can feel it, which at least means he is not paying any attention to his Henri IV's plinth. Amina must not be involved. But her body, beside Theo's is helping to block the camera at the St. John's end of the room. Dion angles herself in front of the bar end one, reaches into her grandmother's bag for a small bottle of smelling salts and, unscrewing the lid, risks glancing up. Salin's eyes are shifting from her father to Theo to Amina.

Now is the weakest moment in Operation Henri IV. There is no way around it. No time to worry about what Salin might be thinking. Dion uses one hand to hold *Yiayiá's* skirt up like a tent, as if for modesty, unfastens her old lady diaper with the other. Wipes the area with the warm cloth. Takes out a bottle of talcum powder, splashes it on her grandmother's nether regions. Lifts the bottle filled diaper out of the bag. Hopes no one registers the thump as its weight meets the skirt covered floor, and slides it up between her grandmother's legs. Pretends to fasten it, lowers the skirt. Braces herself for Salin's interruption.

It does not happen.

"There, not perfect but it'll do for now." She looks up at her father and the Russian. "Can you help roll the blanket under her, so we can wrap it around her to carry her to the car?" Salin instructs his man who, two minutes later, over her father's objections, scoops up a wrapped, Henri IV-carrying *Yiayiá* as easily as if she were a child, and follows his boss, Theo and Dad out to the car. Please may he not twig to the extra seventeen pounds squeezed between the old lady's thighs.

Salin's man deposits her grandmother in the Fiat's back seat, and here now is inspiration. Dion takes off her knapsack, which the cameras will show she has not opened since *Yiayiá* fell ill, and holds it and her grandmother's bag out to Salin who is standing close to the car watching.

"Could you take these for just a minute while I settle her?" So he can feel their lightness while Dion tucks the blanket around her grandmother, gets in beside her, then takes the bags from him.

"Call us as soon as you have news," says Amina, her hand on Salin's arm, her face drawn with worry that would be hard to fake. Good. The Russian's features reveal nothing.

Theo drives down Salin's road, turns onto the tarmac, keeps glancing into the rearview mirror. Dion keeps shaking her head. They reach the highway to Rethymnon and still *Yiayiá* does not open her eyes. Alex keeps twisting around from the front seat to check on her.

"She's okay Dad," says Dion. Theo hears a slight shake in her voice but the old lady looks peaceful and inside the blanket her chest is lifting and falling.

When Alex finally settles into his seat Dion reaches up under *Yiayiá's* dress inside the blanket to dislodge the diaper-wrapped bottle.

At the hospital Theo wheels a gurney out to the car, helps load *Yiayiá* onto it, then stays in the driver's seat while Alex and Dion take her in. Henri IV is now in Dion's knapsack, on the backseat.

He could drive away right now, Dion thinks, assuming a tracker hasn't already been put on the Fiat. Leave them a second time. Take the bottle anywhere. Bury it in a cave. Set himself up for life.

He wouldn't do that, somehow she knows it.

Has Salin discovered the theft yet, she wonders as they wait in the dingy green hospital hallway? Theo's replica is pretty primitive, Salin would have to be blind as a Russian bat not to have noticed it by now. Is his man on his way to the hospital?

"Assume you are being followed, watched, even if you see no one and think the job is done. It can make the final difference, believe me," *Yiayiá* has told them.

They are installed in an examining room, waiting for a doctor, when her grandmother's eyes open.

"You're okay, Mom," Alex tells her, smiling his relief. "We're at the hospital."

"No," *Yiayiá* tries to sit up. "I don't need to be here, I fainted, that's all." Her face looks grey under the corridor's florescent lighting. "Please Alex, if you don't want me to die right here, get me out of this hospital."

Back at the winery Theo and her father help *Yiayiá* into the kitchen. Dion follows with the bag and knapsack. Not until the door is closed and bath water is running does the old lady give her granddaughter a questioning look. Dion shows her a thumbs up.

Her grandmother and Alex are already packed to leave tomorrow for Elafonisi, for a break *Yiayiá* has requested, ostensibly to take the sting out of their contract signing. Leaving her to rest now, Dion saunters out onto the patio with her knapsack, then disappears into the vineyard as if on her way to Theo's shed. Veering into the vines, she finds a hole she dug for it this morning.

Leaving right away would look like an admission of guilt and Salin would find a way to follow. Even so, for sure he is onto them by now. Returning to his study after they left, to put away the contracts, maybe have a drink, he can't have failed to notice Theo's crude mock-up of his prized, two million-dollar bottle of Henri IV Dudognon cognac. Maybe his man didn't come after them to Rethymnon because he came here instead, to search the winery and instal surveillance devices Theo says will be too sophisticated for them to find.

Nine-tenths of creating anything flawless is good follow-up preparation. Theo kept trying to talk them into selling Henri IV on the Dark Web, for Bitcoin, a cryptocurrency that can not be marked or traced. Thieves and gangsters use it all the time, he said, trying unsuccessfully to explain how it works, how once they receive the untraceable Bitcoins online, they can convert them into currency through a bank. But *Yiayiá* insisted on having nothing to do with Bitcoin and banks.

"They exists only in computers that can crash and die and only God knows what else. And how am I supposed to buy flour, fava beans with these Bitcoins? We will pay Leonid Salin in cash and receive a receipt that cancels our obligation to him. That's what money is for: To settle financial debts."

"Yes but it's so much safer in a bank," Dion argued, "and transfers are so easy."

"My point exactly. So easy, by computers which Leonid Salin can access anytime. Also people who work in banks, who have loved ones, can be bought. We will deal in cash."

"But how do we explain cash, right after he's been robbed?"

"Explain to whom?" said *Yiayiá* in the old, caustic voice Dion used to fear. "Does someone ask Leo Salin where he gets his dollars? We have money, we repay what we owe with a lawyer present. That's all. Where we got the money is our business."

After she has rested *Yiayiá* moves into the sitting room to watch television.

"Mind if I turn this off?" Dion hears Theo's voice from the kitchen, then her grandmother's clipped responses.

Next he visits her father, who has closeted himself in his lab. Alex will be telling Theo that only he himself can decide who and what matters to him, and that he is welcome to stay in his shed/studio as long as it's all right with the rest of the family.

Dion turns up the Bee Gees' "Staying' Alive," playing through the patio speakers, hopefully to muffle anyone's unforeseen comments.

Theo and she have exchanged no words. Anger at his arrogance in turning up unannounced wants to take her over but she is too grateful to let it, feels like a rattle being shaken. And Operation Henri IV is a long way from over.

Yiayiá eats very little supper. Dion helps her get ready for bed. Not into bed though. She'd like to have a little chat with Gio first.

"Don't worry," she squeezes Dion's hand, "we will be very quiet."

Theo is working his way through a pile of tomato-stained spaghetti dishes at the kitchen sink, his back towards her. Covered now in jeans, a sweater, wool socks against November's damp cold, he radiates nothing of the man under whose touch she lay naked. Sunshine, sea and sex do not appear to live in the same world as crime.

She needs to take her father out onto the patio, to tell him what really happened today, because if the police show up he will likely be charged as an accomplice and nobody is more morally correct than Alexander The Grape. Kokanakis Wines is his work of art, his marriage of love with nature's power. Its survival has to be on his terms. Confiding in him will give him the right to rule against the next step, to demand that they return Henri IV. If he does, they'll have to obey. Her job now is to get him to think through who he's dealing with instead of instinctively taking shelter inside a brittle set of old beliefs that no longer apply.

Let him get a good night's sleep before you dump this on him, caution urges.

No. Timing is as crucial now as it is to paper morphing into a textured canvas or grape juice fermenting into wine or sex taking a body out of its habit-imprisoned mind, and Dion finds that she knows as surely as a plant knows to push up through the cold spring ground, as the sea tide knows to rise, that she must talk to her father immediately.

Theo must have read her thought, she can see that in the way he turns from the sink as Alex walks into the kitchen wearing an ancient leftover-from-Canada bathrobe over his pajamas, towelling his head of thick grey hair.

"Can you come outside, Dad?"

Theo hands him his barnyard coat, he and Dion pull on jackets hanging on pegs by the back door as, looking tired and befuddled, Alex lets them usher him out into the night. The light outside the door shows them dead-brown leaves still clinging to one of the plane tree's low branches.

Standing just beyond it at the far edge of the patio, whispering, Dion takes her father through her removal of Henri IV from Salin's villa. Shovelling words into his fatigue, watching his wild eyebrows furrow as he listens.

"We were going to sell the bottle on the Dark Net but *Yiayiá* doesn't want us to use any kind of computer technology—"

"What," Dad's eyebrows shoot up. "Your *Yiayiá's* in on all this?"

Dion nods, telling him that the sale of Henri IV's diamonds will repay Kokanakis Wines' loan to Leonid Salin with interest before the contract deadline and fund at least one year's production and living expenses. The rest will go to the winery's neighbours here in the valley. People like Irina's granddaughter, who is trying to raise a baby alone with no job and barely enough to eat, will receive a thousand euros in an anonymous envelope. Dion will store the bottle's gold and platinum covering for sale later.

It's dark outside and cold, and both Dion and Theo are so intent on bringing Alex on side that their brains do not respond to the sound of a car door or the ticking of boots on the driveway beyond the fermentation room.

"Hello?" Amina's slightly husky, musical voice sounds out of the darkness just before her body activates outdoor lights above the fermentation room and drive shed doors. Wearing a soft green wool poncho, she looks like a model. Behind her Salin is carrying a bouquet of freshly cut blue and white flowers that must have come from his greenhouse. "We rang the showroom bell, but... What are you all doing out here?" She crosses the patio towards them. "We came to see how the patient is doing. I can't bear the thought of *Yiayiá* suffering, and Leo's worried about her too."

A tsunami of anger shakes Dion. A hand, Theo's, closes around hers. She hangs onto it, breathes, tries to search their faces. The lights are behind them though, all she has is their silhouettes. The Russian has the advantage and she can feel his eyes slicing into her psyche and how long until her father's hair, sticking up in spikes, and his bathrobe and bare legs set off a cascade of questions? Anger, such a poor mask for fear. But no police appear behind them. No other reason can explain this intrusion. She lets go of Theo and steps towards Amina, towards the light, where Salin can see her clearly. Away from her father.

"*Yiayiá's* going to be fine," she says, "thank you for asking."

"It was another panic attack then, like before?" Amina asks.

"That's right, that's all it was, thank God," Dion replies, "from the stress." And is it night that's deepening creases at the outer edges of her friend's eyes and at the corners of her mouth? "I just put her to bed. She needs sleep, and so does my father." And please Alex, don't accidentally blurt anything. She looks at Salin. "My grandmother won't be up to signing anything for awhile but there's still time."

Salin hands her the flowers and, thanking him, she tries to sound as if this were not the most dangerous night of her life.

"I'm sorry but I'll have to say goodnight," says Theo. "Alex was on his way to put the chickens to bed but," he puts a hand on her father's arm. "I'll do it."

"What a crazy day," says Amina, watching Theo move away into darkness, pitching her voice to reach him. "You'll never guess what else happened. Remember that diamond-studded bottle of cognac Leo had on a pedestal in his study? Someone stole it today!"

Is she playacting on Salin's instructions so he can gauge their responses? Dion tries to dissect the lightness in her voice. If she is, thank goodness they're out here, unreadable in the dark. Or, married for twenty years to enormous wealth, does Amina really think the heist is a lark? Dion watches her profile swivel towards the barn. "Leo thinks you made the replica bottle, Theo."

He's no more than a moving shadow now, which stops, his face visible but unreadable as he turns back to them.

"I'm an artist Salin, if I'd made a replica of something you wouldn't see the difference. Anyway I haven't been around here in weeks, not since the harvest." He turns away, his voice receding as he rounds the corner. "I would have thought a man who does what you do would know that."

Her father coughs. Dion takes his arm.

"Come on Dad, you must be dead on your feet, and the last thing you need right now is to listen to this crap."

"Cameras don't lie, Dion." Salin's voice, soft in the darkness, points to Operation Henri IV's second unavoidable, irremediable weakness, about which there is nothing she can do, except hope he is bluffing about the level of her visibility on camera. "No court will dispute my video of you taking the bottle and putting it in your bag."

Planning can't cover every eventuality, *Yiayiá* has told her. Something always comes up and when it does your best move is to go with it the way a martial arts expert accepts a thrust, turning its energy back on the attacker.

"What?" she says, as if confused. "Are you suggesting that while my poor grandmother was lying comatose on your floor I stole a bottle of your brandy? How can you think that way?" Telltale heat is flushing into her cheeks but he can't pick that up, and hearing her voice, Dion can not believe how naturally adept she is at this. "You were right there and—" as if she had just thought of it – "didn't you even hold my knapsack and *Yiayiá's* bag?"

Alex's bushy eyebrows are still knitting themselves together. Now, standing there in his bathrobe and coat and wet hair, his head begins to shake.

"If you came here to accuse my daughter of stealing, Leo, you should leave right now. Our home doesn't belong to you yet. But if that is not so, if you really did come out of concern for my mother, then come on inside, have a glass of *raki* and toast my ninety-four year old mother's resilience." Giving the bastard the chance to choose the path of sincerity. Dear inimitable, unpredictably wily Dad. Yes, coming inside would allow Salin to question and examine them, but what thief of a two million-dollar bottle sits down to drink with his victim?

Amina takes the Russian's arm and holds it close against her breast. She will stay or go, whatever he wants.

"I think we will not disturb the Kokanakises further tonight, my dear," he says. "Perhaps we may visit tomorrow."

To put a pen into *Yiayiá's* hand and convince her to sign his contract before Dion can claim that her capacities are too diminished. To stop her and Theo from taking Henri IV anywhere. To spread lethal poison on the doorknobs of their home?

"We'll call first," Amina tells her.

Dion's body feels like a choppy sea, her thinking splashing, in danger of tipping. As soon as Salin's headlights recede down the road, she pitches his flowers and any tiny unfindable microphone they might contain into the bushes behind the plane tree. A roosting bird flaps up into the darkness. A rumbling starts inside her Dad. Dion goes to him.

"Oh dear." Alex uses his fingers to wipe away tears. Dion tries to see his face.

He's laughing!

"I was afraid you'd make me give the bottle back!" she hisses.

"Pfff," he says, sounding like his mother, "does a bee give its nectar back to the flower? Does an ant return our crumbs? No chicken." Something new in his voice comes to her through the darkness. "Nature's patterns repeat and repeat, and I've told you before that some of those patterns are powerfully destructive. You see it in ivy, underground in fungi, in dandelions cracking pavement if they have to. In people for whom enough is never enough. But invasive greed forces other plants to find new, better, stronger patterns in order not to be choked out. When a rabbit population overruns its habitat the weed it likes best turns toxic, did you know that? We will not return Henri IV to Leo. Neither will we sell the bottle to some collector on the Dark Net though, because your grandmother is right about that." He looks from Dion to Theo, who has just re-emerged from the darkness. "What worries me is you two. This problem belongs to my mother and me. You both have lives, futures that must not be tainted—"

"No Dad—!"

"Alex," Theo steps forward, "you know that once Dion and *Yiayiá* have a plan it's no use arguing, right? And I'll be with Dion every step of the way from here, that's a promise."

The vines' wide leaves, no longer turning sunshine into food for grapes, are becoming yellow and brown, beginning to shrivel and fall. Still, enough of them are left to shield *Yiayiá*, Dion, Alex and Theo and the wrought iron patio table they have carried out into the middle of the vineyard from unwanted visitors, cameras and listening devices. A Haydn violin concerto playing through the patio speakers will further obliterate their voices and is fitting accompaniment, says Alexander the Grape, for the imperial European beauty sitting on the table between them. Its six thousand five hundred diamonds glitter even in November's weak mid-morning light.

Who says cognac cannot be enjoyed at any time of the day, he says?

Dion has called Amina, told her *Yiayiá* is still too weak to receive visitors – only a partial lie. Sitting beside Dion now, wrapped against the cold in a patterned green and beige wool shawl, *Yiayiá's* shoulders have a new droop. Her mind is clear though, and stubborn. Henri IV Dudognon's makers did not select premium grapes to make cognac using a three-hundred-year old family recipe only to have it locked away, she declared this morning. Alex agreed.

"Ready?" He scans his yellowing vineyard, the olive and oak trees beyond it, then the barnyard, patio, driveway before taking out his pocket knife.

No! Dion wants to stop his knife's blade from breaking the seal between Henri IV's diamond-studded stopper and the bottle's gold and platinum coated body, from demolishing the bottle's value as a cognac connoisseur's collectible. But they've been over this: "Value, what is that? Who determines it?" *Yiayiá* said. "Real value is only what a person pays for something. And even then, transfer euros from this bank account to that bank account and what have you got? Numbers, digital castles that can be built and then demolished like that." She snapped her fingers. "Value is only realized when you're holding money in your hand. So we empty the bottle, extract the diamonds, gold, platinum and sell them for cash. That's what this bottle is worth to us."

Now nobody breathes. Alex looks down at the squat, knobby two million-dollar bottle. *Yiayiá's* hand crosses the table to cover the one with which he is holding the bottle. Dion has never seen that before.

"Okay," he clears his throat, presses his blade into the bottle's neck. Henri's seal cracks. Bottle in one hand now, its stopper in the other, Alex pulls, grunting, pulls again. Finally pops open the vacuum that has protected Henri IV's contents for one hundred years. Raising the bottleneck to his nose, he breathes in, then runs his fingers down the bottle's diamond-studded, gold and platinum sides and looks at his daughter.

"Life distilled, into diamonds we can touch, brandy we can drink, that's richness, Dionysia."

A square-based crystal decanter he bought with his *Prix D'Or* winnings usually sits on a plinth in the showroom, where light will pick up the hues of whatever wines Alexander the Grape wants to display. Henri IV Dudognon's cognac has an amber glow as Alex decants it.

"Hmm," her father holds the filled decanter up towards the lackadaisical sun then sniffs the cognac again. "It needs to rest now." Leaning down, he parks the decanter against the trunk of the closest vine, out of sight of the house. Dion will guard it while wrapping Henri's bottle in a tea towel and returning it to her knapsack. *Yiayiá* will nap and Alex will put their suitcases in the Fiat while Theo uses a scanner his Boston friends advised him to buy in Iraklio to check the Fiat and his motorcycle for tracking devices. The barnyard crew have already been looked after this morning and Georgina will come up once a day to feed and water them.

An hour later the mood almost feels holy as they resume their seats around the table in the middle of the vineyard. Alex pours Henri IV into four snifters. They raise them.

"*Yamas*." Appreciating the history that has produced this treasure.

"*Yamas*." Celebrating a theft perfectly executed. So far.

"*Yamas.*" Praying their next moves against a Russian hacker who has access to every computer network on the planet, every ferry manifest, surveillance camera, every source of dollars, will be successful.

Yiayiá, Dion and Theo watch Alexander the Grape's reverence as he swirls the cognac in his snifter, takes in its bouquet once more, then tips it into his mouth.

iii.

Theo's scanner has found tracking devices on the Fiat and on his motorcycle, probably planted by Salin's man last night. He parks the little round disks side by side in the driveway. It won't buy them much time. Salin will come to the winery today sometime, but at least he won't know where they've gone. Alex leaves his phone in the house, has a disposable one Dion can call. Watching him drive off with *Yiayiá* for a week at Elafonisi, Dion waves as if this were a holiday, relief that they will both be safe now making her almost giddy.

Theo's motorcycle takes them up the road to Rethymnon. His back feels familiar but also distant, fleece and his leather jacket insulating him from her. They have not discussed his having left her without even saying goodbye. There has been no time, also no need. The fact of it is statement enough: When this job is done he will leave again, this time for good. To paint his painting – if he hasn't abandoned it – somewhere else. Their summer, her posing, his sketching, their trips and swims, picnics and discussions, are all over.

As Theo leaves the highway, following the road down into Rethymnon, empty Henri IV, hidden under food, underwear and an extra sweater in her knapsack feels like a bomb on her back. At any moment, should someone stop them, it could blow up her life.

He parks down by the harbour. They walk up into the shopping district through old town streets that are nearly empty. She tries not to show that she is checking behind her, ahead, around corners, until they reach her favourite cafe. Still open, its patio overlooks every entryway to the square. They can splurge safely on souvlaki and beer until dusk makes it difficult for anyone to follow them down to the back of Rethymnon's harbour, where Kiri's father, a fishermen, will dock his boat before a night of fishing. Still they are both on edge, Theo getting up every few minutes to check the street.

The night sea is black, unusually calm. Fish are caught, several of them grilled on a portable deck stove and eaten with wine Dion has brought. Kiri's Dad produces a bottle of *raki* and even inside her shivering fear, as the boat's gentle rocking, its engine's drone and the fishermen's banter puts her to sleep, Dion knows that this night, these tough, kind men and the smells of sea and fresh fish will light her memory for the rest of her life.

When Theo shakes her a bright half moon is guiding them towards the lights on Iraklio's fish wharf.

A mangy dog follows them into the city's pre-dawn streets. Theo shoos it away but it stays with them, just out of reach, smelling their fish dinner probably and the provisions in Dion's knapsack. A second dog joins it, then a third, all of them lean, strong, used to cadging scraps, a walking billboard announcing their presence if Salin has found out where his mother lives. Because although Theo and Dion too have left their phones at the winery, he will know by now that they are not there. And defeat is not in the Russian's playbook.

Dodging between shadowed store and apartment entryways, running through alleys, they cover the few blocks between the harbour and a tiny turn-of-the-last-century foyer in Theo's mother's apartment building.

"Wait here," Theo whispers, "while I get the key to her workshop."

"What if she wakes up?" A geyser of anxiety brings bile into her throat.

"She won't. I've been sneaking home in the dead of night since I was twelve." He bounds soundlessly up the stairs.

His mother's workshop, upstairs in a nondescript industrial building, consists of one room. Smelling its potpourri of metals, dust, cooked food and his mother's cologne yanks Theo back to his childhood, before Boston, when he would nap on the couch or play video games while at the counter at the other end of the room his leather-aproned mother worked with pencils, pliers, torches, tools kept in a wall cabinet behind her. Tanks, an oven, a shelf full of design books, a safe full of gems, precious metals are packed into every other square centimetre. At the door end of the room an old couch and coffee table share space with a small bar fridge, a hot plate and a sink. Pillows and a blanket are still piled on the couch. Sometimes in the days of large orders his mother would bring dinner for them and work through the night. Now all of the workshop's smells are old, stale.

Some gem suppliers don't question the provenance of brilliant-cut diamonds if the price is right. You learn these things by hanging out, listening, watching, and as soon as he reached his teens, before he left for Boston, Theo was already badgering his mother into showing him how to use an oxi-acetylene torch. Now, wearing his mother's apron, face shield and thick gloves, he secures Henri IV in a vice above a heavy ceramic crucible.

"The torch will melt the metal enough for me to pick out the diamonds," he tells Dion.

When they're cool enough they'll pack them into sacks she has sewn then clipped onto the bottom of her brassiere, two in front, two under her arms, and into the waistband of her jeans. Six thousand five hundred small and unremarkable diamonds.

As Theo's flame heats the workshop and sparks fly up around his visored head in the dark and diamonds clink into the bowl and Dion makes coffee, new slimy-horrific questions slither into her mind:

What does she really know about this man/boy? Modelling, swimming, fucking, that's all. And where's he been all these weeks? Has he returned to bilk a ninety-four year old woman, her hapless son and lonely middle-aged granddaughter out of diamonds, gold, platinum? Is she about to become his mule?

Trust no one, said *Yiayiá*. Who also sat with Theo at the table in the vineyard, drinking Henri IV's cognac.

Theo works with his flame. Sitting on the couch, Dion watches him pause to sip his coffee. She is no longer his model or his playmate. So what other reason could he have for doing this?

Friendship. She feels its warmth. Or is this too a needy illusion?

Faith is a delicate thread, easily snapped, but it's all she has to hang onto. And she is so tired.

When Theo wakes her, just after dawn, Henri IV has been denuded. Four bowls of diamonds sparkle under the counter's work light.

Dion turns away from him to take off her sweater, t-shirt and brassiere under the workshop's bright light. He would like to say something, she can feel it, but what? Anyway there's no time. He starts loading diamonds into the little sacks so she can clip them into place.

"They're going to be heavy."

Full, the diamond pouches tug down on her bra straps.

"You're going to have to do me up," she says. Her back feels warm under his fingers as he pulls her load into position then fastens her brassiere's clasps. She unzips her jeans. "Can you smooth these full pouches while I'm wearing them?" He reaches down inside her jeans. The back of his hand grazes her groin, her thighs, her bum. Questioning?

She lifts his hand, puts it away from her.

He glances around the workshop, making sure there is no trace of their having been here. Looks exhauasted.

Dressed now in her coat, her knapsack on her back, Dion looks as normal as she did coming into the workshop but, loaded with diamonds, her body feels too cumbersome almost to walk. And for sure the Russian has deduced by now that they've gone to Chania or Iraklio to catch a ferry to Athens, to convert Henri IV into the euros they need. Thank God he won't be able to pry any information on their whereabouts out of her father and *Yiayiá* – neither he nor Amina knows about the Elafonisi guest house and her Dad will use only cash for gas. Salin will have somebody watching the ferries but may not have guessed that they have taken the bottle apart, given how much more it's worth intact, so if they hurry, he might miss them before they meet the Athens diamond dealer Theo has found.

She wishes she could wrap a single diamond with a note for Theo's mother: '*Efkaristo*' (thank you.)

Theo takes her to a thin strip of sand nobody climbs down to on the far side of the harbour's ancient stone seawall. Digging down at the base of the wall as a boy, he had found a loose stone which, pulled out, created a cache he often used to store his sketching money so no one could mug him for it. If the stone is still be there, Henri IV's gold and platinum body, hidden in a plastic bag, will be safe in the hole behind it until they return from Athens. She keeps watch while Theo digs. No one is anywhere near here this early on a weekday morning in November. Sauntering away from the spot, Dion gulps in the cold sea air, trying to add sangfroid to a toolbox she's going to need now.

Passengers at the ferry terminal are bundled into coats and scarves against what might soon become rain. They stay within sight of the mainstream, sit over coffees and breakfast pastries in the lounge, her knapsack snugged into her lap as if there is something of value in it. Just in case. Theo sits close beside her.

No one bothers them. Of course they don't. Waiting until they reach the city, following them to their dealer would be the most efficient play.

Dusk is leaching what little light is left out of an overcast sky when they dock at Piraeus, cross the port's tarmac with a stream of passengers going down into the Metro station, and board a subway that will deliver them into Athens' city centre. It is not crowded. Theo shows her their stop on a map in their car but Dion suddenly channels Teddy's Perfect Robbery and jumps up to get off one station earlier. Theo follows, surprised, as she heaves her diamond-laden body up the stairs, finds a women's washroom, makes sure it's empty then hauls Theo in after her, into a cubicle, where she climbs up onto the toilet seat.

"You too."

They are standing body to body when the washroom door opens. Someone comes in, tinkles, flushes, runs a tap, leaves. They jump down, giggling, then wait until a train pulls in before dashing across the platform to get on. No one appears to have followed them.

It works, Teddy! When finally they come up out of the Metro recent rain has left a metallic smell in the salty air of a cracked-pavement neighbourhood.

The diamond dealer's office is on the second floor of a walk-up building sandwiched between a grocery store and some other business, both closed now. Its grimy window overlooks the empty street below. Puddles glisten between cars lining both curbs. The man behind the desk is wearing yesterday's shirt under a suit that saw better days a long time ago. Files, papers, what must be reference books, yesterdays newspaper, a mug of half drunk coffee, a small sports trophy are a jumble on shelves behind him. A beat-up safe sitting in the corner and framed photographs showing him shaking hands with what must be local dignitaries are the only indications that this is a supplier about to buy thousands of euros worth of diamonds. Theo introduces them, then gunfire Greek erupts between the two men.

"No no no," Dion raises her voice, puts up a hand. "In English, please." A diamond supplier must have a grasp of the international language of business.

"*Parakalo*," He effects an apologetic smile. "Please, sit." Two wooden chairs have been drawn up to the desk. Theo takes a small cloth pouch out of his pocket, tips a handful of sample diamonds onto a cloth the dealer lays out and, putting on a pair of jeweller's magnifying glasses, snapping on a desk light, the man finally looks as if he knows his trade. "How many?" he asks after awhile.

"Five thousand," says Theo. "For now." The dealer looks up at him. Says nothing for a long moment. Dion's heart sounds like a tambourine.

The dealer offers a price in Greek. Theo throws up his hands, delivers a diatribe Dion does not need the language to understand. The dealer smiles slightly, a cat playing with a mouse whom he suspects is trapped by circumstances. And all at once Dion has had enough of this, and of being scared, and of men who want to take take take.

"Look," she tells Theo, "thanks a lot for setting this up, but maybe I'd be better off taking the diamonds to London, where I'll have no difficulty getting a decent price." Which might possibly be true if she had any clue about where to go, how to do that, and how to wire the money to Crete in time. "Or," she looks at the dealer, "you can have all five thousand of them right now, in return for four hundred thousand euros in cash. No duties, taxes, no records. She nods at the pile of diamonds he has been examining. "Their value speaks for itself." It must do, given Henri IV's valuation.

"Four hundred thousand in cash? Impossible, lady."

"Okay." Dion gets up, addresses Theo. "Not sure why we bothered coming all this way." Is amazed at the brusqueness of her voice, its subtle ferociousness. So is Theo, standing now, goring the dealer with a glare.

"You think you're the only jewelry supplier I know in Athens?" he says. "We came to you first because of your reputation but," he turns to the door. The dealer sighs theatrically.

"I might be able to find you one hundred and fifty thousand euros at such short notice." Her head and Theo's shake simultaneously.

"Three hundred thousand or we leave right now," Dion tells him. It's way too little, a bargain for him, a sign of her desperation. But. "No bargaining."

The dealer unleashes a long string of what sounds like Greek hopelessness, recrimination, resignation. Theo does not reply. Dion looks at the man, unmoved.

"I need a day," he says at last, in English.

"And we need assurance," Theo nods at the safe. "We'll leave you these samples, you give us ten percent now."

"Five. It's all I have here."

Accepting feels like defeat but inside Dion's clothes the diamonds are dragging at her brassiere cups now, a weight belt bloating the waist of her jeans. Lumbering back down the dingy stairs, she feels every one of her forty years.

No one is lurking in the street but that means nothing. Who knows who bankrolls this dealer, who will follow her and Theo to take the diamonds? Theo ducks into an alley to consult a burner phone he bought in Piraeus. A five-star boutique hotel just below the Acropolis, the kind of place tourists or lovers or business people on expense accounts frequent, has a room. They zigzag through alleys, do another Teddy in the subway. Pay for their hotel room with cash.

As soon as the door closes she heads to the bathroom, takes off her clothes, soothes welts left by the diamond bags on her chest, back, belly in the shower, then swaddles herself in a soft terry towel robe. Outside their bedroom window lights in the Acropolis, birthplace of democracy and economy and psychology and so many other Greek-named ideals and institutions, bathe its three-thousand year old Parthenon. This room is a safe niche, a respite before the dangers facing them tomorrow morning. Because now that the diamond buyer knows they are carrying diamonds, who else does?

The bed is fresh-white, full of pillows. Theo has gone out for *gyros* and beer from a take-out place down the street.

He'll come back alone, for sure he will. She sees him with her family, with the blow torch, with the dealer, with her here. He will come back.

After dinner he piles her loaded brassiere and jeans into the bed. She snuggles down beside them wearing only her underpants. Theo takes off his shoes, takes a pillow off the bed, looks at the floor.

"No." He had no sleep at all last night. She pats the other side of the bed. "There's room for you here. And I promise not to attack you."

He hears her joke, does not respond. Strips, showers. There's a small bottle of complimentary *raki* on a little side table. He brings it to the bed, sits up against the bed's headboard and she would love nothing more than to bury her terror in his arms. He drinks straight from the little bottle then hands it to her. Smooth, warm as a hug, the *raki* is soon gone. She lies back, pulls the covers up to her chin.

"Please," Theo says, "don't go to sleep yet. I need you to listen."

He tells her about waking in his boyhood bed in Iraklio on her birthday, hearing his mother tiptoe around her kitchen, not to disturb him. She shouldn't have to tiptoe, not for the sake of an unkept, unshaven, probably stinking asshole. Who'd been lying there for weeks, eyes closed, his brain trying to erase Dion, so close in his bed the morning after Kokanakis Wines' harvest feast, her body smelling of smoke and sex and wildflowers, her sleeping breath on his cheek. His head throbbing with hangover, his mouth dry, still he had wanted only to go on filling himself with her. Even though he had told her 'I will never have sex with you.' A lie. Making him a failure. The bold truth of this made clear the other ruinous thing he was doing: Putting his freedom, his future at risk in a crazy scheme with a two desperate women he only met a few months ago.

Leaving the winery that morning, he had no idea where he was headed until his motorcycle took the north shore highway's east ramp, towards Iraklio. Where he found his mother too thin, too proud to tell him she had been ill, had not set foot in her workshop in several weeks. He took his sketchpad into the street, was doing a promotional picture for the fruit and vegetable grocer on the corner when a girl he knew came by. Invited him to a beach party. He took with him a bottle of homemade *raki* the grocer had added to a basket of goods with which he paid for Theo's drawing. Left the party right after it started. Sat on a scrap of beach trying to think about what kind of artist jumps onto the bucking horse of desire he's trying to paint, rides it all fucking night, turns himself into its slave. No answers came so instead of thinking he set out to drown the self he thought he had always been and the self he wanted to be and the self he actually was in *raki*.

Lying beside him now in their Athens hotel bed, Dion finds nothing to say. If they were back at the winery, arguing out on the patio after supper, she'd probably bring up Adam and Eve and their stupid apple story, or Odysseus's trouble with the Syrens. But this is not that conversation, not any conversation, and he has not finished.

When finally he opened his eyes on the morning of her birthday, he knew that people he has come to care about, who really needed the help he had insisted on contributing since day one of Operation Henri IV, would press ahead without him.

"The Dion I know would see no other choice and *Yiayiá* thinks Operation Henri IV is a World War II mission." And he owes her and her family so much, especially after leaving his castle, bringing everything he owned to the new studio Alex has given him at the winery.

Still all this, guilt, remorse, obligation were wrappings only over what had brought him back to the winery.

On harvest night he had intended only to release Dion from a lifetime of frustration, to give her the gift of an orgasm. What his rampant lust did not realize in touching her that night, exploring and kissing a body he thought he knew so well, was that under her skin lay the complexity that had drawn him to her in the first place. Her mixture of colours, luminous one moment then deeply shadowed then light again in some way he could not name, her whites always touched by some other tone, her blacks a little grey or blue or green, never absolute, all of this was beyond his reach unless, coming into her, he could penetrate its very centre. Waking the next morning, he knew something had happened to him.

"Something that scared the bejesus out of me." His hand finds her bare shoulder under the edge of the hotel duvet. "Then, in Iraklio, when the girl I knew invited me to go dancing, drinking and whatever else I wanted at the party on the beach, I found I didn't want to be there. Didn't want anything," his fingers begin to stroke her shoulder. "Except to come back to you."

She looks up at a man she has spent the better part of this year coming to know, who has no side to him, no pretensions. Who's risking everything with her right now. How ludicrous to have doubted him. But fear does that, takes over thought, shapes it into its own image, trusses you up. How foolish of her to have deluded herself into thinking she could ever banish fear. She tugs on Theo's hand. He slides down into the bed beside her, finds her body with his and, after twenty four hours awake, within seconds they are both fast asleep.

Knocking, repetitive, insistent, will not stop. Theo's hand covers her mouth. 2 am says the bedside clock. His breath warms her ear.

"Get dressed." He wedges a chair under the door handle, helps her with the diamond-packed brassiere.

The knocking becomes louder.

She struggles into her jeans. The racket will wake others on this floor. Unless there are no others.

"Open door, please," says a male voice on the other side of it. "I am manager and this is emergency."

Theo shakes his head at her. The bedside telephone rings. Theo shakes his head again.

The phone goes on ringing, the knocking becomes pounding.

Who? Diamond thieves or Salin's men, or both? Dion edges towards the window. They are three floors up. No fire escape.

The knocking stops. So does the phone. Footsteps recede. Foreboding rings through the silence.

"Probably going to get a key." Theo puts a hand on the doorknob, peeks into the hallway. "Quick, now!"

A camera at the other end, by the elevator, will see Theo push open a door to the stairwell. He starts down ahead of her.

"No." Dion points up, Teddy with her again. They'll suspect down so you go up. The hotel has another storey above them and there must be a fire escape somewhere.

It's a fold down one, to guard against thieves, that clatters as it drops them into a stone-lined alley that looks as old as the Acropolis. Freezing dampness penetrates Dion's sweater and anorak as they run into the safety of darkness up here under the Acropolis walls, above lamplit streets patrolled by city police who all have wives or husbands and babies and debts, according to Theo.

"If even one has morals that can be corrupted, we'll be fucked."

Stone arches in an ancient amphitheatre just below the Acropolis gates are in deep shadow. Theo finds a cranny where, sheltering close together, they try to use each other's body heat to ward off hypothermia. Still, by the time the first weak rays of morning light enter the amphitheatre and she gets to her feet, Dion's hip joints are creaking with cold, like one of those Greek drama hags who would have wept and wailed on this stage two thousand years ago.

The only movements on the streets come from cats, dogs, maybe rats. Fresh bread smells lure them lower down the hill to a bakery.

"Sorry, we closed," the baker says in English, eying Dion. Theo launches into a Greek story about robbers, the cold, the fact that they can pay.

"Ah, *ne, ne, ne*." (Yes, yes, yes.) Gesturing them in.

Coffee in a back room, cheese and honey pastries just out of the oven – a favourite Athenian breakfast – returns prickles of feeling to her wooden fingers and toes. She fantasizes about sliding down under the counter, curling up to sleep. But once the bakery opens every minute they're here will endanger their benefactor. Because whoever was responsible for last night's raid on their hotel room will be trying to follow their trail, and will not stop until they have what they want.

Athens' homeless, coming out of wherever they have sheltered for the night, pay no attention to two more unfortunates in their midst. Neither, they have to hope, does anyone else, until the flee market stalls roll up their metal grills. Theo takes her into one, finds her a black skirt and shawl, a cheap, hideous beige and black checked coat, a black purse and a string shopping bag. Putting them on in the store, her own jacket in her knapsack under her coat, she hides her hair inside a kerchief knotted under her chin, trades her red sneakers for cheap second hand shoes. Walking out, her hunchbacked body sags, matching her outer self to her inner hag.

Theo left while she was paying. "Meet me in the street." And there he is, wearing a New York Yankees baseball cap and bomber jacket, new jeans, white sneakers and a brand new backpack. He's also carrying a briefcase: a techie on his way to a meeting.

Splitting up is the safe move. So now, on her own for the first time, loaded with diamonds, armed with nothing more than a burner phone, Dion has to suck up her terror, act like an aging Athenian woman out shopping, and traverse Athens alone. All she can do is keep breathing, be ready to run until finally in an alley ten blocks from the diamond dealer's office, there he is, a baseball-capped beacon in the choppy sea of her fear.

Behind overflowing trash bins reeking of rot they stuff Dion's coat and shawl into her knapsack, put his baseball cap and jacket into his, then unclip the sacks containing five thousand diamonds from her brassiere and jeans, and load them into Theo's briefcase. Disappearing into the Metro, getting on a train going the wrong way, they watch to see who else gets on, then off at the first stop where they do a third Teddy, checking again before boarding the right subway. No one follows and, climbing the stairs to the dealer's office, they try to look as if this were an everyday transaction.

Counting diamonds and money takes all morning. Are the thousand-euro bills marked? The only person who would do that, to link the euros to the diamonds, is Salin and all they can do is hope he has not caught up to them here. The dealer's eyes remind Dion of documentaries she has seen about carnivorous pythons as he watches Theo load thirty banded packs of ten one-thousand euro notes into the briefcase.

"Do you have a washroom I could use?" she asks. Because the dealer will think they are heading from here to a bank. If he or those bankrolling him are the same people who hammered on their door last night, who want both the diamonds and their money, now is when they will make their move.

"*Ne, ne, parakalo.*" The dealer points to a closet down the hall where the toilet has no seat and the sink, stained by a dripping tap, looks as if it hasn't been cleaned in a decade.

"I might as well use it too," Theo tells him. "It's a long ride back to Piraeus." The dealer smiles.

"You will take a little time in Athens first, no?"

"I wish," Theo shrugs, "but computer companies don't leave time for sightseeing."

A camera surveilling the hall will register Theo following Dion into the bathroom but no seeing eye will watch them fill the empty diamond sacks with bill packs and attach them to the band of her brassiere. More bills expand her bum inside her underpants; more money fits beside the fifteen hundred diamonds still attached to her jeans' waistband. The last two packs go into her socks. So that, carrying the empty briefcase, they can walk safely out of the building. No one they can see follows them into the alley they visited after yesterday's meeting.

Emerging from its other end, elderly, hunchbacked Dion does not acknowledge Yankee, briefcase carrying Theo as both make their way to the Metro.

All they have to do now is make it safely through the rest of the day. If the diamond dealer is a crook he will conclude that they made it to a bank by now. Hopefully Salin's people will not catch up to them before they reach Piraeus.

"Stay away from the wharves there, and from me, but not too far from me," says Theo. So she wanders the streets, finds a fruit and vegetable stand, spends as many minutes as she can get away with choosing fall greens, a pomegranate, potatoes, then saunters from street to street, carrying her full string bag, as if she were on her way home. She can't stop for coffee or take a break in a *taverna*. Women in Crete who look like her don't do that unless they're with family or a friend. By mid-afternoon, her fingers and toes freezing, Dion parks her shopping bag and herself on a bench across the street from a travel agency where Theo will eventually buy last-minute tickets for two separate cabins on the overnight ferry to Iraklio, one of them deluxe, in her grandmother's maiden name: Dionysia Ionna Aramenis. *Yiayiá's* birth certificate is so old the paper was easy to scratch in a crease where her birthdate appears, then alter from 1926 to 1956. Weighed down by diamonds and money, Dion can easily pretend to be a woman bent by sixty-four years of living. Looking at her watch, she hobbles purposefully away. And knows as certainly as she knows her real name, that even though she's seen no evidence all day, someone is watching.

iv.

A woman wearing an expensive trench coat, hiking boots and a wide-brimmed hat that hides most of her face stands under a lamp standard on the Piraeus ferry terminal's tarmac pier in the November dusk, watching passengers board the overnight ferry to Iraklio. Bodies speak – arms swing or jerk or don't, legs strut or glide, backs stoop or sway or stiffen, heads poke or tilt or duck – and it is his fluency of movement that gives away the identity of a small American-looking man wearing a baseball cap and jacket and carrying a briefcase. Further down the line, near its end, a hunched, broken down-looking woman in a cheap coat, an old-lady kerchief and a shawl is shuffling along close behind but not part of a mother and daughter family. As she steps onto the ferry an overhead light catches the side of her head. Highlights a hanging strand of ginger hair. The woman in the trench coat attaches herself to the end of the line.

Beside the foot passengers trucks carrying food and products and machine parts not otherwise available on Crete are growling, expelling fumes as they inch forward into the belly of the ship. Ferry staff at the entryway require passengers to haul their luggage up a flight of metal stairs to the passenger decks. Dion stays close to the mother and her clearly ailing young daughter in front of her. At the top of the stairs an embarkation officer sitting behind a desk in a reception area is checking tickets. No name plate or lapel pin identifies the bald headed man in a black turtleneck and suit jacket standing behind him: Salin's man!

What will Theo do? The money and diamond sacks, wet with sweat now, are sticking to her chest, chafing her thighs. Should she turn back, take a ferry to somewhere else all alone—?

'No,' snaps *Yiayiá's* voice. 'Find a way to force his hand, expose him here, where you have some protection.'

Halfway up the stairs Theo is joking with a group of young soccer players. It does not matter if Salin's man recognizes him, ferry staff can ask Theo to open his briefcase. All it contains now are new sketch pads and paint brushes. The mother and daughter start up the stairs. Dion wonders if they can hear her heart hammering.

'You are a sixty-four year old woman with a birth certificate to prove it,' *Yiayiá's* voice reminds her. 'You're allowed to look flustered.'

She tucks a stray strand of hair into her kerchief and tries to scrape together a smattering of German words she has picked up from World War II movies and from tourists here in Crete: *Bitte*, *Jawohl*, *Nixt*, *Danke*. But it's no use. Baldy will see who she is. Though he won't be able to do anything about it before she reaches her cabin.

The woman in the trench coat at the back of the line sees the check-in table from the bottom of the stairs and Leo's man standing behind it.

How she laughed at Leo's face when he realized what Dion and dear *Yiayiá* and Theo had done, when she saw the camera's video of the hooded thief, and Theo's replica of that hideously knobby, gold and platinum, diamond-studded trophy bottle, and Leo's rage. Later that night, after they returned from taking flowers to *Yiayiá* at the winery, she was brushing her teeth when her phone pinged. 'Come,' a one-word text message. Leo did that sometimes when he was downstairs having a nightcap. She looked into the bathroom mirror, rubbed a little rosiness into her cheeks. Her hair's shiny black waves didn't need more than a few strokes of her brush and she had already changed into a white silk nightgown, his favourite. Down inside her body anxiety was a spice she likes with a man like Salin. His assistant would have retired for the night and the house was warm. No need for a robe. Her high heels were still by the bedroom door. Sexy fun would make up for laughing at his loss.

Salin was sitting in one of the leather armchairs in his study, facing away from St. John, towards Henri IV's plinth, now empty. Seeing her in the doorway, he patted his lap. Daily sessions in the gym upstairs have given him hard abs. She loves to fit her body against their contours, anticipating the press of his lips, the feel of hands that know how to make her moan, break free of her mind, her life. Now she smelled brandy as, pulling her nightgown strap off her shoulder, he took one of her nipples into his mouth, his teeth closing on it, just enough to hurt a little before he kissed her neck.

"Did you help them take my bottle?"

"No, Leo!" She tried to turn, to face him. His arm tightened, holding her where she was, his free hand moving up between her legs under the silk.

"Did you know what they were doing and help them?" The tone of his voice warned her against lying.

"No," she cried, "help them how? I was upstairs."

"Are you sure?" He slid a finger inside her.

"Yes, Leo!" Unfurling the hand holding her down, she took one of its fingers into her mouth, bit down on it. "Don't you think you would have been able to tell if I was involved?"

"You laughed."

"I did." She wiggled her body against the finger inside her, laughing again. "What they did was priceless, you have to admit that."

"Priceless?" She felt him harden inside his slacks. And then she was on the carpet, no more room for words until he was spent and she was a sobbing, sated body. Who finally saw that her life could mean something other than endless engagement in the politics of pleasure.

On the other side of a barricade at the bottom of the ferry stairs the ship's innards lie in darkness down here on the vehicle level. A driver jumps down from his truck. The ferryman watching over the foot passengers turns to chat with him. Amina slips around the barrier and disappears. She's a hiker, she'll say, showing cargo pants and a fleece under her trench coat to anyone who questions her, in urgent need of a washroom.

Dion's body wilts as she takes her ticket and birth certificate out of her purse and hands them to the bursar. Head down, she watches him match her grandmother's maiden name with his manifest. Behind him Salin's man says nothing.

'That doesn't mean he's deceived,' warns *Yiayiá's* voice.

The mother and daughter move off towards the ferry's lounge, probably to spend the night on the floor under a blanket the mother is carrying. The bursar hands back Dion's papers and gives her a key, saying something in Greek, pointing towards an elevator.

"*Dankeshun*," she mumbles, gathering her purse and papers, forcing herself not to look up.

Her deluxe cabin is at the far end of a narrow corridor. Staterooms next to her do not appear to be occupied. At the near end passengers are settling into large group cabins, men on one side of the hallway, women on the other. A camera watches her close her door.

A complimentary bottle of Cretan white wine sits in a bucket of ice. She reaches out to pick it up. Stops.

"Don't touch, eat or drink anything," Theo warned this morning. So she sits on the floor, listens to the thump of the ferry ramps being secured, the hum of its engine reversing away from the wharf.

Caught in a floating trap with Salin's man, she is also behind a locked door, and on her way home with three hundred thousand euros in cash. Her father and *Yiayiá* will return from Elafonisi and a lawyer who handled their winery's incorporation will meet them all at the winery with the requisite paperwork. If she can get herself and her load off this ferry. Outside her cabin's porthole Piraeus' lights are receding. Night has arrived. She would lie down, spend it here on this floor, but she has to meet Theo on the vehicle deck to plan Operation Henri IV's last, crucial step.

Trucks debarking in Iraklio, Crete, a domestic destination, do not need to go through customs but for sure Salin's man will check them. Before they drive off. Once their tires are on dry land drivers on a schedule will refuse to stop. So how to use this?

'Every eventuality, every security system has a weakness," *Yiayiá* told her the morning they sat together in the sea at Elafonisi. Timing is the difference between success and catastrophe.

Dion unlocks her cabin door, peeks into the hallway. Empty. She stays close to the wall, passes the group cabins, comes into a foyer where passengers are unpacking suppers, drinking coffee, playing cards, looking at their phones, where older women are interchangeable. Staircases on each side of the ship lead down to the ferry's vehicle deck.

Cameras watch it from both ends. Dark spaces between bumpers at midship will be harder to surveil. Theo finds her hunkered down between two transport trucks. And never has she been so glad to feel his body beside hers.

They need a covered but accessible vehicle they can jump out of once they leave the docks, at a traffic light in the city. They can not risk using Theo's motorbike again but Theo's Ukrainian friend Kiri will meet them in his truck. He knew his father was going to give them a lift in his fishing boat, he told Theo on harvest night. "And there's nothing I would like better than to help you fleece a Russian."

A rusting tarp-covered truck about a quarter of the way down the deck looks older than Dion. She starts towards it. In the back a jumble of used engine parts smells of metal and oil and grime.

"We can hide somewhere down here on the deck. You can boost me into the back after they've searched it, just before it drives off."

"Come on," Theo pulls her away. "We can't risk alerting anyone."

Under the stairs to the upper decks, beside buckets of sand and other docking paraphernalia, coils of mooring lines are thick as a person. Dion squeezes herself between them.

"This might work."

"Shsh!" Theo must have the ears of a bat. Not until the door to the stairs on the other side of the deck opens does Dion hear footsteps. Two sets. Theo pulls her out of her hiding place and through the door into the near-side stairwell.

Up on the night-berth deck men and women in the group cabins are coming and going with towels, toothbrushes, getting ready for bed. Theo goes into the men's cabin. Dion locks herself into her cabin and returns to the floor. A sack of diamonds jabs into her groin, packets of money itch against her waist, poke into the top of her bum but, exhausted to the point of nausea, she is ready to sleep even inside her anorak and hideous coat on this ferry carpet.

Someone knocks on her cabin door.

"Madam?"

She does not reply.

"Security check. Open please." Not loud.

Please Theo, be near the men's cabin door, listening. Ready.

"Madam! I come in now." A key turns in the lock. The door opens: two men. To check security? Salin's man and a ferry official push into the cabin. She scrambles to her feet.

The probability of this moment has terrified her ever since their planning sessions in the winery kitchen but now fury gushes into her limbs.

"*Voítheia*!" Help! She screams loud enough to alert the captain on this and any other passing ship. "*Voítheia*!" Running, hiding, thieving, needing, how dare anyone put her and her family in this position! Help! Over and over, startling her assailants. Salin's man reaches for her but her fist is already thumping the wall: "Help somebody, please! I'm being attacked!" She bounces her body off the dresser, knocking over the ice bucket. "Ouch! *Voítheia*!" A little scrap of her brain pulls her sleeve down over the hand that now plucks the possibly contaminated wine bottle off the dresser before it can roll onto the floor. She raises it. To do who knows what because she feels like she's flying, the way you do when you leap off a cliff, thin air dictating whatever comes next. The ferry official backs out of the door, one arm up, protecting his head. Leaving her trapped in here with Salin's man. "Help!" She screams again before he can close the door, her voice laced now with genuine terror.

Mumbling has already started in the corridor as men and women in nightgowns, pyjamas, tank tops and track pants come out of their cabins, clog the passageway, box in the ferry official. Theo pushes through them in time to keep the cabin door open.

"What? A woman is not safe even in a luxury cabin?" he shouts in Greek. Dion does not have to fake letting go of the bottle, crash landing on the floor, half in, half out of her cabin, crying now. Theo reaches down to help her up, puts his arm around her. "What kind of ferry is this?" he asks the official.

"Yeah," another passenger shouts. "Keep these assholes here and call the captain." The crowd, men and women, form a solid barricade in the ship's narrow hallway. No one remarks on how odd it is that a youngish woman is wearing a black wool skirt and shabby coat over an anorak and jeans.

A mistake has been made, the captain tells her, ordering his bursar to take her attackers to his office. The ferry service is very sorry, her ticket will be refunded and perhaps in the meantime she will accept a different cabin?

"No." Trust no one — she can feel *Yiayiá* watching — not the captain or the passengers.

"She'll be safest here now," says Theo, "with us. Right people?"

"*Ano, ano.*" Yes, yes.

Theo volunteers to take the first shift guarding her door and as soon as peace returns he and Dion slip away. Down into unmonitored stairwells, they thread their way through crew-only parts of the ship, into a passageway deep inside its bowels that also has no cameras, to an unoccupied cabin that contains nothing more than a single bed and night stand.

Sitting on the bed, they listen. The ship creaks. Nothing outside moves. Theo looks at his watch.

"There's a few hours left before we land. Why don't you take everything off and get into the bed."

She doesn't want to. Needs to be the way you are in a fire drill, everything packed and ready to run. But money pouches are poking her, sticking to her skin, dragging at her clothes, and she's So Tired. And she can tuck the pouches in beside her. She peels off her coats, knapsack, sweater, t-shirt. He unhooks her loaded bra. Her jeans hit the floor with a thud. She looks up at Theo, who looks like a demented New York Yankees pixie, and tries to smother a sudden gust of laughter.

"*Voítheia!*" she whisper-giggles, standing naked, hugging herself in the tiny cabin. He pulls her into a quick hug, then lifts the covers so she can slip into bed.

Nobody has seen her knapsack under her coats. She watches Theo dump everything out of it then take the money sacks and diamonds out of her jeans and brassiere and pack them into the bottom of it.

Somewhere under the cabin the ship's engine thrums reassuringly as Theo leans over her to wedge her knapsack between her body and the wall. His wiry body is so close, and it feels like a lifetime has passed since last night, when he explained why he left her for all those weeks after their harvest night. Not because she's old and he's twenty-eight and ashamed of his appetite and ready to leave again as soon as this is over.

He tucks the sheet and blanket around her and now his day-old, slightly rank scent brings her memories of him arranging her nude limbs in the golden sunshine on their beach below Hora Sfakion then sitting over his sketch pad, so intent the world around him could dissolve and he would notice nothing but his model and his drawing. She sees him laughing when she mimicked the way he rams the entire end of an ice cream cone into his mouth. Arguing with her about words and life and right versus wrong. Insisting on playing a part in this heist. Nudging her knees open on his sleeping bag by the fire on harvest night. Leaving his life in Iraklio to come back to her. He sits on the end of the bed.

"May I?" One of his hands finds her foot under the covers, caresses it, then her ankle, moves up to massage her calf muscle. Her body unclenches. His hand moves to her other leg.

"No," she lifts the covers. "Why don't you get out of those smelly clothes."

His body feels chilly against her breasts and belly and legs as she holds him. Holds onto him as a different cascade of images releases: her screaming for help in the deluxe cabin, the look on the face of Salin's man as she pounded the wall, picked up the bottle, the ferry man's horror. She feels herself trembling with laughter too wild to let out, that has nothing to do with anything funny.

"Shsh," Theo hugs her.

She burrows into his warmth. His penis comes to life. His mouth opens hers. Then pulls away, in case here in a stolen cabin in the bottom of the ship, pursued by a man who will employ every power he owns to see that they do not take what's his off this ferry, he is mistaking her fatigue and need for protection for desire.

Her body answers by finding his mouth again, her tongue playing with his and she loves the strength in his knee pushing her legs apart so his fingers can find her private, secret places. Lets him wipe her mind clean of everything but this moment, and this time she is an active lover, cupping her painting-model breast, offering it to him. Groaning as, sucking her nipple, he ignites lightning that spreads up out of her pelvis into her heart, which surrenders to it. His penis twitches in her hand as her body arches towards his. Tips off the edge of the real-time world and she would cry out except here is his mouth covering hers, sharing her breath as he shifts his body to come between her legs. Which wrap themselves around his back, her vagina pulsing, pulling him as deeply as she can into who she is as his thrusts explode them out of their separate selves.

He stays inside her, neither of them willing to leave this hallowed glow.

A change in the engine's thrum wakes her. They're slowing down! The cabin has no porthole but they must be close to the ferry harbour at Iraklio. Theo is not in the bed. Panic stops her breath.

No need, the cabin light is on and he is already dressed, a new, sweet smile telling her that the love they made was not a dream.

Her old lady cover is blown but the knapsack must stay hidden. They repack her body with money and diamonds and she puts on the black skirt and coat over her jeans and anorak. Then, sitting thigh to thigh on the bed, they run through their debarkation strategy.

Salin's man will have bought his freedom from the ship's captain. How many other staff members has he co-opted? After searching departing vehicles, one man will have to watch that deck while the other checks disembarking foot passengers.

Divide to survive. Theo will go down with her now to hide under the stairs. Will watch with her as Salin's minions shine flashlights into the eyes of truckers waking in their cabs as the ferry docks, and bribe them if necessary for permission to search their loads. When they have finished, and just before the vehicles drive off the ferry, Theo will see her safely hidden behind oil-smelly, freezing cold pieces of machinery in the back of her getaway truck. He will then ditch his baseball hat and jacket, not the briefcase, and walk off the ferry as a foot passenger to meet Kiri, who will be waiting in his truck. Forcing Salin's man to choose to pursue him and the briefcase through the streets of Iraklio.

She doesn't like any of this, Theo baiting Salin's man and how many others waiting on the dock — maybe Salin himself — and her alone in the back of a truck with a body-load of money and diamonds going who knows where. And having to ditch the black skirt and coat, get out of the truck safely.

'So you don't like it,' says *Yiayiá's* voice. 'Who are you to have the luxury of liking everything you do in life? Do what you have to do to get the money and diamonds off this ferry.'

Early morning is lightening the truck deck's gloom when the ferry's engine gears down again. Behind the coiled lines underneath the stairwell the night's salt-metal chill starts Dion shivering. Theo holds her close against him, so much more at stake now than money and diamonds. Luck and fate and all the stars in the universe will have to align if they're going to clear this last obstacle. His arm tightens and she hears it too: footsteps in the stairwell above, heavy, male. The door onto the deck squeaks as it opens. She scrunches lower behind the coiled ropes. A flashlight beam arcs past their corner and moves on.

Dozens of trucks and cars will be in a hurry to drive off as soon as the ferry's barrier is lowered. Two flashlights now are sweeping the deck, stopping at car windows, probing the undersides and open backs of trucks.

A shadow detaches itself from a pile of coiled landing lines a few metres away, and crosses the space between them.

"It's okay." Whispered. "It's me." Amina's voice. Neither of them speak, move, breathe. Amina squeezes in beside them. "I know you're here." Her voice is barely audible. "I followed you earlier."

"Why?" Theo's voice does not sound friendly.

"To save you, idiot! You think Leo and his man are just going to shrug when they see you two get off this ferry? Not after that little scene you pulled last night, D." A giggle escapes her. "I came to help."

So she knows they took the bottle. Is she here for Salin? The lightness in Amina's voice rankles Dion. 'Leo thinks you made the bottle, Theo,' she said the night she and Salin came to the winery, right after the heist. As if it was all a lark.

"Help how?" says Theo.

The flashlights reach the unloading end of the deck at the ferry's stern. The ship's engine growls, reversing. Getting ready to dock.

"Whatever you need," Amina says, lightness gone now. "Dion saved me Theo, that's why."

Chains are unspooled outside the ship's deck. Nobody speaks. Amina expels a breath.

"Look D, if there's one thing you learn in a harem it's how to read people and I know I haven't been around much lately but something in you has changed in the last few weeks. I thought it was just that you don't like Leo, what he's doing to the winery, and God knows I don't blame you for that but then, when you took the bottle I understood. Your secrecy with *Yiayiá*, the way you'd stop talking when I came in all made sense. And I thought 'good for you!'"

She does not detail the sexual aftermath, for her, of their heist, tells them only that "things happened" that gave her a window into her relationship with Leo Salin, who has never appreciated any more about who she is than she has herself. So does not know about her facility for languages, and that when her Saudi husband started fostering business partnerships in Moscow a couple of years ago, she amused herself by Googling Russian words she kept hearing: hello, goodbye, thank you, please, taxi, travel, tickets. When Leo's man called him away from lunch the day before yesterday, the urgency in his Russian tuned in her ears enough to pick out their names and 'tickets' and 'Iraklio' and 'port' before Leo disappeared into his computer office.

"I have always looked past his work, you know that," she goes on. "'Computer programming is boring,' he says whenever I have asked about it and: 'I don't want to waste our time together explaining it.' And it was so easy to accept that, to sunbathe by the pool, take the little red Mini he bought me out for a spin or to visit you all at the winery. Now, however, what was he going to do to my two best friends in the world when they got off the ferry?"

Last night's glow, still alight, brings Theo's impatience into Dion. Amina is still talking.

When a life-changing decision pops up to your mind's surface you better bring it to shore before fear sinks your resolve, she tells them. She learned that in Istanbul. So: 'Gone hiking,' read the note she left Leo. 'Need some time to think about us.'

"Hiking, you?" says Dion.

The ferry deck bumps against the wharf.

"I know but I wanted to be vague, not to give him a destination. So see?" She finds Dion's hand and takes it in under the trench coat to feel a thick fleece jacket and the kind of cargo pants hundreds of tourists wear to Crete. "I bought them yesterday in Athens. Leo won't like that I've gone, probably has a tracker on my car, but if he's searching for me maybe he'll be distracted from you, I thought. And maybe there'd be some other way I could help you too. So I drove to Chania and caught a flight to Athens, then took a car to Piraeus in time to watch you get on this ferry."

"And Salin's man didn't see you board last night?"

"I snuck on through the truck deck."

"We have to go," says Theo.

"Please wait just one more minute," urges Amina. "If anyone can catch you it's Leo, and if you're carrying anything stolen from him you'll go to jail. He'll make sure of that. So I'm thinking, if Leo has come to meet the ferry I could surprise him, jump into his arms as if he were here for me—"

"No Amina!" Dion cries. "You cannot be involved in this. Your life has been ruined enough and if Salin ever thought you were complicit—"

"What ID did you use to fly to Athens?" Theo sounds as if he doesn't believe her.

"My passport. I know, my Saudi husband might still have people reviewing ferry manifests all over the Mediterranean but at a certain point I do have to take responsibility for who I am, you know? As soon as I get off this ferry I plan to visit a lawyer, get rid of that marriage."

The ferry men are working the mooring lines.

"But you're still going back to Salin today." Theo states it as a fact.

"Yes. And if he dares to even suggest that my leaving had to do with your theft I'll tell him he's right, it did because his suspicion of me in his study the night of the heist is why I left. A relationship between equals cannot be built on suspicion, threats, control blah blah blah. And he does want me to live with him."

Metal plates at the end of the deck, that will bridge the crack between ship and shore, clatter into place. Daylight is chasing the shadows even in here now, bringing with it smells of oil and seaweed. Truck engines cough, whine, roar. Exhaust curls into their hiding place.

"Come on Dion," Theo's voice is urgent, "we have to go. Now." But:

"What if Salin doesn't buy it?" Dion pictures her friend trapped inside that villa—

"Not now, D." Theo's arm tightens around her shoulder, nudging her out of their nook. "If we're going to do this it has to be right now."

Do this: ride alone with thousands of euros and telltale, incriminating diamonds. Dion breathes in the oily darkness. Does she believe Amina's story? Because her friend is right, if she's caught—

"Wait," she tells Theo."No one knows Amina's on this ferry. Salin will know that she drove to Chania but will have no reason to expect her to be arriving here. Is there not some way we can use that?"

"Yes, do it, please!" Amina's whispers.

Desire: Dion sees a hawk diving, herself lying with Theo on harvest night.

And then last night.

Trust no one, her grandmother warned. But you trusted Gio up in the mountains, *Yiayia*. Her grandmother's image smiles: Yes I did, with my body before I knew any better. And my body was right.

Love, the endpoint of human desire, the light of human life, lives in the present. Her every cell is alive with its power in this moment, and Dion finds that she knows who and what to trust. Sees Amina laughing when they stole Henri IV. Because she loves their taking hold of life and shaking what they need out of it. That's why she made this trip, Dion knows this as surely as day follows night. Also:

Yiayiá: There is always a weakness, you just have to find it.

And Teddy: When they think you'll go down, you go up.

And her Dad: What we tend with love makes whatever comes next.

"Quick," she whispers. No need to second-guess. "Take off your clothes, Amina. We need to switch bras and pants and coats. Theo, give us room."

"There's no time, D!" But she is already shrugging out of her coat, her anorak, pulling her sweater up over her head. She lands a kiss on Theo's mouth.

"Unhook me."

Five minutes later, just before the driver of the beat-up metal parts truck starts to inch forward, Theo tosses a stone across the deck. The ferry man watching the trucks debark looks towards the sound, does not see a woman in a trench coat boost another woman wearing filthy jeans and an anorak up over the truck's tailgate, into the darkness under its tarpaulin.

Vehicles clatter over the metal plates, leaving the ship. Dion and Theo watch the truck bearing Amina, all their money and the diamonds follow a tall transport truck off the ferry.

"Text me where to meet you," said Amina, shrugging into Dion's heavy brassiere.

"No don't!" said Theo as Dion pulled the laden bra across Amina's back and fastened it. "For sure he's got your phone tapped. Which means he knows you're on the ferry, which means he's here. So give me your phone. You'll have to leave it on the ferry. We'll meet in the lobby of the Kronos Hotel, by the old harbour, as soon as you can get there." Enough light was reaching the vehicle deck for Dion and Theo to see Amina's smile.

"If I'm not in the lobby look for me in the washroom."

Back up the stairs, Dion and Theo watch foot passengers debark as Amina's truck joins the line of vehicles crossing the ferry port's tarmac towards the exit. No one stops it.

A black sedan with tinted windows is parked just inside the port's gates. Standing by it, sleek in a camelhair coat, Salin is watching, waiting. Close enough to supervise, not close enough to be seen to be involved in whatever is necessary to get what he wants. Dion's heart pounds.

Kiri's red truck is on the street just outside the gates.

Hurrying down the stairs, holding hands, they mix with the departing crowd of passengers on the dockside tarmac. Halfway to the gate Salin's man rushes them from behind, knocks Theo to the ground.

"Hey!" she shouts. Passengers around them stop, step back. Salin's goon yanks the briefcase out of Theo's hand and his knapsack off his shoulder before anyone can react.

"Stop thief!" she cries, looking around, trying to attract attention. "Hey!" A man she hasn't seen before is yanking her knapsack off her back.

Salin's man looks around them, daring anyone to challenge him. Normal people carrying luggage, trying to get home or to work hesitate to take on two thugs. Salin's man opens the briefcase. Paint supplies spill out onto the ground. And now here's Kiri, running towards them, shouting. Theo struggles to his feet, yelling in Greek for someone to get the port police.

Amina's truck leaves the port's gates, eases out into the traffic. Taking with it Dion's family's only hope for a future.

On the other side of the parking lot Dion sees Salin watching his men dump dirty clothes out of their knapsacks. Kiri arrives, pulls Salin's man by the shoulder, lands a punch. The man backs away, hands raised, empty knapsacks on the ground. The other man's hands pat Dion's body before anyone can do anything about it.

"Stop!" she yells again, pushing him away. Port workers, ferry hands elbow their way through the crowd. Theo gets up.

"Here," he holds out his arms. "You want to frisk me too while we wait for the cops?"

Salin's man's dislike for Theo comes out in the roughness with which he catches hold of him, frisking him as he turns him then gives him a push towards Kiri. It all happens in a matter of seconds. Salin's goons walk away. Dion watches the Russian open the door of his SUV and slide inside. Moments later his man drives off as if he had nothing to do with this ruckus.

Fear, always lying in wait, wanting centre stage, does not partner well with untried trust. Riding between Kiri and Theo in the Ukrainian's truck, Dion watches shop keepers raising their metal grills, putting out crates of oranges. She pictures Amina wedged between engine parts in the back of a truck reeking of motor oil and mould and yesterday's grease, wearing a sweaty bra and jeans packed with hundred-euro bills and diamonds. Where and when will she feel safe enough to climb over the tailgate?

Dion had planned to jump down at the first red light, into the startled stare of the driver behind the truck, and then flag down a passing taxi, the safest way to navigate Iraklio's busy streets unseen. Amina's has no adult experience in the rough and tumble world. Hiding in the back of the truck, is she cool, laughing inside herself at the whole adventure, or have her sweet intentions turned to jelly?

Please God or Zeus or whoever else is here, please help Amina manage it without turning an ankle or falling or getting run over or drawing attention to herself.

She has not betrayed them, does not plan to return to her car in Chania and drive away to some other future of her own, that much Dion knows with unassailable certainty. And from within that certainty, she sends love and strength and thanks to her friend. Because Amina was right, without her help there was no way they could have pulled this off.

If they have. Salin's car does not follow Kiri's truck but she lost track of the second ferry thug. Kiri takes Dion and Theo to a bar down by the fish docks. And if there's one thing Dion knows it's how to Teddy them out of the reach of a possible tail. Once they are back downtown they join the crowds relaxing in restaurants down by the harbour. Let anyone who wants to watch them eat, drink, laugh. Saunter up the street to the Kronos Hotel holding hands.

Tomorrow, when the tide is low and they're sure no one is watching, they might take a stroll along the scrap of beach below the seawall.

The Angels' Share

In cellars where aging
ripeness breathes
evanescences we humans,
trapped within our senses,
can not apprehend,
mould paints black designs
on casks and beams
while the angels take their share
of every new creation.

March brings late afternoon sunlight to the floor of Dion's gully above the stream bed beyond the vineyard and the olive and oak groves. Winter storms have washed away the spiders' webs. Up on the mountainside sheep bells keep her company as she spreads her rug a year after the day last spring when Theo entered her life. Lying down, she lifts her t-shirt to let the sun shine on her belly. Will not take off any clothes until Theo joins her, until she's faced him with her news.

They have the winery to themselves now. Theo has spent most of their off-season winter days painting, using the showroom as a studio, but this is the right place for a conversation that must have nothing to do with the future of Dionysia Wines.

Before her father left for America, to see Amina safely through negotiations with her parents in Philadelphia and with a divorce lawyer, Alexander the Grape renamed the winery 'Dionysia' to honour both *Yiayia* who, reassured that her family was now safe, went off to join her beloved Gio the day before New Year's Eve, and his daughter, who saved his life's work, and represents its future.

Yiayia had smiled her assent when Theo hung his painting of Dion above shelves behind the showroom counter, facing the door to the street, just before a Christmas party the winery hosted for the village and wine critics and media from Chania and Iraklio and Athens (Amina's idea.) A mix of line and colours on textured paper, the painting 'Dionysia' suggests so much more about a female nude lying in the breaking surf and offering her breast than the eye can take in. Gazes, comments, commissions and requests for drawings and other paintings of her mounted on the showroom walls have kept Theo busy ever since.

One day in January a scout from a gallery in Athens stopped by.

He wanted the painting, said Theo's unique technique radiates something so much deeper and more nuanced than physical desire, but Theo wouldn't part with 'Dionysia.' Has no desire to go to Athens, attend an opening, pretend to be polite.

Why does he need to hang onto the painting when he can have the body/soul of it under his fingertips whenever he likes, Dion wonders? Because often, while winter rains were running down the showroom windows and the street outside was empty and no one was visiting, real-life Dionysia would set the mid-morning coffee tray on the showroom counter and brush against him, letting him know that under her sweater she was not wearing a bra. Or, while below them in the wine cellar the angels tipsily took their share of Alexander The Grape's first batch of brandy, she might remove his paintbrush from his hand and sit in his lap. Loves yielding to the feel of him, to his touch, to who he is, how he takes in the world and what he does with it. Loves the little world they are making here together. Theo is twenty-nine however, an artist on his way. At some point he is bound to get restless, she thought.

Wrong, Theo told her one day. They had just finished making love on the bed in his studio shed when rain started hammering on its corrugated tin roof.

"Uhoh." Theo leapt up, naked as a Grecian god, dumped paint brushes out of an old pickle jar and placed it to catch a line of rain drops splashing onto the floor, his mouth quirking into a smile. "Looks like we'll have to spend the rest of the afternoon here."

And just as suddenly as it had started, the storm outside stopped. Came inside her instead. Became a deluge of tears Dion had no way of damming.

"What?" A filament of winter light on Theo's curls, his eyes, his chest threatened to break Dion's heart. "I thought I make you happy?"

"Oh yes yes, my love, you do that every single day." She reached out to him. "So happy." But the tear storm intensified. He held her against him. She cried herself onto a shoal of sadness. "I'm so sorry, darling Theo." She traced the lovely line of his jaw. "It's just that I... I'm...

Sooner or later you'll leave me again, this time for good. I know that, and do understand—"

He pulled away. Her heart wanted to stop. But now here he was kneeling on the bottom of the bed, taking hold of her feet, bending her knees up, spreading them. Kissing the insides of her thighs then looking at her as if to penetrate her with his eyes, his face as serious as it was when he was painting. Leftover rain dripped into the jar.

"I'm not going anywhere, D. The only home I want is right here, with you."

That home is secure now. When Amina came out of the Kronos Hotel's washroom, looking bedraggled in Dion's travel-stained clothes but also gleeful, Dion and Theo whisked her up to a room they had paid for with cash, in *Yiayia's* name. Two days later *Yiayia* sat at the kitchen wearing Amina's pink silk blouse above her black Cretan skirt, a stack of euro notes next to Kokanakis Wines' expiring contract with Leonid Salin. Waiting for Salin to sign the receipt Theo's uncle's lawyer had prepared, that expunged their obligations to the Russian 'computer specialist.'

Salin knows where the money came from but the police told him the videos his cameras took did not point conclusively towards anyone, and hadn't he been right there in the room when they were recorded?

After the signing Alex brought his crystal decanter out of the showroom.

"Will you join us in a toast to our future, Leo?" he asked. "Let go of bygones? I've come upon a nice little brandy." Dion will never forget *Yiayia's* full-out grin.

Salin looked at his watch, declined and left. And they spent the rest of the day sharing leftover euros amongst envelopes addressed first to Kokanakis Wines's grape growers and harvest helpers, then to every village resident.

Amina stayed on at the Kronos Hotel for a week then took a bus to Chania, picked up her car and made peace with Salin.

"I just want to see if what I have with him is worth anything," she told Dion at the hotel, "if I can find the man I fell for and bring him out again, maybe out sailing, under the moon."

Salin was edgy on her return, not entirely convinced of Amina's innocence in his loss of Henri IV.

"The theft and your leaving me, the timing of that, and losing your phone on the ferry," he said, confronting her one morning in his heated, glass-enclosed garden room. "I don't believe in co-incidences."

"You don't have to," she told him, looking up from her phone. "Your suspicious, hurtful treatment of me after the theft is the reason I left you, Leo. I'm hoping you'll come to see that I'm worth a whole lot more than that."

"Maybe I'll see how much more by selling you back to your husband."

She let her laughter ring through the room.

"Come on, you'd miss me if I was rotting in a Saudi Arabian cellar, admit it." Leaning across the space between them, she picked up his hand, kissed his knuckles then put his middle finger into her mouth, sucking on it as if it was a lolly pop, her eyes telling Salin there was nowhere else she'd rather be. "If not, you'd have sold me by now."

He put his free hand on the back of her head, pulling her close enough to slide his tongue into her mouth. But stored away behind his sexy strength and her arousal she glimpsed vindictiveness, ambition, confusion, greed, and beyond those a well of need a person could drown in. She started spending more time at the winery.

"I've always envied you and Theo you know," she told Dion one night over their bedtime cup of herbal tea. "Your struggles with sex and money and paint, how you'd go up and then down, all of it so... unprotected." Their heist, and her part in it, let Amina taste a free, no-holds-barred life she had only glimpsed once before, for a few minutes with an Australian admirer. Now she longed to hear, smell more of it, taste reality, get down and dirty by herself, for herself.

"I have a business degree for God's sake, isn't it about time I did something with it?"

"Like what?"

"I dunno, something to do with climate change. Maybe I could start some kind of carbon-eating collective in the U.S., something simple, adaptable." She looked sheepish. "Your father has taught me about fungus, and I saw this documentary about how powerful it is, always pushing, pushing, eating carbon, transforming, creating. Check it out, D. Mushrooms might save the planet."

Dion helped her plan her exit from Salin's closely watched universe then drove her down to the Elafonisi guest house, where she would be safe. While she was waiting there, until Alex was free to make the trip to America with her, Amina developed a business plan for the Dionysia Winery.

Now, after settling Amina safely in the United States and visiting his brothers and sister, who had reconnected with him in Crete after *Yiayia's* death, her father is exploring new investment opportunities for U.S. and Canadian vintners interested in his climate-conscious, nature-nurturing wine production methods.

"Wineries in Oregon and on Vancouver Island are interested in hiring me as a consultant," he emailed last week. "Teddy loved the U.S's west coast, and Vancouver Island, its ancient forests and wild sea, remember? So I think I might take the jobs, to be with him for awhile, and with your mother." She and Theo know enough to tend his grape vines until he returns.

Once her fungus farm is up and running, Amina wants to visit Alex in Canada, and maybe expand into seaweed on Vancouver Island.

"Seaweed's one of the oldest life forms on the planet, D," she wrote, "also one of the healthiest foods. And if I do that I'll also be able to keep an eye on Alex." Maybe Dion and Theo could meet them there when the time is right. Dion sees her smile. "The world is a small place when you're free."

Flowers in the pots at Salin's front gates are dead now. There's no sign but his villa is on the market, according to Theo's uncle's lawyer, who goes fishing with a Rethymnon real estate attorney. A new, pressing project for the Kremlin is the reason Salin has given for selling it.

Pfff, said *Yiayia's* spirit. Bullies who lose always leave the sandbox.

Dion often talks to her grandmother, finds love and solace by kneeling in *Yiayia's* vegetable garden, breaking up soil as hard as her grandmother's favourite tone of voice while the old lady tells her how to make the earth ready, then put this year's seeds in her mouth before planting them, so her saliva can tell them what nutrients she needs them to create. Preparing a supper casserole in the kitchen, Dion lets *Yiayia* know that who she was and what she loved and thought and did have saved her granddaughter, and given her a future here on her family's ancestral land in Crete. In Canada too, when the time is right. Now that she's gone, the old lady has to listen.

"There's one thing I'm not sure about," Dion told her the other day while stoking the fire in the Aga before putting a *boureki* casserole into the oven.

You're pregnant, said *Yiayia*.

Dion flopped into a chair at the kitchen table, a wave of nausea rising.

How can you be surprised, said her grandmother? Have you two ever once used any form of birth control?

"Did you?" Dion shot back in a way she never could when her grandmother's body was here.

Her belly has begun to swell. She may be forty but she and her baby are fine, said the doctor. Now she has to tell Theo, who hasn't noticed yet. Of course he hasn't, he's twenty-nine, easily duped into thinking her nausea is due to a winter virus. And she, who would love nothing more than to have a baby with Theo, has not yet found courage enough to get the words out.

Not because he won't want to marry if she wants to, and take on fatherhood, stay up all night, change pooey diapers. No, the problem is her own. Because no matter how she rationalizes what she did to save the winery, the fact is that this baby's mother is an uncaught criminal. And in a world that is becoming increasingly hazardous, our consciences are the only measure of ourselves we can rely on.

Pfff, says *Yiayia*, short on patience as always. People throughout this valley, who have suffered so many years from poverty and austerities, did you not see their faces when they opened an envelope with their name on it, and found a packet of Salin's euros? What we did with our pasts sets our futures in motion, Dionysia, that's what matters. I thought you'd know that by now.

Outside the gully March's late afternoon sunlight is almost horizontal now.

Do you have to measure yourself, asks a voice that does not belong to Teddy or Theo or her father or *Yiayia*, that is hardly even a voice, more like air-fuelled light that comes from no fixed point, from inside of her but also from the stream bed poppies and thistles and the shushing oak leaves?

Dion looks down at her body, feels her heart beating. Love is streaming into her billions of cells, all of which are working collaboratively, miraculously together to create a new person while outside her gully the poppies begin to glow in the sunlight. Love for Theo, for her baby and herself, for Teddy and *Yiayia* and her father and Amina. For the life that is hers, thanks to this sunlight and all the laws that keep its forces balanced, so many laws of gravity, action and reaction, thermodynamics, laws old as Earth itself, that no human can break.

She shifts onto her side on the rug, hopes Theo gets here in time to see this golden light. Strokes her swollen belly.

"You're going to love yourself," she tells her baby, "your body, whatever shape it is, and your mind and the spirit you share with every other living being so that, whatever the future holds, you can make your own best choices."

Footfalls shuffle through dead leaves on the bank above her gully.

"Is there room in there for me?" Crouching on the stream bank, Theo is backlit by sunlight.

She smiles, keeps her hand where it is. Watches his mind connect with it.

"No!" He crawls into the gully, his curly hair tickling her belly as he kisses it. "Hello in there." He looks up at her, awed. "I wonder who we've made."

He will paint Dion's lines as their baby grows, Theo tells her. Will go to sleep with his hand on her belly so that whoever is inside her will know, through Dion's skin, that he is right here, waiting.

And, thinks Dion, her love joining with Theo's will bring light into all their baby's cells as they grow and divide and decide who to become, while the angels keep watch.

Acknowledgements

I wrote this novel with help from sources too numerous to name. These include the sun, sea, vines and trees and all those who live with them in harmony and competition. Humans I would like to thank especially include:

In Crete, Anna Maria Kambourakis and Vasilis Kokologiannakis, owners of Chania Wine Tours, storyteller friends Alan Fairest and Carola Poppinga of Myrthios, and Dourakis Winery.

In Britain, Hilary Boyd, author, and editor Kate Rizzo of Cornerstones Literary Consultancy.

In the United States, story master Michael Hauge, books and lectures by Caroline Myss, Dr. Daniel Siegel and Dr. Bruce Lipton, and publisher Paul Cohen and book designer Colin Rolfe of Monkfish Books' Red Elixir imprint.

In Canada, poets Florence Treadwell and Lea Harper, the late Mary Breen, artist Jill Segal, baker/papermaker Graham Thoem, editor/agent Barbara Berson, retired financier Anne Brown, Ariel Hudnall and Nicole Magas at Serif, reader Kelly Anderson, and most of all Grant Collins without whom this book would not exist.

www.ingramcontent.com/pod-product-compliance
Lightning Source LLC
LaVergne TN
LVHW091043080826
845145LV00002B/606

* 9 7 8 1 9 6 6 2 9 3 3 0 9 *